CHAINS

MATTHEW LEDREW

CHAINS

CORAL BEACH CASEFILES

Published in Canada by Engen Books, St. John's, NL.

A CIP catalogue record for this book is available from Library and Archives Canada.
ISBN: 978-1-989473-27-6

This book is a work of fiction. Names, characters, places and incidents are products of the author's imagination or are used fictitiously. Any resemblance to actual events or locales or persons living or dead is entirely coincidental.

Distributed by:
Engen Books
www.engenbooks.com
submissions@engenbooks.com

First mass market paperback printing: April 2013
Second mass market paperback printing: November 2019

Cover Image: Shutterstock
Cover Design: Matthew LeDrew

For
Ellen

PROLOGUE

It always starts off small.

They say that even an ant can start an avalanche, and now I know it to be true, even if I don't quite grasp how yet.

It all started about ten years ago, with an event that's more common in today's society than most people realize: with the abuse and neglect of a small child, only five or six years old at the time. That child's name was Derek Smith.

He wasn't beaten or accosted or molested like some of the suffering children in this world, but the abuse was no less real and its effect no less grand. His father and mother worked, one a journalist and one a grade school teacher. As a result, little Derek never got the attention he deserved and needed to develop as a child. He was raised by the media around him as opposed to those that loved and cared for him. Surrounded by third-person-shooter video games and movies that glorified acts of terrorism, he grew up callas and unable to distinguish between right and wrong, or recognize the effect of his actions upon others or to empathize with the harm he caused them, feeling only whatever the event brought to him at the time, which quickly away like a autumn leaf on a spring breeze.

As the time with his parents became less and less, he reached a breaking point when his mother passed away at the age of eight. Now his workaholic father was his sole support system, and proved lacking. So with his father working harder and harder at getting that Pulitzer prize to prove himself worthy to his only son, Derek worked to make sure that his father would get it: and began murdering the people of Coral Beach, Maine in an attempt to get his father that award-winning story so that they could spend more time together.

It was in that act that... that...

...

..

.

Cathy Kennessy stopped typing and watched the curser blink at the end of the line. She frowned as it winked at her from where she had left it after the end of the word that.

It was early morning, roughly five am, and the first bare hints of sunlight were beginning to perk their way above the trees that stood beyond her bedroom window. The air in her room was cool enough to make her breath show when she exhaled, and she had snuggled her feet into fluffy red slippers to protect them.

She shifted her focus from the blinking curser to the clock in the lower right hand corner of the screen and then back again, let out a huff of frustration, then brought one red-painted fingernail over the backspace button, as if threatening her writer's block to come undone.

"What are you doing over there?" Mike Harris chuckled from his place snuggled into the sea of pillows that covered her bed. He pressed pause on his DS for a moment and laid it atop his chest, then squinted his eyes to see what she was typing across the room. "'Surrounded by third-person-shooter video games and movies that glorified acts of terrorism'... hun, what are you writing? 'Derek Smith : The Unauthorized Biography'?"

Cathy smiled, turning around on her chair to face him, giving him a smug look. "Something like that."

Mike snorted, then turned his game back on and started to play, the three-note melodies of the game humming away once again. The game was nearly enveloped by his massive hands, which occupied her line of sight and prompted several inappropriate thoughts. His forearms and shoulders were no less large or broad. He had always been strong, something that she had always guessed was a trait amongst his birth parents, but in the last few months he had been pushing himself to be bigger and better than everyone else. Especially since winter set in, he had been spending a great deal of time at the school gym after hours training himself, and now he was positively rippling.

He paused his game again and looked past it to Cathy, her eyes still lingering somewhere in the vicinity of his tricep muscles. He raised an eyebrow to her and pretended to be annoyed at her ogling of him. "Can I help you?" he asked impatiently.

Cathy's gaze jolted up toward his face, as if only now realizing that she had been staring. She laughed, and then a wry smile began to curl its way up the edges of her lips. She stood up slowly and made her way over toward him. "I'd rather help myself," she said in a hushed, deep voice. She leaned over him and opened her mouth and brought it down until it was just above his, letting it linger there for a moment as her hair fell onto either side of his face. His breath quickened the longer she waited before actually making contact, and when she finally did the smooth wet sensation of her lips drove shocks through his entire system, her tongue leaving her mouth and entering his just once, briefly, before she broke off the embrace. His eyes still closed and mouth still open as she backed off ever so slightly, watching the as the effects of her kiss lasted even after she had stopped. Putting both her hands on the bed for support, she got off of him and then moved back to her chair.

"Um..." he said when his brain became a little less foggy and his ability to speak returned. "Was that your fantasy, or mine?"

She smirked, giggling at him. "Let's go with both."

"You're a cruel girlfriend," he reminded her as he sat up against the wall and let his feet dangle off the edge of the bed. He fixed his suddenly too-tight jeans to be more comfortable.

"I try." She flashed him a goofy smile that always made him laugh, then turning back toward her laptop and starting to backspace over what she had just written.

Mike watched her as the words erased one by one, except for the first two paragraphs, leaving it at :

It always starts off small.

They say that even an ant can start an avalanche, and

now I know it to be true, even if I don't quite grasp how yet...

"I'll ask again," he sighed, switching off the game and laying it on his lap. "What are you doing?"

Cathy turned and gave him a look of dismay. "How many lives have you saved in the past few months?"

His head bobbed back a second, shocked by the suddenness of the unexpected question. "I don't know-- a dozen, maybe? I don't really keep track."

"And what about Xander, how many has he saved? Or taken, for that matter? That's if you don't count the whole thing with Alpha, when he pretty much saved the world, so, like, seven billion lives right there."

"What are you getting at?"

She laughed, in such a way that let him know she thought that question was absurd. "He - saved - the - world - once!" she said, pronouncing every word slowly to hammer home the point. "I know all those video games and comic books and science fiction novels and all that make that seem like no big deal-- but it is, Mike. I mean I don't think anybody has actually ever done that before. Or since."

Mike's brow tightened toward the center, as he started to understand. "I guess it is a big deal. But that still doesn't explain what you're doing."

She frowned and touched a hand against the soft skin between her neck and her left shoulder, tracing a finger around the intricate network of scars that were only now covering themselves over with a fine layer of flesh.

"Ah," Mike smiled, nodding. "It's about that," he said, motioning to the wound.

"No, it's not -- it's --" her eyes cast downward, then back up to meet him. "When the Womb attacked me, my whole life flashed before my eyes. I know how cheesy and fake that sounds, but -"

"No," he interrupted, his voice as soothing as he could make it. "It's not at all."

She smiled. "Anyway, that was the first time he ever attacked me... alone, you know? And on my way to the hospital, even though I wasn't hurt that bad, all I could think was that it could have been worse. It could have killed me, right there. I starting thinking that I'd never get to see Trina grow up, or tell my parents how much I loved them, or get to move in with you, or tell Xander that I forgive him. All the people we've seen die since September, you would think that I would have learned not to leave so many things undone."

"You wanna move in together?" he smiled stupidly.

She gave him a look, then continued. "I know there's nothing I can do about that. I know that if I die, you'll find some way to explain all this -- madness -- to my parents so that they understand. But what if we all die, Mike?"

He sat up now, leaning close enough to take her hand and run his thumb rhythmically against the back of it. "What?" he asked patiently.

She tisked, unsure of how exactly to get her point across. "What if you, me, and Xander all died? At once?"

"That's -- not going to happen, sweetie."

"Oh, really?" she laughed, taking the statement as an insult to her intelligence. "We almost did when the Tee's attacked the school. And when Zakron came after us. That thing could have easily killed all three of us. That's not even considering that two of the greatest serial killers in the country have a serious hate for all three of us, and one of them is out there somewhere right now!"

"Shh --" he calmed, stroking her hand until she lowered her voice, mindful of her little sister in the next room.

She got off the chair and knelt on the floor, snuggling in close to him. She draped her arms around him and rested her head on his stomach. It was less soft since he'd started working out regularly, and she found she missed the comfort of a little fat. "What if we all died and nobody knew? Nobody knew why or for what... or what we'd done and the lives we'd saved? What if nobody realized how close the world came to ending once?"

"I get it," he smiled warmly, touching the side of her head. "I do. I get it now."

She smiled. "Thank you. So, I decided I'm going to write a book. A novel, really. Kind of like those dramatic reenactments from Unsolved Mysteries."

"Yes, because our lives need the added drama."

"Shut up," she teased, giving him a little slap before kissing him quickly, then moving back to her chair. "I mean I know most of what happened, either first hand or from being told, but there's some stuff I'm going to have to make up. Like, there's no way of knowing what Hale might have said to O'Toole behind closed doors, so I'll make it up. But I'll make it sound real -- y' know?"

"I gotcha," Mike nodded, then thought for a moment. "I like the line in that case. The whole 'ant and the avalanche' thing. It suits it, I guess."

"But--" she coaxed, wanting more feedback than that.

Chains

"I think it's wrong to start the story with Derek. It's not supposed to be about him. And the way you were writing it, you would have written yourself to an end in like, four more pages."

She frowned, looking back at the horrid blinking curser. "Actually, I already had," she admitted. "But isn't that where it all starts, with Derek? He's the one who killed all those people."

"Yeah, but that's one of the reasons it shouldn't be about him."

"Well, I'd make it about Xander, but that 'd be too hard. There's so little we know about where he actually came from or how he was made yet, it'd just confuse who-ever read it."

Mike motioned in agreement. "Why not write it from your point of view? That 'd be simplest."

Her brow furrowed as she considered that for a moment, then looked back at the screen with confidence. "Yeah... I could do that. Tell the whole story from my side of things. It's going to end up that way whether I try to or not, seeing as I'm the writer."

"Exactly. And that way, you can put in how you feel about stuff. You can put the font in italics and do like a voice-over monolog or something, like: 'Star Date 0.8765.765.9, I was making out with Mike, when --'"

She shot him a look. "No Star Trek now please. I'm not in the mood."

"I thought you liked Star Trek?"

She rolled her eyes at him, dangling her fingers over the keyboard again.

He took this as a sign that she was starting again and

picked up his game.

After a pause to collect her thoughts, her fingers once again began to flutter over the keys.

... It always starts off small.

They say that even an ant can start an avalanche, and now I know it to be true, even if I don't quite grasp how yet.

The Factory. The Factory was a local arcade where we all went to hang out when there was nothing better to do, which was just about all the time. It existed in this limbo where nothing happened and everything happened. Couples became couples there, and often became singles there as well. There was money and there was change at a time when it seemed like everything was changing. It was a giant living room outside our parent's homes, always loud and exciting and neon.

Jamie Dawkins leaned over one of the many pool tables which adorned the club, raising an eyebrow as he tried to figure out his shot. His leather sports jacket crumpled and scrunched noisily every time he moved, impeding his ability to shoot. Many times he had pushed up the sleeves, but they always fell back down almost immediately. But he dared not take it off. His brother had worn that jacket when he was captain of the Coral Beach Cougars, and his father before that. Now that he was finally the captain it barely ever left his back. Some even said he showered with it on...

She stopped, her shoulders falling.

Mike glanced up, taking a quick scan of the screen. "That sounds good."

"It's crap," she corrected flatly. "It's going to come into my point of view in a second. I couldn't think of where to start it, so I figured right before Jamie died would be as good a spot as any. And I'd have to spend a little bit of that time introducing Jamie and everyone else, so I thought maybe I'd do it from my point of view, watching the two of you play pool at the Factory that night -- but it's stupid."

He winced, remembering the pain he'd felt when he heard of Jamie's death as though it had just happened. "That's great, baby," he said, swallowing back hard.

She turned to look at him with regret, then quickly pressed save on the word document and closed out of the program, then walked over to him. "It still tears at you, doesn't it?" she asked, though it wasn't really a question.

Mike's eyes grew distant for a moment as he stared off at nothing, then turned back to her as she sat down beside him. "No, it doesn't," he admitted, raising up his arm so she would be able to snuggle in against his chest. "And I think that bothers me more than anything. There's been so much since then, that it seems..."

"Small?" she finished for him, reaching one hand up inside his shirt to keep it warm, then running her nail around the groves of his familiar frame.

He nodded, but did not respond.

She opened her mouth to continue, then stopped. There really wasn't anything to say. As horrible as it sounded, it was true and she knew it. The death of Jamie Dawkins did seem small now.

They sat in silence for several minutes until the glowing red letters of her clock read five thirty. She turned to Mike, whose eyes were closed but she knew was not asleep, and poked him twice in the leg. "Come on," she coaxed, then waited for him to move.

CHAPTER ONE
DISCOVERY

It watched her from the corner of its eye, her every movement reflecting off its opaque, aqua-marine retinas. She was holding a tiny plastic statuette of a bird sporting a green Mohawk. After examining it carefully for a moment she placed it back atop her dresser along with several others, including a duck that was smashing an electric guitar in grand Who-style and a long-tailed mouse playing the maracas.

She turned toward the window and looked almost directly at it, not quite right into its eyes but close enough. She lingered, and it thought that perhaps it might have been spotted. It let go of a frustrated grunt into the cool fall air, which became visible in the chill and traveled up past the leaves of the tree on which it stood perched. She stared out the window, then turned back toward her bed. She moved the pillow and pulled back the covers. She should have been in bed hours ago.

She had light blonde hair with white highlights, which had made her head shine like a halo. She was beautiful and graceful, sweet and innocent. Somewhere deep within the creature's mind it remembered someone else that had fit that description, although it couldn't quite remember who just now.

There were stuffed animals all over a shelf near the ceiling, the bright colors of each drawing its gaze. It focused in on a red one in particular, turned an odd purple in its always-blue distorted vision. There was a hole in the wall that had been hastily patched, about the size of a quarter, and an old stereo that looked as though it might have been handed down from an older sibling. It rested atop a bookcase, the lower shelves of which were decorated with Baby Sitter's Clubs, Harry Potters, and Chronicles of Narnia. The creature regarded them with some degree of fascination, then turned back toward the girl.

She was wearing a floppy nightgown now with a faded printing of a teddy bear on the front of it.

The creature jumped off of its branch, its black, scaly form glistening in the starlight for a moment before landing on the roof over her window with a soft thud, digging its talons into the tiling and tar.

The noise, no matter how slight, made the girl jump. She looked around her room, then out the window into the trees, trying to find the source of the sound. There was none to be seen.

She picked up her copy of Harry Potter and the Prisoner of Azkaban and lay on her bed for thirty minutes reading it before she had assured herself that there was nothing in her room that was going to jump out and hurt her. She laid the book on her night stand and turned off her lamp, shrouding the room in darkness. She rolled over and closed her eyes and went to sleep.

The creature's eyes opened, their blue-green glow illuminating the room surrounding them. The eyes were all that were visible of it now, here in the blackness, if the girl had been awake to see.

It reached out quickly quietly as it crept ever closer, bring-

ing a claw ever so lightly up -- up -- raising it to just the right height. With one lightning fast motion, it brought its arm down, digging it deep into the girl's chest. Her eyes snapped open and she opened her mouth to scream. The creature's hand was already there, holding the noise in as it ripped upward agonizingly slow, spilling blood onto clean sheets --

Cathy awoke with a start, hot sweat flying off her forehead. Her breathing was labored, drowning out even the roaring winter wind outside, which shook the whole upper floor of the house down to the very last nail. Her full lips gasped for air as her nightmare slowly eased its way out of her mind, the bane of consciousness forcing it away.

She pushed her covers away, her warm body sticking to them where flesh was exposed until only her flannel pajamas covered her. Her chest heaved and her hands shook as she struggled both to remember and to forget what her mind had just been experiencing.

She looked out her window and realized that it was dawn. The sun was almost invisible through the clouds that constantly threatened to snow. There was a defused glow over the trees and buildings outside, bathing everything in light, making every wind-swept snow drift visible.

It almost looked peaceful.

She put her feet down on the cold carpet that lined her spacious room. She stood there wriggling her toes for a moment, an exercise she was convinced forced her feet to get used to whatever temperature they were in (and that Mike was convinced was just plain crazy). Satisfied that she was as warm as she was going to get until her father got up and turned up the thermostat, she walked over to her closet and opened it, her back turned to the rest of the room.

She stopped, her eyes growing wide.

She heard a sound behind her, a long, scraping slice like the sound of metal against metal. She closed her eyes in a silent prayer, then turned around slowly.

The room was empty. She knew it was for a fact, now. A few months ago she'd arranged the furniture into the corners and asked her parents for a new bed, one that you could not fit a person under, but went straight to the floor. She's told them that she liked the idea of having all that space to do her exercises in, but in reality it was for reasons just like this, so that she could be quickly assured there was nobody in her room that shouldn't be.

Allowing her dark eyes one last sweep of the room, she turned back to the closet and ruffled through the shirts she had there, settling after a moment on a black tank top that said dumpster across the front of it in glitter. She threw it hanger-and-all against the bed, then tapped her finger against her lip for a moment while deciding on her jeans.

Gripping each door of the closet in a hand she closed it again (it so rarely got left open these days) and headed toward her vanity.

There was a tickle in the back of her mind, a memory to do something that had almost reached the point of habit, but not yet. She opened her jewelry box and took out a small silver packet with twenty-eight pills in it, each in their own tiny blister-pack bubble of air. She snapped one small pink pill out and pressed it between her lips. She swallowed it without water and the ritual was done, the twinkle in the back of her brain quelled for another day.

She removed her top, and her shoulder cried out in pain when she did. She craned her head awkwardly to look at the scar on her left shoulder, administered by one of the Tees months ago and never having healed quite right. She tisked, then reached for the shirt she had picked out and slid it down over her head.

She stopped again when it was almost completely down over her, swearing that she heard something.

-Nok - Kock-

She turned toward her bedroom door even though she knew that wasn't where the sound was coming from. She glanced briefly at the glowing red numbers on her alarm clock. It was not yet six in the morning. Mike shouldn't be picking her up for school for at least another two hours.

-Knock!-

That one was louder, and she decided that she had better go down and see who it was before one of her parents woke up and did it, because if it was Mike at this hour it would be the last time he would be allowed to knock on the door until long after Christmas.

She moved down the stairs with the speed and grace of a pedal on a breeze, her long black hair continuing in that direction as the rest of her turned toward the front door, released the latch and turned the knob, then opened it just a little.

"Shouldn't open the door... without asking who it is first," Xander Drew said, leaning his entire body against the doorframe. He was covered in blood and snow. "Never know who might be there."

Her eyes grew wide and she opened the door the rest of the way. Xander fell and crashed onto the hardwood floor, slamming his teeth against it as he did so.

CHAPTER TWO
SEARCH

Mike wriggled his toes inside of his size eleven shoes, hoping that it would somehow force his feet to adjust to the cold -- or at least ward off frostbite as he walked knee-deep through a snow drift that seemed to go on for miles in every direction, pulling his parka tight to protect against the freezing wind.

He stopped a moment and looked at the ground around him for footprints or any sign that somebody had been there before him. He turned off his flashlight, realizing that he no longer needed it.

Strands of his hair had become frozen together, making them now just stems of yellow icicles coming out of his scalp. He shivered against a biting wind and wished to high heaven that he could get the Friends theme out of his head. It had been stuck there for several hours.

He saw a police officer about ten feet away, just coming into his peripheral vision. The tall man had a pot belly and still held his flashlight out in front of him, apparently not yet having realized its uselessness in the dawning hours. He held a smoldering cup of coffee in hand and brought it to blue lips at regular intervals.

Good, Mike thought to himself. *One of the officer's wives must have put on another pot.*

At the thought of it, he could almost feel the warm liquid traveling down his throat, thick and sweet with far too much sugar and just the slightest hint of cream. If he was lucky they'd still have some real cream, which had made the entire experience nothing short of perfect. The fat from it made the warm from the coffee last hours instead of minutes.

Licking his lips, he forced his eyes away from the coffee and back to the wilderness ahead, a frown making his cracked, freckled cheek-bones smart. He stumbled once against the mounting snow, then pressed forward.

It's been twenty days, he reminded himself, feeling his foot dig into the virgin powder. Realizing that it was now morning, he corrected himself. *It's been twenty-one days. Twenty-one days since Derek escaped, and since then nobody has gotten a look at him.*

There had been sightings. Many, to say the least. It seemed that for the last twenty-one days, every time a shadow moved in the night or a sound was heard echoing from the winter darkness, it had been Derek Smith back to finish the job he'd started months ago and kill them all one by one. But as for somebody actually seeing him... that had yet to happen. And in a town where there was more than one thing out there to make noises in the night, one could hardly pin ones hopes on them.

What there had been, however, where signs of his presence.

The night after he broke out there had been a break-in at The Factory. His fingerprints had been found all over several of the video game terminals. One even had a spot of his blood on it, though god only knew how he had come to shed it.

The night after there had been two occurrences. One had taken place in the city morgue. One of the coroners had come in to close up for the night and had found the body of Derek's father strewn across the operating table. The body had been ripped apart, much like many of Smith's victims months ago -- and his hand was missing.

That same night, an old man answered his doorbell only find a flaming brown paper bag left on his porch. It was a childish prank that Derek, Mike and Tommy had often played when they were young, filling a bag full of a dog's excrement and putting it on a doorstep. When the man would try to stomp out the fire, he would get it all over his shoes and legs.

Only this time, when the man had attempted to put out the blaze the aforementioned hand had been inside, causing the elderly man to go into cardiac arrest. He died short hours later as doctors attempted to revive him.

Somewhere deep inside him, Mike knew that Derek had gleaned a sick sense of self-satisfaction from that incident in particular.

Having come a few feet over the snow bank he took another look around, squinting against the wisps of air that made his eyes water and want to close. Again, there was nothing. No sign of life whatsoever, except the occasional squirrel. He sighed, the air forming a cloud as it came out of his mouth, hanging for a moment before rising up and eventually disappearing. It was what Mike feared the most. That, like his breath, Derek was just hanging around for a moment or two after being released -- and that then he would disappear, and the only thing left of him would be a town that would always be gripped in fear.

He heard the snow crunch just over his right shoulder. He turned and clenched his gloved fists in one quick motion, but his grip automatically relaxed when he saw Officer Banner holding out a paper cup filled with coffee toward him, the cup balanced precariously in his thick mitten.

Mike nodded in thanks as he took it carefully, not wanting to spill a drop of the precious liquid.

"You looked like you could use it," Banner said, watching as he took a cautious first sip. "You've been at this all night. There's bagels waiting at the parking lot when you get back. If you wait a bit, the wives are talking about putting on some ham and sausages -- maybe even a boiled egg or two. You should head back and get some."

Mike nodded. "I will. Believe me, I will. I just want to get this quadrant mapped off first. We need to know where he is." He took a much longer gulp of the java.

"Slow down, son. You'll burn your mouth off like that."

He was right of course, and Mike could already feel the numbness of liquid burn all over his mouth. But more importantly, he could feel it in his gut and chest. Still, he slacked off.

"You're the only one out here besides the wives not wearing a badge, son. Why're you doing this to yourself?"

"How much ground have we covered since you gave me my last cup?" Mike asked, not responding to the question.

"At least two miles. We'll know better in a few minutes, when all the squad leaders radio in their reports."

Mike shook his head and bent down to look over the snow at eye-level, looking for any inconsistency in the sea of white. "He wouldn't come out this far," he grumbled to himself.

"I don't know," Banner grinned, tipping back his parka with his thumb to look up at the rising sun. "I've seen them come out further than this. When we were huntin' down the Snakes, they were stretched out over miles keeping in contact somehow -- the furthest one was twenty clicks into the north wilderness, almost to Canada. We felt lucky that we'd nailed him before he made it, too."

"I didn't say he couldn't," Mike corrected, handing the now empty cup to the officer. "I said that he *wouldn't.* I don't think Derek would come this far out -- away from people. It means he has to go farther to play his little pranks -- plus he likes to be near the aftermath. Likes to watch the masses talk and scream and be paranoid. It's his favorite part."

Banner eyed Mike for a moment as he rose to his feet and brushed the snow off of his pant leg before it set in and made him more moist than he already was. "You knew him, didn't you?"

Mike nodded, but did not look back. "He was one of my best friends."

There was a long silence then as Mike stared into the

wilderness with his fists tight, daring Derek to jump out at him. To attack and get it over with. To end the wait. The silence was interrupted by a snow bird singing its morning praise and scraping its talons against the bark of a nearby tree. Mike sighed, then turned with the officer back the way they'd come. He winced in pain and brought a hand to his right side to stop it at the source.

Banner regarded him with a look of even greater concern then, but decided not to voice it, as the both of them imagined the taste of ham, sausages -- and maybe boiled eggs, too.

But inside, Mike was looking around, taking in every square inch of land as they walked back, studying for any place that Derek could be hiding -- any place he could start looking when it came time again.

𝄐

Cathy lay Xander's head upon the inflatable back rest that had adorned the downstairs bathtub since her sister Trina was an infant. He fought it for only a moment, then relaxed his neck against the foamy material as she loomed over him, the ends of her black hair tickling his face and chest. He opened his eyes for the first time since he had collapsed in her hallway. It caught her attention and she returned the gaze with soulful brown eyes. He was trying very hard to look alert, but both pupils were lazy and one eye was open further than the other, then they switched, like scales that could not reach balance.

"Are you hurt?" she asked curtly, trying to disguise the pain she felt at seeing him like this. She avoided continued eye contact by removing his socks. She had managed to coax his pants and shirt off of him while he was throwing up in the toilet, but had had to explain to him several times not to remove his underpants. She still wasn't sure he understood why.

"N... No. No," Xander replied, his thick brown hair weighed down flat against his head with congealed blood, making it look blackish red. "'Mjus all fucked up."

She glanced back at the bathroom door to make sure it was locked tight, then grabbed a towel from a nearby shelf and rolled it into itself, forcing him to lift his back and then using it to raise it slightly. "Why is that?" she asked, her confusion making the stress and concern show through a little. She pushed some of the hair out of his eyes, making no attempt to hide her disgust as long tendrils of bodily fluids stuck to her fingers. "I thought that after you -- after Black Womb -- went out, you were supposed to get all (what's the word?), *rejuvenated* or something?"

He nodded, which visibly took a great deal of energy. "It usually comes out when I sleep, so I feel all rested. Last night it forced itself out. I tried not to go to sleep, but it came anyway. So I didn't sleep, my mind didn't go to sleep. It just -- it took over."

She nodded, tending to a few parts of him that seemed to be extremely strained... his wrists, neck, and the femoral artery in his leg she'd come to learn was very tender after a transformation. She didn't even think he realized that yet. She reached out and turned on the faucet, pouring hot water into the tub. If it had just been him she would have made it boiling, but as she pulled up her sleeves she added a hint of cold for her own benefit, grabbing the softest cloth she could find as she pulled the lever for the shower head to turn on.

"Did you kill anyone?" she asked, fighting to keep her voice even as the carefully dabbed the blood off of his hands, watching as it was discarded and floated along the top of the water all the way down the drain.

He closed his eyes, and after a moment, a single tear escaped one, turning red upon contact with his still spattered cheek.

She was wearing a floppy night-gown with teddy bears printed on it.

He nodded.

"Was it anyone we know?" she sighed, he voice wavering now.

"No," he replied after a moment, his voice solemn. "I think -- I think it was a child."

She dropped the washcloth without realizing it, her mouth pulling inward and making her chin wrinkle. She forced herself to pick the cloth back up and continue. "Oh."

"I think it was looking for Derek, but it found her first. I remember it like it was a dream -- it was remembering the way Derek killed Sara, then it was remembering the way Sara looked when she died -- then, the way Sara looked when she lived, as a child... and then it saw a child that looked like that..."

He looked down at the water, the level of which was rising steadily as the blood poured off him, revealing the pink skin underneath. It crossed his mind to just slide down and let the water envelop him. To open his mouth and breathe deep of it and let it fill his lungs until there was no life left in him. "I want this to end, Cathy," he said, his head snapping in her direction. He made full, open eye-contact with her.

Her tears came easily now, as the comfort of her bed upstairs seemed so far away. "I know," she choked, reaching out her arms in an embrace that he gladly accepted, bringing her body close to his, getting soaked as the boiling water poured down -- but could not wash away their sins.

Nothing could.

CHAPTER THREE
CUP

August Styles took a brown paper bag out of her locker, then opened it and pushed her face down in it to see what her mother had packed for her today. It was a turkey sandwich (not real turkey, the kind that came from a can and got mixed with mayonnaise), a can of off-brand cola and a Jell-O pudding cup, complete with small plastic spoon.

She smiled a little as one of the more obnoxious boys in the school walked past her and purposely bumping into her. Her body slumped against the sharp metal door for a second, then she righted herself. She ignored the boy and turned down the top of the bag, placed it carefully into her sack, then closed the locker door.

The locker had no lock, which some said defeated the purpose, but she could never remember the combination anyway and she could always see it from her classroom. Besides, the only thing she kept in there were two pictures, her lunch, and her gym clothes. She looked at the door for a second, almost absent-mindedly, then turned toward class. They were learning more about trees to-day, and she had always loved in when they talked about things that grow.

August was fifteen, had blonde hair, and blue eyes. She was short, and quite chubby to match, but was usu-ally wearing a rather large smile, one that was infectious to anyone else that saw it. She was happiest when she was at school, but she also liked doing things afterwards too, with her mom and her friends. Her clothes rarely matched, but she found she rarely noticed and absolutely never cared. She was friends with all the teachers, and most of the students.

She also had Down syndrome.

That was the technical name for what made August a little different from most of the other people at Coral Beach High School. Her mother told her that nobody was exactly the same, and that she just had the special honor of her difference having a special name.

Now she walked to her classroom and sat down at her desk near the back. Mrs. Foxx, their teacher for everything except gym, was at the front of the class going through the attendance sheet of who had been on the bus but was not in class. She had short brown hair and thick glasses that curled upwards at the ends into points with little sparkles on them. She was usually smiling once class started, but not right now. Right now all her wrinkles seemed like they were trying to stretch down and escape from her face, like they did every day when she was doing attendance.

There were three other people in the room. There should have been four. One was missing.

There was Tim, he was her best friend. He was really

smart, and he had shaggy brown hair and glasses that re-minded August of the bottoms of Coke bottles.

There was Robyn. She was younger than them. She was only twelve. She was really pretty, August thought, and she liked to draw things while she was in class.

Cory was here today, he was big and always had a smile and was laughing and trying to make jokes, even though Mrs. Foxx once told him that his jokes "Were not in good humor." He had glasses too, and a buzz-cut hair-do. People called him Buzz sometimes and it frustrated him horribly.

The only person missing was David, but he was miss-ing a lot.

The classroom itself was full of colors. There were plenty of things on the wall, a few height charts, Robyn's drawings, and hand-prints each that of them had made on their first day of class. August's hand-print was purple. She had always liked purple. There were different spheres hanging from the ceiling, each one a different color. They were the different planets in the solar system. There were four computers lining the far wall, one for each of them. Tim's had a program on it where you could type some-thing in and a purple monkey would say it, which Au-gust had always thought was funny. Partly because it was purple.

August opened her science book and turned to the part about trees. There was a picture of an evergreen there, and she thought for a second about how pretty it looked, tak-ing up the entire height of the page.

All at once her stomach started to hurt. It felt like it had done a flip inside her. Her face crunched in pain and she bent over in her desk.

"August?" Mrs. Foxx asked from the top of the class, holding her dry-marker and getting ready to write something on the board. "August are you okay? Do you need to go to the bathroom?"

August nodded. Her face was already very pale.

Mrs. Foxx nodded.

August got up and made her way through the brightly colored door. The other three students watched her go.

A worried look came over Tim, stretching out his thin, long face.

Reverend Robert Gallagher moved quickly to one side as August bumped past him, nearly falling over as his entire weight shifted from one foot to the other. He steadied himself quickly, then turned to frown at the child as she bolted down the hallway. He considered calling out to her and telling her to slow down, but decided not to bother, instead turning and continuing his walk toward his office.

He wore a dark blazer with suede patches on the arms, the kind of suit which looked like it should be worn with a tacky tie... but no tie was there, only a paper-white collar. Carrying his briefcase by his side, he appeared quite the oddity to anyone who did not understand his specific place at Coral Beach High School. He was aware of the contradiction, to the point that he had decided to poke a bit of fun at it, putting an Ichthys on the side of his briefcase.

Gallagher had been brought on board as the newest

Guidance Counselor to help console the youth at Coral Beach High through the everyday trials of adolescence as well as the often remarkable situations that presented themselves in this particular facility. He recalled Principal Shnieder saying those exact words to him, just as he passed a section of hallway where the molding and paint were slightly discolored. It had been replaced after an eight foot tall black animal had broken through it and attacked several students.

All the same, Gallagher had taken the position with a degree of pleasure. He had been trying for years to get young people into his church to console them and help them, only to find that young people were not interested in faith.

"When you can't get the world to come to you, you go to the world," he chuckled softly to himself as he turned the last corner before his office door, situated very close to both the bathroom and Shnieder's office -- one of which he regarded as a dumpsite of dung, the other where it was created.

He lifted his right arm high, revealing the watch he had been given on his tenth anniversary with the church. He let out a guttural sound as he realized that he was going to be late again. He rubbed his tired, bloodshot eyes and made sure once again that his balding head of hair was not wild and crazy. He quickened his pace, so much so that he barely noticed Xander Drew sitting against the wall outside his home-room, waiting for classes to begin.

He afforded Xander a quick nod, which was not returned. The gesture (or lack thereof) didn't seem to be an act made out of unkindness. The boy simply seemed to be off in his own little fantasy world -- and not a particularly happy one at that.

Adding it to an ever-growing list of mental notes, Gallagher finished the last few strides to his office, his name freshly painted on the glass front.

The child in him couldn't help but wonder what new challenges the day might bring him.

Cathy stared at the open window of Chem room 103, examining the snow-covered trees and buildings that surrounded the school with a concentration she'd never had before, wary of the things that could be hiding behind them.

When she turned back to Miles' lecture she realized that she must have drowned out more than she thought as she picked up half-way into a sentence on a topic she did not remember him starting.

"... a chemical element that has the symbol Tc and the atomic number 43," he explained, marking the letters 'tc' and the number '43' in bright pink on the dry board. "The chemical properties of this silvery grey, radioactive, crystalline transition metal are intermediate between rhenium and manganese. Its short-lived isotope 99mTc is used in nuclear medicine for a wide variety of diagnostic tests. 99Tc is used as a gamma-ray free source - -"

"Gamma rays?" Tommy interjected, as though he had only heard those two words.

"Yes, Thomas. Gamma Rays. A form of electromagnetic radiation or light emissions of a certain frequency produced from sub atomic particle interaction, such as radioactive decay and electron positron annihilation; most are generated from nuclear reactions occurring within the interstellar medium of space. However, as I was about to say, technetium is a gamma-ray *free* source of beta particles, which can be used to treat medical conditions such as eye and bone cancer."

Tommy was thoughtful. "So, if this is a gamma-free source of this, then there must be a way to get it that had gamma rays, right?"

"Yes. It's still used in some countries."

"For medicine?"

"Yes," he smiled, delighted that he'd caught the boys attention. He had been trying to for several months now.

"Wouldn't that turn people into the Hulk?"

The smile left his face. "No, Thomas, it would not."

"Sure it would," Tommy urged. "That's how the song goes, isn't it? Dr. Banner, belted by gamma rays, turned into the Hulk, Ain't he unglamou rays!"

"Banner didn't turn into the Hulk *because* of the gamma rays," corrected a scrawny kid with thick glasses and bad acne near the front of the class. "The transformation of the gamma rays latched onto a long-dormant personality inside his brain caused by his multiple personality disorder."

Tommy pondered this a moment. "Ok, so what if someone with multiple personality disorder was hit by gamma rays --"

"That's not what gamma rays are used for," Miles spat."Now if you want to consider this discussion, I suggest you drop this course and join 'flights of fancy 101'."

Tommy stared blankly at him a moment, then leaned

over toward the person next to him and whispered, "Why wasn't that on my course sheet this semester?"

Miles' head fell, and he let go a long sigh, rubbing the bridge of his nose.

Cathy turned back toward her desk, opened her exercise book to a fresh page, and began to write.

Tommy Irons watched the pool game from the other side of the Factory, taking a sip of his Diet Coke and playing with the tips of his gelled hair, which always seemed to be just a little too long to be spiking up, but he did it anyway.

She couldn't remember if Tommy had actually been at the Factory on the night Jamie was killed, and the more she thought of it the more it made her head hurt. She remembered seeing him there that day because Mike had punched him in the arm a few hours before. Had he left right after that? She wasn't sure. After a few moments of going back and forth on the subject she decided that it didn't matter all too much and to just leave it alone, continuing the paragraph from where she had left off.

He wore a big grin across his face, and together with his pointed chin it always made his face appear to be the shape of a heart. He was tall and lanky with long legs that ended comically at his big feet that looked like a clowns on him. Next to him, Fred Windsor (who everyone called Sud) slurped his own Diet Coke.

Sud was short and bulky and still caught in those awkward years when some parts of the body seem to be growing faster than others, his arms hanging further down than they should have. This was exaggerated by the baggy sweaters and jeans he seemed to wear perpetually. His head was always shaved, except for a five o'clock shadow around the ears, and made his brow seem all the more pronounced, punctuated by a deep scowl and beady eyes.

Apart they were both likely targets of a snicker or two, but together they were outright hilarious, one tall and skinny and the other short and big. They looked like they had just stepped out of an episode of Fat Albert. Both men were almost always misunderstood by their friends and peers. It was easy to misinterpret Tommy's crude comments and Sud's constant mimicry his friends as signs of stupidity and inauspiciousness, but in fact they were just trying their best to do what every kid at Coral Beach High was trying to do : fit in. And most days it seemed like they would do anything to do it.

That's why he picked them.

"Hey, guys," smiled Derek Smith, as he walked over to the three of them.

If she had been uncertain as to whether or not Tommy and Sud had been there, she flat out *knew* that Derek had not been there. Nobody could be sure, but it had been accepted that he had been in his house, while all this was going on. That he'd watched as Jamie had been attacked by Genblade and Spider -- and that in the opposite direction, the Black Womb had been watching as well, both young killers learning *how* to kill by watching two of the best. But she wanted to get Derek in as soon as possible, and she'd wanted someone to come over and start talking to Tommy and Sud. At first she was going to use Grendel, but had decided against putting him in, at least for now. She wasn't going to say he was never there, but she saw no harm in lying by omission when it came to the man that had hurt her so much.

She tapped her pencil against her pad and her mind began to drift. She felt horrible that at the same time that her friend's life was at an all-time low, her relationship with Mike seemed to be hitting an all-time high again finally.

She stopped tapping her pencil as she remembered how far she and her lover had fallen the last time they had gotten so close, and suddenly became very, very afraid; her pupils dilating and her lungs growing short of breath.

Even though she was trying to make a conscious effort not to think it, her brain screamed at her: *What else could go wrong?*

Xander let his head fall back and thud against the painted brick of the school corridor.

"Ow," he said emotionlessly. He was sure he could feel the impact reverberating through his skull, as if it were an echo in an empty room. *Your mind is an empty room,* he snickered to himself sarcastically.

The bell to end home room shattered the quiet of the corridors. It was only then that he realized just how 'turned up' his enhanced senses had become in the silence, the sudden noise making him cup his ears so tight they formed suction.

Classmates poured out of their classrooms, heading off to the first classes of the day like sheep moving from field to field, each one moving past him without paying him any notice. He watched their legs and feet pass by one by one, recognizing a few of them by what they wore and guessing the rest. They passed him as though he was a statue, until eventually one pair of legs stopped squarely in front of him.

He didn't need to look up to see who it was.

He was so tall that Xander couldn't see his waist. His ripped blue jeans were baggy and rolled up at the cuffs. They were soaking wet from the knees down and led into new brown boots, the kind that you had to lace up every time. Xander had always hated footwear like that. If he could have gotten away with wearing loafers or velcro-laced shoes every day and not had Cathy kill him, he would have.

"Mike," Xander regarded, still not looking up at him.

Mike sighed, then knelt down until he was just a little above eye-level with Xander. "How's it going?"

Even though Xander had not altered his gaze, Mike had placed himself in a position where he would have to shift his vision to break eye contact. In doing so his entire body became uncomfortable, as if the illusion that he was in fact a part of the wall had been destroyed. "Been better," he answered, his voice low as he found a new point just beyond Mike's head to stare at.

Mike nodded slowly. He glanced at the clock on the wall and decided that he had a little time before his Biology teacher got irreparably mad at him, then sat down next to his friend. His legs cracked with relief as the hours of pressure he had built into them was relieved. "I hear you there," he sighed, letting his own head fall back against the brick. "Ow."

Xander took deep breath through his nose, then exhaled. A confused look passed over his face, his brow furrowing in deep thought. He turned slightly toward Mike, taking in another, shorter breath. "Have you been in the woods?"

Mike nodded. "Out helping the cops look for Derek."

"How's that going?"

The look on Mike's face said all that was necessary.

"That good, huh?" Xander groaned, turning back toward his staring spot on the opposite wall.

"Every day we don't catch him, the area he could be hiding in expands just a little more. We're just lucky that the public transportation departments are working with us, not selling any bus tickets to people who match Derek's description, or we'd already have the entire country as a search zone."

"And you're sure he's on foot?"

Mike raised a hand, counting each point off on a finger as he made them. "No public transport, no stolen vehicles, nobody stupid enough to pick up a hitchhiker matching his description. Unless he's learned to sprout wings and fly, Derek Smith is still somewhere in the Coral Beach Coral Cove area."

Xander nodded. The silence between them became palpable then. It was tradition among good friends. One told what one did last night, the other told theirs. So when it was obvious that it was Xander's turn to speak, the silence became a very tangible thing.

"I bumped into Cathy coming in," Mike said finally, breaking the quiet. "She told me what happened."

Tears welled up in Xander's eyes, but he pushed them back. "Have the police heard anything yet?"

"Not when I left, no," he replied, resting a hand on Xander's shoulder. "They'll probably blame it of Derek. It fits his usual M.O."

"That's a great comfort," Xander said sarcastically, unable to fight the tears now as they dribbled down and pitted against his dark green shirt. "That I won't be blamed for killing a young girl -- again. Really, a weight has been lifted off my shoulders."

Mike's entire upper frame seemed to fall into the lower. "We know now that it's possible for you to get control. All we need to do now is - "

"Control?" Xander yelled, whipping his arm out from behind him. He let the force of the motion carry through to his fingertips, thrusting a three-inch long serrated talon from each one of them, an action accompanied by a quick sucking sound and a dribble of blood from the digits. "Is this what you call control?" He brought the razor-sharp shards of bone up to his cheeks and dragging them down, making four ridged slices.

"Jesus!" Mike screamed, grabbing Xander's arms and pulling them back. As he watched in horror, the flesh on Xander's face seemed to take on a life of its own, bending and shuffling until the cuts became scars, and then the scars gave way to the pale flesh he had started with, marked only by a few thin trails of blood.

Xander slumped back into his relaxed pose. "I don't even have control over whether or not I bleed," he said, his voice filled with despair and hopelessness.

Mike watched intently as the claws slowly reverted back into Xander's fingers, refusing to relinquish his grip on his friend until they did. "Then we'll have to find something new. Something to reign it in. We'll get there, man. We will."

Xander turned and was about to say something very unsavory in response to Mike's well intentioned words when he stopped, his gaze shifting past him. "Cathy," he said, his voice immediately warmer.

She smiled down at him, big and bright, with ruby lips and pure white teeth as she approached the pair. She regarded Xander first, then bent down and kissed her boyfriend, lightly, on the lips.

Xander closed his eyes and gave his head a little shake, his still-enhanced sense of sound picking up the wet smacks of their lips pressing together, something that was disturbing enough to him without his powers amplifying the experience.

"How are you?" she asked Mike. "Did you eat anything today?"

Mike nodded, allowing himself a smile. In truth, even in the horrible situations their lives had managed to become wrapped up in, he couldn't keep it off his face whenever she was around. "Yeah. Some of the wives made a big breakfast for everyone."

"Sounds good. Keep it up," he grinned. She turned to Xander, her expression more serious and concerned, the smile smaller and pasted on now. "And you?" she asked him, her eyes sparkling with the pain she felt for him.

He wiped the sleeve of his jacket across his face, drying the blood and tears. "I'm fine," he lied through his teeth. He wondered if a lie was still a lie if all parties involved knew the difference.

She nodded, agreeing with the truth behind the statement if not the statement itself. She reached out and hugged him tightly, kissing him briefly on the cheek. When their bodies parted she tweaked the kiss away with her thumb, giving him another grin.

The three of them sat in silence then, each trying to think of something to say.

"Oh," Cathy said, reaching into her book-bag and pulling out several pages of paper, all folded together neatly, and handed it to Mike. "Here. I was reading this article the other day on dietary supplements, and how some of them can actually reduce the risk of heart disease. They were saying that..."

Xander turned his head until it faced almost perfectly forward and stared at his spot on the wall again.

"... eems pretty cool. I saw something on CNN like that, said with just a little gene..."

Slowly their conversation started to drone away from him, their voices sounding more and more like they were underwater, until finally it was just a hushed mumble, like the teachers on the old Peanuts cartoons.

"... thought about us, because if we were, you know, ever going to..."

Xander got up suddenly and without a word. He pushed himself off from the wall and walked down the hall the way Cathy had come, shoving his hands deep into his pockets.

Mike and Cathy turned to watch him go, waiting until he was long out of sight to say anything.

Mike turned to her, a puzzled look on his face. "What was that all about?"

She frowned, moving in close to him, putting her back

against the wall. "We're losing him," she said softly, no longer feeling the need to hide the pain she felt. She never felt the need to hide anything from him.

He wrapped his arm around her instinctively, pulling her close into a lover's squeeze. "I know. I can't figure a way to pull him back either -- and with everything that's going on, I don't have time to think of one."

"We have to help him Mike. He needs it. More than that... I don't want to think about what'll happen to us if we can't keep him from going over the edge."

Mike raised his eyebrows. It was the first time he's heard her vocalize any sort of worry that Xander might hurt her, although he'd suspected that she'd thought it before. Not knowing what to say, he turned his head and kissed her on the top of hers.

Huffing, she bent her head back and knocked it against the brick wall. "Ow."

CHAPTER FOUR
FAITH

Calla McFadden stood alone in the smoker's section just off the south wing, brushing ash-stained snow from side to side with the long heel of her leather winter boot. She did this over and over again until there was a semi-circle of clean flat snow big enough for her to sit in, and then did, pulling the tail of her coat down. Her face had a healthy roundness to it, along with the rest of her. Her eyes seemed too big and sparkly for her head, her mouth a little too small and cutesy, both outlined by generously sprinkled freckles. Her hair (naturally a light brown) was mostly jet black and straight now, with one curled lock that hung in the left corner of her face dyed hot pink.

Samara Reynolds was standing next to her with her arms crossed defiantly in front of her chest. She wore a padded vest in lieu of a jacket, her hair done up in a bun with long stands spider-webbing out the back of it. A few similar strands hung down in front of a slender face, giving her a spiteful look. She watched as Calla reached into her pocket and withdrew a small plastic bag that she opened and started picking through. "What do you think you're doing?"

Calla looked up quizzically, as if completely unaware that she was doing anything out of the ordinary. She smiled politely and tilted her head to one side in a way that Samara had come to recognize meant that she was about to say something either very patronizing or very condescending. Or, in this case, both. "I'm rolling, sweetie. What are you doing?"

"I know that," Samara huffed, crouching down to be on the same level with Calla but not actually sitting, her eyes darting back and forth for any sign that they might be seen. "Why are you doing it here?"

Calla looked down at the clumpy green substance in the baggie, then back up at her friend, an annoyed and comically exasperated expression on her face. "Because when I do it at home, my parents get mad."

"I think they'll get mad when you do it here too, Cal."

She shot the shorter girl a look. "All the crap that goes on at this school, do you really think they're gonna get on my case about possession?"

Samara nodded slightly, conceding to the point as she lay her back against the wall and relaxed a little.

Calla pinched the marijuana and sprinkled it onto a thin piece of paper she'd taken out of her jeans pocket, dipping her hand back into the bag twice to get more before deciding it was enough. She turned to Samara expectantly, who reluctantly produced a single flattened cigarette from her vest. Calla rolled its tip back and forth between her fingers, sending tobacco raining down onto her concoction until the paper appeared full enough, then licked along the inside edge until it was damp and rolled it together, the glue holding properly as she twisted both ends so that nothing would come out. "There, see?" she smiled at her friend, holding up the joint between her thumb and forefinger triumphantly. "That's how it's done."

Samara rolled her eyes and plucked the bone from between Calla's fingers, then placed it into the top pouch on her vest.

"Hey, I was gonna smoke that," she fake-whined, pouting out her tiny lower lip a little.

"Come on, Cal. We've got Geometry. What's with you, anyway? You've smoked *maybe* three times in your life. Suddenly, what, you're a pothead now?"

Calla scoffed, bracing herself against the bricks as she got up. "Just trying to enjoy life, that's all," she murmured, brushing the snow off of her jeans until there was hardly any there anymore. "Speaking of which, we gotta find us a couple of guys. It's been a while since we've really partied, y' know?"

"Excuse me, I have a guy."

"That's not what I'd call Travis."

"Shut up!" Samara laughed, slapping Calla's arm. "Come on, we gotta get to class."

"Fuck that. Gimmie back the smoke," she demanded, though in a pleasant tone of voice, putting her palm out and motioning with her finger for the joint's return. "I'm gonna stay out here myself a while, if you're going in."

Samara tisked, tapping one foot against the ground as she pulled out the rolled up square of paper and placed it in Calla's open palm.

"Thank you very much," Calla beamed, her cheeks shining in the morning light when she did so.

"Whatever. I'm going to class. You need some serious help, girl," Samara said, smiling briefly before walking off to class.

Xander stalked the hallways of the school, his hands deep inside his pants pockets. He reached the front lobby looking out into the cold outside. He took a quick glance around the corridor for Shnieder. There were bullet holes in the walls. He stared at them and they stared back, like the gun that had put them there had given the concrete eyes. Walls had always been said to have ears that could hear and mouths that could talk, but now they had two holes for eyes that could see everything. Soon Coral Beach High would just sprout legs and walk away from him, he thought, transfixed in the dead gaze or the stone.

He pulled a cigarette pack and a lighter from either pocket and started toward the front door.

Outside the wind blew fiercely, making his coat dance and flap at his side. He barely noticed it, instead fighting against the breeze to light his smoke and using the small porch of the school for what little cover it provided. Finally the cherry lit and he took a long drag, feeling his tension melt away as his throat burned.

The healing factor made every puff feel like his first, his esophagus healing between breaths.

After a moment he stepped off the balcony and down the concrete stairs, fearful that the Shnieder was still about.

"Hello my son," came Gallagher's warm, instantly recognizable voice. He smiled up at Xander from just around the corner, leaning against the school in his winter coat.

Xander turned, surprised. "Father? What are you doing out here?"

"Not killing myself with those blasted sticks like you are, I'm happy to say."

Xander immediately threw the smoke to the ground behind him, pretending as though he had no idea what the holy man was talking about.

"Last night I was so pleased when I'd made my way through all the student case-files... and when I walked into my office this morning there was a whole new pile, marked M through Z'." He smirked. "I decided I needed some air, no matter how bitter it might be this morning."

"M-Z... so, you've read mine, then?" Xander poised, failing to hide his interest in the subject.

"Yes," Gallagher smiled, looking down at an odd shape he was unconsciously making in the snow with his feet. "In fact I was hoping to get you into my office if I got some time today... but now I guess that isn't necessary."

Xander raised an eyebrow, cautiously strolled over to the older man, then leaned against the school next to him. "What about?"

Gallagher opened his mouth to speak, then stopped. After a moment of continued silence, he chuckled to himself. "You know, in my line of work I get to listen a lot, and then I give my opinion and best advice, if it's warranted and appropriate... it never occurred to me how hard it was to start a conversation."

Xander grinned a little at this, and his face felt weird in

the expression, his suspicion of the good Reverend melting away at his clumsiness. "Just say it, Father."

"I'm worried about you, boy," he said, needing to get the words out as quickly as possible lest he trip over them again. "Tell me... are you feeling all right?"

Xander bit his lip, and now it was his turn to look down at his feet. "I don't know how to answer that, Father."

"A few months ago in my chamber, you told me you felt as though God had forgotten you... do you still feel that way, Alexander?"

The use of his full name made Xander flinch. He'd been named for a saint by the nuns that had overseen his adoption, and since then he'd never been comfortable with it being said by members of the clergy. It felt too formal, somehow. "No..." he said, meaning for it to be both the beginning and the ending of the sentence, then he continued. "... No, lately I feel as though God has been paying far too much attention to me."

Gallagher raised an eyebrow, then caught the child's meaning and nodded. "The Good Lord does test us all, my son... though I would agree, he seems to test some more than others. And there has been so much death..."

"They're the lucky ones," Xander interrupted, saying the words before his mind could filter them out.

"Excuse me?"

"All the people that I've buried -- I've noticed something about them. Most of them didn't deserve it. They were innocent. They were purity."

"Nobody deserves to die, my son."

Xander shot him a look. "I think you and I both know the difference of that, Father."

Gallagher said nothing in response, which Xander took as an agreement.

"What I've come to think is that death is God's reward for good people. He takes them out of this earth, so that they don't have to live in it anymore. I look around and I see all these people living here, so afraid of dying... but I'm not, Father. I'm afraid of living forever. Of watching all the good things in my life lift up to the heavens... because I know that if I'm right, I'll never get it. I'll never be released from this world."

Gallagher looked at him astonishment for a moment, then smiled.

"Something funny?"

"No," he grinned. "But I was going to ask how old you were, not to demean your sentiment."

Xander smirked, then let it fade. "Sometimes I do feel old."

Gallagher nodded, then patted him on the back. His body was angled as though he were about to leave. "My son, understand that when I say this, it is not as a faculty member nor as a priest. I wish to give you my best advice... as a man. Is that all right?"

Xander looked up, hopeful and a might curious.

"Find relief in the Lord, my son. No matter what you believe... I have never seen it steer anyone wrong."

Gallagher turned and walked up the concrete steps, clouds of breath spiraling over his head every time he exhaled on his way back into the school.

Xander stood there in the snow for a moment, his brow furrowed as he bounced the idea in his head over and over again. His head rose slowly as a flash of inspiration sparked in his head so bright that his eyes lit up. A smart, sinister grin played over his lips as he laughed at his idea, then jumped out of the snow onto the pavement and headed back up the stairs into the warm.

CHAPTER FIVE
WITH

August Styles sat in the bathroom floor with tears streaming down her young face. There was cold water touching her hand on the floor, but she made no attempt to move it as she leaned against the dingy toilet, comfortable for the first time in what seemed like days.

Her chest quivered a little as her breath slowed from the breakneck pace they had been going, each one throbbing in her throat, strained from countless urges and heaves.

There was an odd taste in her mouth, like the tang of a penny, and her sinuses were assaulted with the scents of human waste and pine cleaner, stuffing her nose and making her eyes water even more.

Her stomach wretched again and she thought she might throw up for the tenth time, but instead it slowly calmed itself, like water brought to a boil then allowed to cool.

There was a clacking together of heels and tile floor moving steadily in her direction, and she turned away from the open stall door, hiding her face and trying not to get noticed.

The girl walked by at first, but then the sound of the heels stopped and the tall brunette stepped back a pace, looking in at August sitting on the floor. August recognized her instantly as Jennifer Bradley, a girl from her grade that wasn't particularly nice to her.

Jennifer glared at August for a moment, curled her lip, then grabbed the handle to the stall and closed it, leaving August alone once again. The sound of her heels moved away once again.

August's gut turned and she buried her head in the toilet and threw up again.

CHAPTER SIX
CHAINS

"This is a stupid idea." Cathy frowned, squinting through the gaps in the dried plywood and watching the sun set for the evening. Her arms were crossed across of her chest and her hair fell in two straight lines on either side of her down-turned face. Her bottom lip stuck out as a visual act of her dismay. "I just want to state that for the record."

"It's not a stupid idea," Xander heaved, wincing just a little as he watched Mike clamp the first large, metal cuff onto his right arm. It pinched his skin a little, and the jolt it caused wasn't altogether unpleasant. Thick, sturdy chains traveled from the half-inch-thick bonds to three huge copper circles that were screwed into the wall and then out the other side where a second cuff hung, waiting to be attached as well. "It's a smart idea. Waiting around for the bodies to pile up, that, was a stupid idea."

Cathy's frown only increased, her lip sticking out even more.

"As long as we're putting it on the record," Mike said,

careful of his tone when dealing with an obviously already frustrated girlfriend. "I think Xander's right. We've tried everything else to keep the Womb in check, and right now we do not have the time to devote to watching over it all night. This seems like the best option."

"Thank you," Xander smiled, giving Cathy an over-the-top nod to flaunt his victory.

"Whatever," Mike shrugged, picking up the left restraint. He pulled it to its fullest length, making Xander's arm jerk back to the point that it might have bent backward. It made Cathy flinch. In her mind, she could hear her friend's joints straining.

Mike clamped the second restraint shut with a loud clack that echoed off of the halls surrounding them, then gave them a firm tug on each side to make sure they would hold before stepping back a pace. He gave it all a once over, then nodded.

Xander's arms were stretched out as if he were on a crucifix.

Mike brought a hand up to his mouth as he surveyed the situation, a thoughtful look coming over him as he looked down at the base of the apparatus. "You sure we don't need the feet as well?"

Xander looked down, shuffling his legs in every direction, trying his best to get free to test the restraints. "I really don't think so," he said, still trying to get free. "It shouldn't be a problem. And, call me a whiner, but I don't want any uncomfortableness that isn't necessary to getting the job done."

"Cool," Mike nodded, holding up a key ring with two pairs of keys on it, one for each cuff and a duplicate. He took off one set and handed it to Cathy. "Come morning, if I can't make it over here to let him out I'll call you on your cell."

She nodded, unable to look at either of them. Her expression had gone from frustrated to angry as she snatched away the key.

"Make sure you leave it on..."

"*Okay*," she stressed, giving him the hint to drop it, which he did. Finally, after huffing twice, she turned to Xander. "Did I hear you say that this was Gallagher's idea?"

Xander nodded.

She raised an eyebrow at him. "One Guidance Councilor's a serial rapist, another worked for a evil genetics company that manipulated events for months to try and recruit you, then the third tells you to chain yourself up in an old church... and you listen?"

Xander smiled. He looked around the abandoned Catholic church, which the residents of Coral Beach had used until the back end burned down in the sixties. That part had been boarded off, but when the repair crew discovered that the entire place was rank with asbestos, they'd decided to just close it up and build a new one (which Gallagher now presided over). The rings that held his bonds to the wall had once held a large two-hundred pound cross there. It had hovered just slightly off the ground before some teenagers had stolen it and tied a freshman to it, setting him naked in the middle of the baseball field several years back.

All of the pews were empty and most were falling apart, just like the rest of the place. Many of the stained glass windows had been beaten in with rocks, but the confessional was still mostly intact, something that Xander found disturbing for some reason. "He didn't exactly put it like that," he said finally.

"How did he put it then?" she demanded.

"He told me to find relief with the lord."

Cathy's eyes widened slightly. Mike snickered. He'd seen that expression on her before.

"And *that's* what you took from that?" she said, taking a step closer and rapping him on the head with her knuckles.

"Ow. Stop it," he grimaced, trying in vain to bend his head away from her attack.

"What are you, dysfunctional? That is the most fucked up logic I have ever heard in my entire life! What is *wrong* with you?"

"Are you done?" he asked, as she finally stopped hitting him.

She sighed, shaking her head and making her hair dance in all directions. "Yes. Yes, I'm done. I just wanted it noted that this is -"

"A bad idea. Right, got it," Xander interrupted.

"Do you want us to stay until you transform?" Mike asked, putting his key in his pocket as he grabbed up his parka, already prepared to go out in search of Derek again. He winced a bit when he did, his side still sore.

"No," Xander said, forcing cheerfulness. "I don't think I would with you here anyway. I'd never go to sleep, and that would defeat the purpose."

Mike nodded, then took Cathy by the shoulders and led her out. Neither looked back, even as they snuck back out the front doors, closing them as they left with a loud slam.

Xander stared at the spot where they had disappeared, trying to get as comfortable as he could... and waited.

ᚠᚩ

Gallagher ran his fingers through his silver hair, ruining the comb over that he'd labored on in the faculty washroom just thirty minutes before. He stared at the pile of files in front of him, which seemed as though it was only growing.

When he'd been a child, his grandmother had told him stories about the Devil. She'd said that you could never rest when fighting the Devil, because it would never rest. Didn't have too. The Devil would just keep coming until it got the upper hand. Right now, he felt that the Devil was being represented primarily by file folders.

"No wonder the last three went crazy," he mumbled to himself, finishing off another spot of coffee.

A few minutes ago he'd finished a file on a particularly troubled young man named David Walton. A solitary boy, he was prone to jolts of enthusiasm and loud behavior, and was constantly striving for the attention of others, often causing him problems with the faculty and the rest of the student body.

Before that, there had been Evan Lucas, a young man with questionable social skills who seemed to be taking a darker spin on his adolescent misgivings around females. Both O'Toole and Shnieder had separately marked him on their observation list.

Prior to that had been Nick Carry, a student who had

always been the victim of ridicule, something to do with his appearance. That child hadn't even been seen in several months, with some reports stating that he'd gone to another school, but there was no record of the transfer ever happening.

He heard a sound up ahead of him, finally pulling his tired eyes away from the mountain of files that seemed to be growing out of his desk.

Leaning against the doorway to his office was a pudgy blonde girl with a long face. It was dirty and covered with that certain sparkle that could only be left by tears. She sniffed and turned her head downward as soon as he made eye contact with her.

He smiled, although there was pain and pity in it that he tried to hide, rising from his uncomfortable chair. "Can I help you?" he asked, motioning for her to come in if she wanted too.

She took a step forward, and now he could see the tiny white speckles of vomit that dotted the corners of her mouth.

"Are you all right?"

August looked up, her eyes welling up with tears once again. Her hands were both planted firmly around her stomach.

"It's my baby..." she sobbed, her voice whined, as she collapsed onto the floor.

Gallagher stood in shock for a moment before moving forward to help the girl up.

There was a tree in the courtyard of Coral Beach High,

pressed against the far wall directly in front of the rear exit. It was a massive elm that had been planted decades ago as a sapling when the town had still been a mining town, and had grown ever since even in times of poverty. There were names carved in it going all the way up, carved there when the trunk was young and close to the ground and carrying them to the sky as it went. Some said there were three generations of sweet-hearts, all on the one tree.

The leaves were green and full of rich veins despite the snow, turned up toward the sun that shone from over-head and nourished it. It sparkled and glowed, its halo stretching out in all directions until the entire courtyard was bathed in its heavenly glow.

CHAPTER SEVEN
PAST AGAIN

Xander took a deep breath, held it for a long moment, then exhaled and opened his eyes once again. Before him all he could see was blackness, without the slightest trace of light to give him any sense of direction or depth, and he blinked once or twice just to make sure his eyes weren't still closed.

The air around him stank like nicotine and old books, assaulting his senses over and over again with its stale odor. His face twitched with every scent of it, yet welcomed it, as it was the only thing letting him know that the void before him was real. There was a sickening taste in the back of his throat that carried the coppery tang of blood, but tinged with something else. It was sweeter than it should have been; with a bitter twist. It was like vomit when the only thing in your stomach had been sugar-water. He cleared his throat, trying to make the taste go away. It only made it stronger, and the sound he'd made echoed off the walls he could not see, his senses telling him that they were both far away and right in front of his nose, the information muddling his already confused brain. He held his breath for a moment, trying not to make any sound at all, so that the *confusion might stop. All at once pressure roared from his central plexus, rocketing into his spine and up his backside, finally exploding out of the back of his brain. He tried hard to scream, but now no sound would come. Had the pain been less, he would have mentally commented on the irony of that.*

After a few more moments of trying to scream, and the unbearable frustration of not being able to, he gave up, hanging his head down to stare at the floor that was took dark to make out, letting out a silent grunt of defeat.

Softly, a silky hand caressed his face, then tilted it upwards. As he looked up, the gentle person brought a cold, wet cloth to his head, nursing a gouge he hadn't even been aware was there. At first all he could see was the red cloth being used to treat him, and it looked huge, spreading up and taking a humanoid form. It confused him, and he hadn't realized how skewed his vision was until he had something to focus on. As his sight slowly but surely returned, he realized the reddish glob in front of him was actually the clothing of someone standing very close. The person bent down, revealing long black hair and soulful dark eyes in the shape of almonds. Her lips were thin and coy, the scent of her perfume unmistakable by those that knew it

Eve Spider looked at him, an intense pity in her eyes that he was not used to seeing. He stared in silent shock upon her beautiful demeanor for a long moment, as she finished wiping the blood from his brow and slid her hand down his face gently. "My poor, poor little Black Womb," she said softly.

He tried to respond, but again, nothing came. He choked back the frustration, sunk his head, then brought it back to her again. He opened his mouth in a silent plea, then shut it again, as if trying to illustrate his disability at this moment.

She nodded her head respectfully, bringing one finger to his lips. "I know... I know. Can't talk, can't move, can't see... can't do anything but sit there and wait. And what happens when you try?"

Pain shot through his body, exciting the nerve ending until they couldn't take it anymore, making him feel cold and numb. Then the healing factor kicked in, and started the whole process again.

"What the fuck!" he exclaimed. His eyes grew wide after a moment when he realized that he was somehow able to form words again.

She smiled at him and waved a finger in front of her, like a mother chiding a child. "Language, little man," she giggled, running a hand over his chest before letting it fall away completely.

He grunted once, almost just to prove that he could, then turned up to glare at her. "Why am I here, Spider?"

She smiled, rising to her feet again, stepping away from him so that he could see her. There was a noticeable tear in her otherwise perfect red gown, draped elegantly over her slender form. It was still there from when he'd killed her months ago, and his gaze lingered on it. "First you have to know where you are, then why you're here will become all too clear."

He sucked in his bottom lip, wanting very much to just close his eyes and ignore her rantings until eventually she went away. After a moment, he deciding to take the bait. "Okay... where am I?"

"Where you've been heading your entire life, and every time you try to avoid it you just end up chained, unable to move, unable to speak. Unable to do anything but sit there in pain and try to deny where you are and the reason for it."

He sighed in discontent. "Did you take a class on how to

answer direct questions with indirect responses, or is it a natural talent?"

She turned and glared at him for a moment, her ankle-length hair spiraling off in all directions from the inertia of it. Her features slowly softened into a coy smile that on any other woman could have been confused with seduction. "Maybe your question wasn't direct enough," she giggled.

Briefly, he longed for the days when she would just show up out of nowhere and slice him with unnecessarily long blades until he was unconscious. "Tell me where I am, Spider," he said sternly, mustering all of the confidence he had in him. Suddenly, there was a brilliant flash of light! Images began parading past his mind's eye, so fast that he couldn't get a clear bead on what was happening. Sara, being stabbed through the gut by Adam Genblade. Mandy with the life ebbing out of her. Sud shot dead in the halls of the school. Tommy beaten and useless. Warren falling victim to Genblade. Julie with her insides on the out. Cathy, laying in her own blood, dying... and Mike next to her, already dead and beginning to turn blue. Between each image were even more images, people he didn't even recognize. An Asian man who looked to be burning alive. A blonde woman crying as she held a lifeless newborn in her arms. A brunette woman, who just looked at him, her eyes full of pity and hate all at the same time. "Stop it!" he screamed, his body wrenching and convulsing with each new impulse.

"I'm just answering your question for you, my silly Womb," she cooed softly.

Suddenly the chains which bonded him were no longer there and he fell a foot or so to the floor, hearing muscles and bone crack with a wet snap even as he did so. His hands finally free, he brought them up to his head and started pounding at it as hard as he could, trying to make the images stop, succeeding only in feeding a migraine. He popped his claws in desperation, each splitting his skin with an audible -shluck- of ruptured flesh. Insane with pain, he brought the claws up to his temples and was about to start to gouge the images out, when there was a pressure against his wrists that stopped them. For a second he thought he might be in the chains again, but when he opened his eyes Spider was holding both of his wrists.

She raised his hands up high above his head until they touched the floor. At some point during the confusion he must have ended up on his back, the sensation being that he had flipped silently, and without feeling it. It was disorienting, a situation only buoyed by the fact that now he was flat on his back with Spider on top of him, binding his wrists over his head with one strong but delicate hand. "Poor boy," she said. "I often forget how young you are. You're just not as ready as you'll need to be for this, when it comes time."

"Ready... for what?" he said through clenched teeth, adjusting his arms against her grip.

"For hell, of course," she said in a teasing voice, swaying her hips about playfully, either side of her red gown on either side of him.

He paused for a moment, looking at her, and then around him. Even though there was still just the blackness, he now had the undeniable sense that he was being watched. That there was somebody else in the room. Lots of people, as point of fact, though he couldn't begin to think who. "You expect me to believe that this... is hell?"

"It's your hell, little Xander," she soothed, rocking her body back and forth, running her free hand from his face to his chest and then back again. "There are billions of hells... as many hells *as there are human souls. This, is yours."*

"So why are you in my hell, then?" he grinned, skeptical.

"Because you killed me," she said, bringing a hand to the slash on her side. When it came back it was covered in blood. "You killed me, and now I get to torture you for all of time. Isn't that just lovely? Think of all the people you'll have killing you by the time you get here for good. All those people you just saw, and oh so many more."

"I don't believe that," he spat defiantly, trying to rise against her but failing to.

"It doesn't matter," she said, her eyes full of mournfulness. "Some things are true whether you believe them or not."

"You can't play with me anymore, Spider. You can't fool me. Most of those people you showed me aren't even dead."

Spider smiled, but not out of happiness. For the first time, it seemed forced... as though she were trying to smile for his benefit. "But they will be, Xander dearest... and soon. And inside, you know exactly how it's going to happen... don't you?"

His gaze became distant and he turned to one side, the images returning to him.

Cathy pushed open the door to the battered old church, its heavy wooden frame moaning beneath her effort. She was about to walk in when she heard a loud, metallic sound echoing off of the tiled walls, and stopped. Even though the sun had been up for almost forty-five minutes, she suddenly became aware of how very dark it was in the dank, run-down cathedral. Broken molding and torn curtains hung from the ceiling and walls, making odd shapes out of the few strands of light that seeped in through the knotholes in the wood that boarded up the windows. Dust floated past the rays of sunshine, stirred up by the door, and were now swirling about like little tornados, making it seem like there was movement when there was none.

She took a deep breath and pushed her bangs back with one quick motion, making sure she had the full range of her sight. It was quiet again now... like a tomb. She stepped inside and closed the door behind her, as gently as possible. Suddenly, from behind her, the rattling sound came again, reminding her briefly of the sound of metal on metal, the sound Derek used to use with his blade as a way to psyche out his victims. The memory brought with it a cold chill that rivaled that of the fresh morning air. Her lungs started to ache, and she realized that she had neglected to breathe out, finally letting go of the tuft of air.

Summoning all her courage she stepped forward, crossing the five meters to the entry point of the main hall as soon as possible.

It was more open here, with more sources of light coming in through the gaping holes in the church's structure. Up in the distance she could see him now, chained up as if crucified.

She remembered when he told her the story of how he'd been crucified, months ago. He'd been on the verge of tears, as if facing the memory were making it happen again. She had, of course, been sympathetic... but had never been able to fully understand. Moreover, her young mind was unable to visualize the scene, despite all of the times she'd seen carvings of it in her grandmother's living room. Now that she saw it, the light coming in on his down-turned head and forming a halo, she felt pity well up anew in her gut. It seemed like such a shame, that it had come to this.

She could see the hair on his head, soaked down with the thin layer of congealed blood that accompanied each transformation each time he completely reverted back to the form of Xander Drew. His clothes were soaked down with it too, and despite the horridness of the image, she felt herself free of the thought that he would be naked, which sometimes happened. His right arm twitched and the chains holding him down rattled, amplified as it refracted off of the walls. She sighed in relief, chiding herself for not realizing what the sound was earlier.

"Xander?" she called out, trying to sound chipper. He was in a bad enough mood already, she wagered. Besides the obvious, sleeping in that position couldn't have done wonders to his back.

He grumbled something indiscernible and twitched against his restraints.

"Xander?" she said, a little more cautiously now as she stepped toward him.

"*Xander?*" *Cathy moaned, trying desperately to hold her intestines in as she looked up at him with tears in her hazel eyes. Blood covered his hands, and as they reached out to help her he found himself unable to retract his claws. Instead of taking her hand, he ripped into the tender flesh of her palm, scattering it against the nearby brick wall... and a stone.*

It was stone where they had once kissed, years ago. They were behind The Factory, he realized. She recoiled in pain, and when she did she faded from his view and into the darkness that enveloped the entire scene.

Xander screamed, thrusting his head back as he twisted under Spider's grip.

"That's it, baby. Scream," she cackled, holding him as she moved her hips back and forth, her form changing from herself to Cathy then Julie then back again as she twisted about. "You know how to get me there, don't you?"

"Please..." he whispered, his head turned on its side in defeat. "...Please, just stop. Let me be."

"I'm not trying to hurt you, Xander," she cooed with a calm voice that belied her malevolence. "I'm just trying to warn you. The man dressed all in white, and the right switch, and the thing you fear most. Six little angels all in a row, sparks will fly, and not just from the one with the electricity, either."

He turned toward her, brow furrowed. "You make no sense, has anyone ever told you that?"

She paused, halting her movement atop him. "Many people," she said after a moment. "But I was pieced together in a lab. How sane would you be?"

"You're insane."

She smiled at him wickedly, then reached around to something on her back. She leaned down and came in close to kiss him, stopping millimeters from his lips. "That may be true... but remember, this is all in your head... so what does that say about you?"

Their lips embraced, and he found himself enjoying the kiss despite the sadism of it... until she drew her sword from the holster on her back and plunged it deep into his right side. Into the heart of the Womb.

Xander thrust forward toward the sound of Cathy's voice, stretching the chains to their limit and letting out a horrible grunted scream through clenched, razor-sharp teeth.

She yelped loudly and jumped back out of his reach.

He stayed there, pulling against his restraints, his arms held at a ninety degree angle as he thrashed and twisted and tried to get at her. He snarled.

"Oh my god..." she said in a hushed voice, her hand raising up to her mouth as she looked upon him.

The black tar that made up Xander's womb form was gone, laying in a dark puddle at his feet... but the transformation was incomplete. His bone structure was still that of the Black Womb, covered so tightly by Xander's human skin that in places it became translucent and she could see the muscle underneath. His lower jaw was skill disjointed and angular to make room for extra, larger teeth.

His face bumped and contorted into the pronounced brow of the Womb, and Cathy saw for the first time just how much it resembled a Neanderthal man. The eyes themselves were his: small, human and blue... but their sockets were larger and slanted upward in a triangle, the remaining space half-covered by bleeding muscle and bone.

"Wom!" he bellowed, and just the tone of his voice and the anger in it made it clear to Cathy that the word it meant to say was not a nice one. She felt fear rise up inside her like vomit, ready to erupt and overcome her.

"Xander..." she said softly, wanting very much to reach out and touch his face, even starting the motion to do so, and then thinking better of it.

He growled deep within his throat, lowering his bile-covered head but never taking his eyes off of her, burning a hole into her with his gaze. "Wommmmmb...." he repeated. For a moment she could do nothing but stare at him, pulling the black leather of her jacket tight around her as he looked her up and down like a piece of meat. As she composed herself she convinced herself that if the chains had held him all night that they would continue to do so now, and she made a kind of sense out of the situation. It was like when you get woken up from a deep sleep, and you weren't quite awake yet - caught halfway in between.

"Sweetie..." she said as soothingly as possible, trying to hide the fear in her voice. "Sweetie, you have to wake up now, okay? It's time to wake up now."

Spider's visage changed to Cathy for a moment, then back to Spider. It was only now that he truly saw how much they looked alike.

"Mmm..." she hummed, licking his taste off of her lips as they finally parted. She released the sword from his gut. "Love you, baby..." she said mockingly.

"Woomb..." he spoke, and as he did, she could see the jagged teeth retracting somewhere into his complex skeletal structure, revealing the normal, human ones behind it. He was reverting.

"Yes, honey?" she asked, finally daring to get close enough to touch him on the side of the face, gently. He twitched once, but she did not flinch.

"Womb hates you," he said spitefully, like a child tossing an insult at an angry mother. The fact that he actually spoke words let her know that Xander was returning. He continued to glare at her, wanting very much to sink his claws into her, even as his brow sunk back into his scalp.

She frowned, trying not to take the words too seriously, but they sliced at her more potently than his talons ever could. Her lower lip quivered. She sucked it back and put her hand underneath his chin, raising his head up to meet her gaze. "But Cathy *loves* you," she said matter-of-fact-ly, leaning in and kissing him passionately on his distorted lips.

There was a pause when he tried to pull away, but she held his chin tight in her grasp, and he was weak from the transformation. Slowly he relaxed, and their lips began to move as one, with each other rather than against each other. Taking subtle cues from the other on what to do that came as naturally as the instinct to breathe.

Spider began to fade away, as the visions had before. As she did she tried to say something to him, but all he saw was her lips moving. Despite himself, a grin pried its way across his mouth as he left her there, in the darkness.

There was a noticeable pop as his jaw snapped back into its rightful place, allowing him to sink into the kiss. His eyes healed over, and he was Xander Drew again. She released his chin and he did not let go. She brought her hands behind his head, playing with the short hairs there and sending strange sensations rocketing throughout his body.

She ended the kiss and looked at him, finally back to normal. She smiled and tweaked him gently on the nose. "Knew that would get you back," she teased, very proud of herself.

He grinned stupidly at her, unsure if he was trying to shake off the disorientation from the kiss or the transformation. Or both. "Thanks," he said, unable to think of anything else.

"No problem," she said cheerily. "Just don't get any ideas. Mike and I are quite happy."

He chuckled. "Wouldn't have it any other way. I appreciate the gesture though."

She nodded and wiping her mouth. She took the keys to the shackles out of her pocket and moved around behind him, twisting his arm to find the hole. "You know... if I wasn't with Mike... I might leave you in these right about now."

His eyes went wide and his entire body became rigid for a second as he tried to turn and face her. "Excuse me?"

She leaned forward to allow him to see her. "Just kidding," she smirked devilishly, then turned back toward the lock. "You're so easy."

He snorted, then closed his eyes. The memories of Spider were coming back to him, as well as what the Womb had done the night before, trying to get out of the chains. She freed his right hand and he used it to rub the bridge of his nose, the intrusion of all those memories at once giving him a migraine. Suddenly he remembered something else, and his eyes shot open. His limbs went limp, allowing her the freedom she needed to free his left arm. "Cathy?" he said softly, looking downward sheepishly, almost shyly.

"Yes, hun?" she responded, fumbling with the keys.

"I love you, too," he said, almost shamefully.

She stopped, smiling warmly at him although he couldn't see. "I know."

Mike stared forward in disbelief, his blue eyes bugging out of his head. If his mind had not been completely blank at that precise moment, he would have imagined that he looked like a complete idiot.

He was standing knee deep in the snow, his toes numbed far past the point where wiggling them could help with the circulation. He had been stupid enough to have worn jeans, and even though he was wearing insulation underneath he could still feel the cold seeping up his legs. His top half wasn't nearly so uncomfortable, a tan parka one of the wives had given him drawn around him snugly. His hair was again brittle, as he refused to wear a cap - another man had appeared to need it more. There were bags under his eyes from lack of sleep, and his breath stank of stale coffee and even staler donuts.

"You're sure?" he said finally, unable to register what he'd just heard.

"Definitely," Officer Banner replied, tipping back his cap and taking a quick glance at how fast the sun seemed to be rising today. "Matches your description perfectly. But our boy was in prison then, wasn't he?"

Mike grew contemplative, tapping his thumbnail against the dimple of his upper lip, lost in thought. "Mmm," he said in a non-answer. After another moment of deadly silence, he smiled at shorter man. "Nothing. Wasn't anything important, just heard it somewhere and wanted to be sure."

Banner raised an eyebrow, then nodded. He cupped his hands around his coffee mug to try and heat them up.

"Shouldn't do that," Mike said as he peeked over a nearby brush out into the clearing beyond, scanning the area ahead for any sign of life.

Banner shot him a look. "And why not?"

"Getting your hands too close to the heat... makes the

pours open up to let it in. Then when you take the heat away they stay open and all the cold comes rushing in. Might heat you up for a few minutes, but it'll make you colder in the long run."

"Hn," he grunted. He did not agree but loosened his grip on the mug all the same.

Mike smiled. His eyes darted around the open areas, until finally he gave a nod to Banner, who nodded back, and the both of them quietly crept onto the next place that appeared safe to scout. Mike glanced at his watch, then up at the sun. *Cathy should have unchained Xander by now*, he thought briefly, his mental image of her serving to warm him up and giving him that odd tingly feeling on one side of his face.

Then he thought of Xander, and what Banner had just told him, and became instantly cold again. *Now what does this crap mean?*

He huffed.

"Tell ya, whole world's gone to hell," Banner grumbled as the two snuck through the dawn into a patch of alders.

"What do you mean?" Mike asked, although he didn't necessarily disagree.

"This Derek piece of shit is walking around free, when they would have given a person just a few years older than him the damn chair."

Mike nodded, sucking in his lower lip.

"That little girl, the one that got killed - - so much death all over the place, and now my wife's niece is giving birth."

Mike stopped in his tracks, squinting quizzically. He

considered the statements provided for a moment, then turned to his compatriot. "Forgive me for going Sesame Street here, but, one of these things is not like the other."

"Huh?" he said, then quickly into his intercom, "Sector F-17 clear."

"Derek, death, carnage... new life brought into the world? How does that fit in with the rest?"

Banner sighed. "Well, for one, she's fifteen,"

Mike felt the guttural pang of pain-filled memories, then forced it back. "Hey man, I know what that's like, but she'll be..."

"... she's also got Down syndrome."

Mike's eyes went wide a moment, for the second time in under ten minutes, when he realized who the man was talking about. "Oh."

CHAPTER EIGHT
MOTHERS

Antony Jones stared blankly at the file in front of him, trying desperately to keep his eyes open as he read the pages. He reached for his morning cup of coffee without looking and almost knocked it over, cursed, then spared a glance at the mug just long enough to grip its handle.

Just a few months ago he wouldn't have had to do this himself. Someone would have briefed him on everything he needed to know. A month ago he had asked his superiors for reassignment as soon as possible. His replacement had been found before he had found a new position suitable, so he had taken up with the local office of Grey, Mercer and Suite in the interim.

He was sweating, like a pig. Coffee always did that to him, but it was a trade off for the forty-five minutes of alertness that it bought him. He shook his face after each sip, sloshing it around in his mouth. It was like a Zen ritual for him, and somehow always managed to make him feel awake. He closed his eyes for a moment, willing the blood vessels within them to stop pounding, then went back to the words in front of him.

His office door opened and a familiar strand of dark red hair poked its way in, followed by the rough-hewn yet beautiful face of Megan Greene. She had been the assistant D. A. until she had accepted the Adam Genblade case that rocketed her into stardom, and lead to her becoming a partner in Mayer, Summers and Soul. She'd always dreamed of being a lawyer ever since she was a child. When they'd met, she'd let her ambition cloud her judgment, and they'd started as abhorrent rivals. But they'd both discovered how not take themselves so seriously, and they'd become confidants. Friends. They'd gone against each other in a case involving Adam Genblade. As it happened the killer had been Derek, and the experience had caused the two to become close, in a manner of speaking.

Everything about Megan screamed of power, and yet there was a softness to her nature, the duel signals usually made those around her (men in particular) quite uncomfortable. Which was alright with her. She'd use every edge she could get.

She watched him, unable to keep the smile from her face as he toiled away, completely unaware of her presence. She relished in this rare chance to be a fly on the wall and watch him behave as he would were she not around. After studying him she raised her fist and rapped twice on the thick wooden door. "Paging Tony Jones," she giggled, mimicking the cheesy entrance that had become a ritual of his. "Tony Jones, are you there?"

He jolted his head back and tapped the button on his intercom. "Yes?" he said wearily, the strain in his voice giving away how sleep deprived he was.

She opened the door the rest of the way, and could now see that his clothes were wrinkled and unpressed. "Well, you're with it, huh?" she said.

He turned, sheepishly taking his hand away from the device. "Hey," he said, running a head through his auburn hair as he turned back to the papers, making it stick up in the back.

"Hey," she replied, the spontaneity of her entrance spent. "New case?"

"Mmm," he mumbled, bringing the caffeine to his lips again. "Disgusting case. Family Court stuff, they're the worst. This is not the stuff I took this job for."

She smiled and stepped around to a quaint art-deco sofa he had placed there to make himself look cultured when clients were in. She sat on it in a relaxed position, legs crossed in front of her. "That's the breaks of working in a small district, Tony. Sometimes you've got to sweat the small stuff to keep yourself in the game."

"Still... this is just too much."

"Hard case?" she asked, unsure herself if she were concerned or amused, and settling for being both.

"No, no... it's open and shut. It's just the filing, the dictation... everything about it is done wrong. Some of these things are hand-written, for God's sake. Who's that new girl? Summer's secretary?"

"Jillian Mayer."

"She should be fired," he grumbled, cursing. "How'd she even get a job here? We used to have standards at this office... I dimly recall."

Megan raised an eyebrow and sucked in her lip, not really wanting to say what she knew was the truth to his question. "She was Natasha Mayer's niece."

He looked up from the papers again, recalling the young woman who had put Mayer, Summers and Soul on the map by initially taking the Adam Genblade case... at the killer's request. "Oh," she said, tapping a pencil against his folder. "Well, she'd still better shape up soon."

She snorted. "I remember tales of a certain D.A. who was so nervous his first day in court that he kept referred to a male judge as Ma'am... just couldn't stop, kept spitting it out, the more nervous he got."

"Those allegations have never been substantiated," he said, raising a finger to punctuate his point, while scribbling on a post-it note tacked to the side of one page. "Besides, I sue anyone who states it for slander."

"Except when it was posted in the office newsletter the day you became D.A."

"Then I sued for libel."

She laughed, and it was a good feeling. But when it died off the two were left in silence for a long moment again. She clicked her tongue against the roof of her mouth, trying desperately to think of something to say. "So, what's the case about?"

He sighed. "Some custody bullshit. Mother against daughter for grand-daughter / son... it's a mess. I'm trying to make heads or tails of it, and it's just not happening. But this mother really doesn't want her kid to raise the grandkid. Still haven't sorted out why."

"Hope you're not up against anyone too good."

"Naw. They put Stack on it. Was appointed by the state."

She rolled her eyes. "Couldn't get anyone to do it pro-bono, huh? Man, she hasn't got a chance."

"Tell me about it. Going to mop the floor with that drop-out."

She was silent for a moment, just looking at him. "This is Family Court, Tone... maybe that attitude isn't the best going in."

He licked his upper lip, put down his pencil, and folded his fingers together in front of him. He took a long moment to gather his thoughts, then finally made eye-contact with her. "Why do you keep doing this?"

"Sorry?" she retorted.

"Why do you keep coming in here like this? Every single day, always with some pearl of wisdom or sharp comment or cute political limerick... why? I mean, I know we said we were going to stay friends, but we're ex, Megan."

The words took their blow, and she stood up to regain herself. "Thought you said you just wanted some time. For work?"

He sighed, giving her a sympathetic look. "We don't want the same things," he said finally.

She frowned, then nodded. "This is about the kid thing, isn't it?"

"You want children, I don't. To me, that's pretty cut-and-dried."

"Doesn't have to be. We don't have to be.. Ex."

He sighed, turning back to the desk. "I have work to do."

She nodded and headed toward the door, her heels clacking angrily against the floor the only indication of emotion she would allow show through. "Fine. Be that way. But I'll be back tomorrow morning to file for an appeal."

He snickered at that and watched her leave. "Duly noted."

She closed the door softly behind her and headed off to her office to start the work day.

He sighed then buried his face in his moist palms, rubbing his face back to life. He turned back toward the closed door to his office, feeling the sudden urge to go after her. He again reached for his coffee without looking, this time knocking it over and spilling its contents onto his desk.

♠♥♠

Gallagher sat with his elbows on his desk, clenching his hands through his receding grey hair. He had loosened his collar significantly a few minutes ago trying to stop his shortness of breath. It hadn't worked, and since then it seemed to have gotten exponentially worse with each passing second, his adam's apple bobbing up and down as he swallowed nothingness trying to get some saliva going in his parched mouth.

He took a deep breath, then slowly exhaled. He composed himself. It was eleven thirty, almost lunch time. His appointment was almost an hour late. He furrowed his brow, checking his wrist watch just to be sure, then glanced at the door to his office, and finally at the brass cross that hung next to it.

He turned to glare at his intercom, nearly obscured by a pile of papers. He groaned at the idea of using it, letting the pros and cons of such an action rattle back and forth in his head for a few minutes, then reached over a pressed the first red button on the left.

"Tanya?" he said, trying to sound cheerful as he held it down. He waited, but there was no response. Finally a dial tone ensued, along with a series of seven beeps. He raised an eyebrow to the machine quizzically, but continuing to depress his finger. After a few rings there was the unmistakable clicking sound of the line connecting. "Hello, Tanya?" he repeated, slightly less cheerily.

"Hello, you have reached the voice mail of... 'Robert Gallagher'... please input your password, now," came an automated female voice.

He released his finger from the button, heaved a loud sigh, then pressed the next button over. "Tanya?"

There was a squeal of feedback as his voice rang over the school's loudspeakers, and he quickly released the button again, pressing the third and last button immediately. "Tanya?!" he barked, using his free hand to again clench his scalp.

"Yes, Mr. Gallagher?"

"Thank you. Did Miss McFadden give any reason why she would miss our appointment?" he considered correcting her on the fact that it was actually Reverend Gallagher, but decided that it would be pretentious.

There was a rustling of papers, and then several clicks on a keyboard. "Miss McFadden did not show up for class today, Mr. Gallagher, nor did she call in sick. Should I put in a call to her home?"

"No, no," he replied hastily, waving his hand to sweep the idea away, until he realized that she couldn't actually see the motion. "That won't be necessary. When is my next appointment?"

"Well, your eleven thirty has been waiting here next to

the office for fifteen minutes."

He fumbled through his own papers, finally coming across the name Jaden Mal, a seventh grade boy here. "Why didn't you send him in?"

"Because you had a ten thirty appointment with Miss McFadden."

"Miss McFadden did not show up for her ten... just send the boy in," he sighed, releasing his finger from the button for what he hoped would be the last time that day (but knew himself it would not), and again made sure that his collar was on correctly.

The door opened and the young man came in. His skin was a kind of tanned brown and his hair dark dark black. Gallagher had become convinced when first meeting the child a few weeks ago that he had been from an inter-racial family, but of course couldn't ask. He was short, and his two front teeth stuck out just a little too far. He wore a green and brown horizontal striped t-shirt with a ketchup stain on the right breast. His jeans were torn and soaked from the knee down from the snow outside. He looked cold. More than that, he looked scared. He always looked scared.

Gallagher immediately felt a swell of pity for the child, walking over to him and smiling warmly, motioning for him to sit. When he did, he placed a comforting hand on the child's knee. "So, what do you want to talk about?"

Xander strained his head to the left as hard as he could,

slowly forcing it more and more until he felt the calcium in his joints pop. He breathed a sigh of relief.

"Kinks?" Cathy asked, taking a sip of her Slush Puppy from an orange straw that fit perfectly between her pursed ruby lips.

He shot her a look, almost laughing. "Yeah. I wonder why?"

"Maybe you slept weird," she grinned, jutting the cup toward him in offering, which he shrugged away.

"Never thirsty after a transform."

The right side of her mouth twitched as she processed the statement, unable to have a frame of reference for what he was talking about. "Always thought you would be."

"Naw. Takes me hours to feel anything after. Womb gives me all the vitamins and stuff my body needs... I think."

She nodded, adjusting the way she was sitting on the cafeteria table, her jacket strewn across her lap. He sat on the chair next to her.

"Can't we go outside?" he asked, his hand tapping against the table uncontrollably.

Her hands sunk as she shot him a disappointed glare. "I'm not going out in that cold just because you're having a damn nic fit," she protested, kicking his hand off the desk. The sound had begun to annoy her.

He grunted, clenching both hands.

She sucked more slush into her mouth as a group of kids walked by, churning it about in her mouth until it melted, making her already healthily-chubby cheeks puff out a little with each movement of the half-frozen liquid. After she swallowed it she smirked and turned back to him. "So if the Womb gives you everything you need, then why do you need a smoke?"

He shot her a deadpan look.

"Seriously," she laughed, loving how much this was getting under his skin. It had been a while since she'd had a chance to seriously bug him. "I guess you don't really have to have one... ever, right?"

"Is this going to be the daily : 'you must quit smoking' speech?" he asked, smirking despite himself. "Because you're early. Usually doesn't kick in until we're on our way home from school."

"That's because you smoke half a pack between here and your house, you freak!"

"Do not."

This time it was her turn to shoot him a look.

His eyes went up in their sockets, the way they always did when he was doing mental math. His fingers also counted. When he finished, he simply leaned forward on the table.

"And?" she asked self-assuredly when he did not immediately present his figures.

"Shut up," he scowled, defeated.

"I believe that's another victory for Catherine Kennessy, Woman-Supreme."

He chuckled. "Woman-Supreme?"

"Uh-Huh," she chimed, giving him a goofy, toothy smile.

"Woman-Supreme?" he re-stated, raising one hairy eyebrow.

"It's my code name."

"You have a code-name?"

"You get one, why can't I?"

"I have two personalities. When you can claim that, you can have a second name."

She thought about that. "I don't know... Mike says I'm like a whole different person when I'm on my period, does that count?"

Xander cupped his hands over his ears. "TMI!" he yelped.

"Huh?"

"Too Much Information!"

"Ah," she laughed. She got a coy look about her, waiting for him to remove his hands from his ears. He did, and she said: "You know, with all the congealed blood you had on you last night, I'd think you'd be used too..."

"TMI! TMI!" he yelled, returning his hands to the sides of his head with lightning-fast reflexes.

She laughed as he kept repeating it, never noticing Mike enter the cafeteria and walk over, bags still obvious under his eyes. "Hey, lover," she greeted, above Xander's yelps.

"Hey," he said as cheerily as he could muster, but a confused mind fueled by lack of sleep was apparent even from that one word.

Cathy smiled. She knew her boyfriend well, and was well aware not to ask what was wrong. He wasn't in the mood just yet, so she simply pouted her lips out toward him.

He smiled, taking the hint and leaning down for a good-morning kiss. After a moment he pulled back, smiled, then gave her a perplexed look. "You taste weird. No offense."

"Xander," she said simply, shrugging.

He raised an eyebrow, considered the context for a moment, then shrugged as well. "Oh... okay then."

"Tmi... tmi..."

Mike pointed a thumb at Xander. "Speaking of which, what's up with him?"

"Apparently he got too much information, or something. I don't know."

He turned from her, to Xander, and then back again. "You were talking about period stuff, huh?"

She grinned devilishly.

He punched Xander in the arm, forcing his friend out of the fetal huddle. "Yo."

Xander smirked. "Yo. You're late."

"Slept in. What about you guys, have any trouble with..." he lowered his voice, suddenly aware they were not alone.

Xander frowned.

Cathy rolled her eyes, dismissing Xander's drama before Mike's mind blew it out of proportion. "He had a little trouble getting up on the right side of his consciousness, but he got over it."

"Hmm."

Xander looked up. "Any word about that girl I saw the other night?"

"Yeah," Mike spat, getting into his down-to-business attitude that Cathy despised. "But not here."

Xander stared at Mike blankly for a moment, fumbling nervously with his forest green t-shirt, his thick eyebrows narrowing in response to what he'd just heard. An unlit cigarette dangled uselessly from his lip, threatening to fall with every breath he took.

"You're sure?" he asked after a moment, having to place a palm against the wall of the smoking section to keep himself from falling over.

"That's what I said," Mike nodded, placing a comforting hand on Xander's shoulder. "But it's definitely true. I trust Banner... and even after he told me, I put in a call to the number White gave me... it's legit. That girl you said you killed the other night... she was killed months ago. Back in September, man."

Cathy's brow furrowed, confused. She stood just a few feet back from pair. She had agreed finally that this would be the most secluded spot to talk about their problems of late, but in her own words had: 'refused to breathe in second-hand stinkiness.' Neither of the men had seen that exact expression on her since Jamie Dawkins had died. It was bewilderment at the sentences coming at her. "So... what does that mean, exactly?" she asked finally, extending her hand palm up.

"Well, it puts more players in the game for her death," Mike pointed out, stroking his chin. "I mean, this girl's death happened when Genblade was still active... not to mention Derek. And the Tee's were still around back then, Bram and Raine. Could have been any one of them, really. There's no reason to assume it was - "

"I remember the taste of her blood in my mouth," Xander interrupted, head turned down and eyes shut as he tried to block out the memories that wouldn't stop coming like a slow leak in a huge dam. "I remember that she still had that new baby smell. I remember... everything." He opened his eyes, locking them to Mike's. "This was me."

Cathy had turned away when he had started to speak. She found that if she didn't see him saying the words, she could distance herself from them. "Again..." she said, pausing to find her voice. "What does that mean?"

All three were silent for a moment, the gears in their minds turning.

"Its hidden things from you before," Mike pointed out. "And it showed you them at a later time, when it needed you to know. Genblade said..."

"Genblade?" Xander scoffed.

"Genblade said that the Womb knew that Derek was the killer, and that it hid that fact from you. Maybe it's the same now," he finished, as if his friend hadn't interrupted.

"No," Xander said, shaking his head somberly. "It means that I'm remembering... that someday I might remember everything that it does, all the time."

"Could this be part of learning to control it again?" Cathy chimed, trying hard to find positive options.

"More like it starting to control me," Xander spat, finally lighting the smoke, to which Cathy stepped away another pace.

Mike snapped his fingers. "Warren!"

"Huh?"

"His hypno-therapy crap! What if he was using it to block your memories somehow? Bring them back at key times in order to control the Womb? We could go through his files, and..."

"We've been through the files a million times. O'Toole had to use a bunch of tricks and schemes just to find out who I was. I don't think he had something this major up his sleeve. Especially not without filing it away for Hale and the Circe's say-so... no, I think this is more just to do with," he paused, pressing his hand to his right side, where the womb-organ throbbed in response to his touch, like a kicking fetus. "... This."

There was a silence then as the three absorbed that, trying to find a place to put it in their heads. Xander sighed, sitting down against the bricks and bringing his knees up close to his face.

He just wanted to curl up in a ball and die.

Feeling a swell of pity, Cathy finally walked over and sat next to him, putting her arm around him and giving him a friendly squeeze. "It'll be okay," she said, ruffling his hair. "We'll find a way to beat it. Last night worked out all right... right?"

Xander nodded, but his heart was not in it. "What about the other thing?" he said finally, wanting very much to shift the focus away from himself for the moment, looking in Mike's direction. "You mentioned something else."

"Yeah," Mike stated, frowning. He bent down in front of them, leaning forward to bring his hand into contact with his girlfriend's, to give her support for what he was about to say. "There's a pregnant girl."

Cathy shifted uncomfortably, even with Mike's support.

Xander shot him a dry stare, puffing smoke through his nostrils. "Not exactly our area of expertise. And don't even try to tell me I'm the father."

"She was fifteen," Mike added, clearing his throat.

"Tragic. But still, there's nothing really sinister in..."

"And she had Down syndrome."

Xander's eyebrows shot up.

Cathy's went wide. "I know who you're talking about!" she said, jaw slack. "We used to be in class together in grade three, before they decided to segregate her into the Special Ed room! It's..."

"August Styles," Xander finished, face still locked in the same shocked position.

"Yeah," Mike said. "And, as you can imagine, her Mom isn't very happy."

"I remember that bitch. She was like a Nazi. A Nazi that Hitler would have been afraid of."

"Pulled my hair once," Cathy added absently.

"August?" Xander questioned.

"Her Mom."

"Ah."

"More than that..." Mike sighed. "... her Mom's making her get an abortion."

Xander's look faded slowly from shock, to a dead-serious look the both of them recognized as him trying to hold back anger. "What?"

"She can't do that." Cathy protested.

"Oh, don't be so sure," Mike sighed. "Mentally challenged, underage, and no idea who the father is..."

"Come again?" Xander spat, almost so fast the words jumbled together. "Am I officially the last person in our school to get any?"

Mike shot him a look. "Not funny, man. The doctor's got to do a rape test on her when she went in for a prenatal exam..." he tightened his grip on Cathy's hand. "They did the old rape clock test... but there was scarring on the upper *and* lower parts of her... well, y' know."

"Upper is consensual, lower means rape," Xander recalled.

"Exactly. This isn't as cut and dried as it sounds. Something's up, and her Mom is rushing it into court asap. If we don't do something about this..."

"...we could have another dead child on our hands," Xander finished, looking downward.

"... there won't be any genetic evidence left in August to find the rapist," Mike said, finishing his own sentence.

Cathy frowned. "Won't work," she said after a moment.

"Why?" Mike said, tilting his head to one side.

"Come on, hun. We've dealt with this before. I've..." she sighed, "... if the girl hasn't talked, she's not going to. And can you blame her? She's got the mental functionality of a six year old. She can't possibly process what's happened to her, let alone open up to us about..."

Mike looked at her. A grin started to play over his face, and he shot a glance at Xander. Xander smiled too, turning and looking at Cathy knowingly.

"... fuck," she spat. "I just got the job of talking to her, didn't I?"

Xander gave her a quick squeeze, then got up and doubted his cigarette and dusted the ash off of his shirt.

"Okay, I'll talk to her. If nothing else, I can point her in a direction... there's all kinds of programs through the school board to help pregnant teens. That weasel Shnieder is surprisingly good with it. He even offered me help when I was... you know."

"Really?" Xander asked, surprised by the new information.

"Yeah. Someone told me his Mom got pregnant with him as a teen, so he tries to help and stuff. Anyway, I'll talk to her."

"You find out what you can," Mike said, squeezing her hand warmly. "Xander, you ask around too. See if Tommy and the rest know anything. Find out who she's close to, who would have had the opportunity for something like this... everything you can."

Xander nodded, scratching his chin. "That sounds good... you can do that. I've got a better idea."

Mike stopped. "And what might that be?"

Xander did not answer, merely started walking toward the exit to school grounds.

"Damn him," Mike said under his breath, as he and Cathy started walking back to class.

ᕕ(ᐛ)ᕗ

Gallagher leaned back in his chair with one hand over his mouth as he tried to stop the other from shaking. A cup of coffee sat on the desk before him, completely untouched and cold by now, a few dribble marks going down the front from where he had raised it to take a sip then placed it back down. Next to the coffee was an equally untouched pack of king-size cigarette's, the plastic still on them.

"Didn't realize you smoked," came a familiarly shrill voice from the doorway. Principal Shnieder was leaning there, taking the last few bites of a banana. He was wearing a plaid sweater-vest over a blue shirt and grey dress pants that almost seemed too long for the pint-sized man, the fluorescent light gleaming off his mostly bald head and making his ears (which stuck out as if by magic) glow red.

"I don't," Gallagher grumbled, leaning his elbows onto the desk. "But I think after this week, I might have to start."

Shnieder smirked a little. "A little overwhelming, isn't it?" he said smugly, scratching his beak-like nose as he did. "I tried to warn you, Robert. It's not as easy as it sounds."

"I know. But I never expected..."

"That's when it'll come, friend. When you don't expect it."

Gallagher groaned, already tired of Shnieder's well-meant Holier-than-Thou attitude. "In the confessionals I hear things I cannot repeat, some that I would not want too... but who would do this? To a child that didn't know any better?"

Shnieder looked somber for a moment, as if trying to push it out of his mind. "I can't tell you, Robert. But you have to remember, this is exactly why we brought you on board. I know it's horrible to say, but this type of thing isn't uncommon. It's just *who* it happened to that is. There have been eleven girls pregnant just this year, and the year is only half over. So many that a few years back I helped set up a program through the school that would help them out financially. I mean, I wish there was more we could do. There just... isn't."

"I understand. I just keep thinking that - "

There was a knock at the door that interrupted him and a student poked her head in to the door. "Principal

Shnieder?" she asked, smiling at him politely. "The secretary said you'd be in here. I need some help with the SADD committee snow-day next week?"

"Of course," Shnieder smiled, nodding at the girl. "I'll be right with you."

He turned back to Gallagher, tapping twice on his desk, trying hard to keep his lower lip as stiff as possible. "We'll talk later."

Gallagher lifted his mug, then turned back to his paperwork for the day.

CHAPTER NINE
DELVE

August Styles sat against the wall of the stairwell between the second and third floor of the school, staring out the nearby window and the snow that clung to it. It took funny shapes, some of it falling onto other parts, making even more shapes. One of them looked kind of like a fairy, she thought. Another one reminded her of a hand. And her Mother... she could see her mother very clearly in the foggy glass.

A tear ran down her cheek, and then another... and another, until finally they were plopping against the floor and dribbling off of her nose, making the skin on her face feel blotchy and red. She sniffed it back, and when she did the breath that followed was a wail, one that echoed throughout the entire set of stairs. It was heard by several people, all of whom ignored it.

She hit herself hard in the side of the face and sank down into herself, looking like a lump of humanity created for making tears. She looked bruised somehow, although there was not a mark on her. It was as if she was the bruise, like it was on her soul, or the small fragile heart that was breaking with every thought that passed through her.

Cathy watched her from the doorway to the third floor. As she did, she couldn't help but be reminded of a child. Even though she knew that they were both the same age, the scene brought an almost maternal feeling out in her, rising up from her gut until it overcame her. August's whole body shuddered in a powerful sob, and Cathy had to do her best not to start to cry as well. "Hey," she said finally, composing herself as she stepped forward. She spoke as gently as possible, using the same tone she would have used on an upset child.

August jumped when she heard the voice, then grabbed her lunch bag and began to move. There was a primal fear in her eyes.

"No, it's okay!" Cathy said, forcing a wide smile. "I was just wondering how you were."

August gave her a long, side-on look, as if sizing the girl up to see whether or not she was dangerous. She sat back down and seemed to relax, but still kept her lunch bag clenched tightly to her chest. "My nose is runny," she said honestly, turning to stare down at her feet.

Cathy nodded, smiling. "Yeah... That happens to me sometimes, too. That's why I always carry these," she said, reaching into her purse and withdrawing a bundle of two or three soft, fluffy tissues. "You want one?" she asked, holding them out.

August regarded the offering with some hesitation, but her nose was hurting more and more, so she reached out and grabbed one. She wrapped it around her hand methodically, then used it to blow her nose. "Thank you," she said, almost a whisper. The strain in her voice could be heard now, and it was obvious that this was not the first crying fit that the girl had gone into today.

Despite her better judgment, Cathy could resist it no longer. She reached out and touched the girl on the shoulder, then leaned in and gave her a warm hug. "It'll be okay, sweetie," she said, holding back her own tears as August started up again. They stayed that way for a long moment, and when they released, Cathy gave her a kiss on the cheek, getting the taste of salt-water on her lips as she did.

"I don't know what's going on," August sobbed, wiping her nose again, only this time with her shirt. "I don't know..." the sentence might have continued, but it was lost in a wail.

"I know, honey," Cathy said, trying hard to think of what to say. "But I need to ask you about how it happened now, okay? I can help you fix it, but I need to know how it happened."

"My Mommy says I can't keep my baby..."

A sharp pang was felt deep within her gut, and she fought the urge to show it. "I heard that, too. I know. You and your Mommy need to talk about that, okay? But right now, I need to talk about the Daddy."

August looked at Cathy for directly for the first time, her eyes bloodshot and puffy. "I don't know where my Daddy is."

"No," Cathy said warmly, placing her hand of the girl's knee. "I need to know about your baby's Daddy." There was a long pause, and she wasn't sure how to phrase the next back delicately. "If you're not... sure... I can help you figure it out?"

August looked confused, her eyes darting about inside her head. Her hands started to twist the brown bag, ripping it in places. "I don't know."

"That's okay," Cathy sighed, pushing a strand of her black hair behind her ear. "I can help you figure it out. Just tell me when the last time you slept with a boy was."

Her brow furrowed. "I never slept with a boy."

Cathy stopped herself from outright objecting to the statement when she realized what her words would mean if someone took them literally. "No, sweetie. Um... the last time you made love to a boy?"

"I kiss Tim sometimes. The last time was at the Halloween dance. He says he wants to be my boyfriend but I don't want a boyfriend right now."

Cathy clucked her tongue against the top of her mouth, struggling now. She knew how she would have to phrase it, but didn't want to say it. "No... no, honey. I need to know the last time you had sex."

August leaned herself back, a little repulsed by the vulgar-sounding word. "I've never had sex!" she said, offended.

Cathy let those words bop around in her head, then finally she thought of the correct wording, smiling. She reached out and touched August's stomach gently. "I need to know when you did the thing that made your baby."

August stared at her for a moment, a sad look passing over her, then looked down at her feet.

Mike sat down next to Tommy in Lit class, even as Mr. Reid was talking about an upcoming assignment based on MacBeth in which they would have to break off into pairs. He cringed at the idea, looking around him for people he was close enough to pair with that might have some shred of understanding of Shakespeare and finding none. He silently cursed the entire idea of the assignment, but decided to keep his mouth shut on the subject.

"Hey," Tommy said to him, finally noticing that he was there. He was leaned back in his chair, something every one of his teachers had told him repeatedly not to do, playing with a toothpick in his mouth. Why he was doing that nobody knew, it was just one of those character traits that Tommy seemed to pick up for a week or so and then never speak of again.

"Hey," Mike reciprocated, nodding a greeting.

"You're late," Tommy said, holding out a fist until Mike held out his own and knocked them together.

"Mmm. I've been told that already."

"Something up?" he almost smiled, using his tongue to position the toothpick between his two front teeth. "Anything interesting?"

"Nothing life and death. You?"

Tommy sighed sadly, yet still retained his smile, which Mike now began to think was fake. "I'm still grounded after the drama a few weeks ago, when... well, you heard."

"Yeah. About that..."

"It's cool."

"Good. Grounded, huh? That must suck."

"Pfft," Tommy shrugged, shaking his head. "I wouldn't be going out anyway. I'm actually kind of glad I'm grounded. Mom picks me up here every day after school and drives me home, then drives me to school every day. Not allowed outside. No outside means no chances for Derek fucking Smith to come at me in a dark alley." He shuddered at even the mention of the killer's name.

Mike was startled, but only for a moment. With his attitude and everything that happened lately, it was easy to forget that Tommy had taken quite a beating in the months since school started... most notably from Derek and the Tee Gang. He nodded sympathetically.

"So, I hear you're actually *helping* the cops look for him?" Tommy asked, raising an eyebrow quizzically.

"Yeah," Mike nodded. "Not much, just scoping out the woods to look for signs that someone's been there. Doing my part."

There was a silence, as Tommy looked the other teen up and down. "No offense, dude - you're killer and all - but I think you should take a cue from me and just lock yourself in your room till the fucker's dead or behind bars."

Mr. Reid shot a look in their direction, but said nothing.

"Why's that?" Mike said, lowering his voice. "Give me one good reason."

Tommy reached out quickly and tapped Mike in the side with the back of his palm.

Mike bent over in pain, fighting the urge to yelp.

"There's one," Tommy said smugly, considering his point proven. "Last time you crossed Smith he nearly gutted you. That's not an experience I would want to repeat, I was you."

"You're not me," Mike spat, a trace of bitterness in his voice as he composed himself. "You handle it your way, I'll handle it mine."

Tommy nodded. He took the pick out of his mouth, licked his dry lips, then put it in again. "Fair enough," he said finally, giving an apologetic look.

Tommy never seemed to apologize for anything. Ever.

Mike breathed heavily, willing his side to stop throbbing. "You heard anything around lately?" he asked when he felt he could speak in an even tone again.

"About Derek? Same as everyone, big load of nothing. Nothing since the old man with the hand... which, by the way, ew."

"Yeah," Mike agreed. "Not Derek. Anything else? Anything you might've heard from the guys?"

Tommy narrowed his eyes at him, taking a long breath and fingering the pick. It reminded Mike of the way Xander sometimes twirled his smokes when he was mulling over something. "You're talking about the retarded girl, huh?"

Mike's eyes grew but he decided not to chide Tommy on the use of the crude term. "The Down syndrome girl, August. Yes, her."

"Heard she got knocked up, but everyone knows that. You must too, or you wouldn't be asking."

Mike tilted his head, conceding to the honest, if not sly, response. "Naw, I'm wondering if you've heard any of the guys say anything. You hear a lot. Anyone been bragging in the locker room? Anyone talking about scoring?"

Tommy shook his head. He leaned in close. "No. Even if one of the guys did it, nobody's stupid enough to brag about something like that. They know they'd get in shit, plus no player wants a reputation for that kind of girl. Hurts the chances with the ladies, if you get my drift."

Mike nodded.

"Why you asking, anyway? This isn't anything you usually get up in people's face about. It's not any murder or a rape."

"I wouldn't be too sure," Cathy said, sitting down between the boys in the row behind and laying her purse and jacket across her desk, leaning on them to get in close.

Both Mike and Tommy turned to her, shocked by her sudden arrival.

"What do you mean?" Mike asked, his hand without delay and unconsciously going to hers.

"Yeah," Tommy said, shifting in his seat to face her now. "I've heard some wild stories, but that isn't one of them. You saying someone forced themselves on the girl?"

Cathy shook her head, wiping her face to make sure there were no tears there. She'd spent the last five minutes in the bathroom making sure, but her face still felt dry from them. "I don't think it's that simple," she said, her voice almost devoid of emotion.

"What?" Mike asked, shooting Tommy a perplexed look, who returned it in kind. "What are you talking about? It's either rape or it isn't, right? Is there something I'm missing? Date-rape? Drugs? Was she tricked somehow?"

Cathy nodded, chattering her tongue against her teeth. "I think so, Mike. She doesn't know what sex is."

"What?" Tommy exclaimed.

"She doesn't know *how* her baby was made."

CHAPTER TEN
PREPERATION

Megan took a sip of the martini she had been nursing for the last hour. The olive that bobbed in the fancy, decorated glass bounced against her nose. She was about to put it down again, when she changed her mind and instead downed the three-quarters that was left to the glass then slammed it down on the mahogany desk, sending an echo throughout the room. "Ah," she exclaimed as the liquor burned her mouth, giving it the after-bite which made her love them so much. One of her friends had told her once that a martini "put hair on your chest" - Megan had thought to tell her that she obviously had never had tequila, but decided not to.

A little red in the face from the drink but by no means drunk, she picked up the tape recorder in front of her and started to rewind it. It contained her own voice-recording of what she planned to use in an upcoming criminal case involving a couple of idiots who'd held up a convenience store. She'd written it, read it aloud to the recorder (while pacing around the room and imagining she was in court), and then played it back, making notes on her first draft as she heard the impact (or sometimes lack thereof) of her own words. This would be the fourth revision. Typically she would only do three, the most ever was ten, but she always kept doing it until she was sure that it was perfect. It was part of her insane need to over-prepare for everything, something that she'd had with her ever since grade school. Pre-school, by her mother's words, although she couldn't testify to that herself.

"Ladies and gentlemen of the jury," came her own voice over the recorder, which she was unconsciously mouthing along too. "The defense is likely to try and convince you today that his clients, Adam Bird and Ron Snelgrove, are innocent. This is an insult to your intelligence, to this court, and to the justice system itself." She smiled at herself proudly at that line. "The question is not whether or not these men are guilty. They are unquestionably guilty, and I shall prove that without doubt during the next few days of trial. The question that you should be asking yourselves is not whether or not they should go to jail... but whether or not they should go for the rest of their lives. While their crime, at face value, in no way indicts a life sentence... think of the terror that this act has inflicted on the lives of Mr. Berkhart?" She made a note on the paper that said 'point to berkhart.' "A seventy-five year old man whose wife died last year, leaving only his store to keep himself occupied. How can he go to work now, after years of loyal service to this *community* and not be afraid?" She made another note, point to defendants, "Is that what you went in for? Two hundred dollars... cigarettes... and few dozen beer, maybe some candy bars... and one life?

Because that is exactly what you two have taken from Mr. Berkhart... you have taken away his *life*. His ability to not be afraid. Just as it was taken from all of us months ago, by the killer known as Derek Smith..."

"Nice," came a voice from behind her. She switched off the recording immediately, then turned to smile at Nathaniel Summers. Nathan was the head of the firm, and had been for the better part of a decade. He collected antique vases and studied anthropology in the small amount of spare time his job afforded, and he'd always loved Megan's smile. "That's genius, comparing them to Smith. You might as well have called the two of them Hitler in this town. It'll get the jury hating them just by association."

"You don't think it's too much?" she asked, biting her lower lip, tapping her yellow writing pad with her pencil.

"Not at all. It's just right. The 'rest of their lives' thing might be a bit much... just don't overdo it. Say it almost under your voice, like a whisper, and it'll be fine." He entered her office fully and closed the door behind him. He was wearing a grey Italian suit that seemed to have been poured onto him it fit so well, and dark sunglasses that seemed to only cover his eyes, none of the area around him. He had short, slicked-back silver hair and a dashing smile he was never afraid to use in court. It did not surprise her that Nate was one of the best the firm had to offer.

Megan looked at her pad, then nodded silently and made the note. When she turned back to him and went from twenty-nine to sixteen in a heartbeat. "So, what's new, Pinky? Any new plans to take over the world?"

Nathan chuckled at that, taking the seat across from her casually. "Actually, I wanted to talk about you."

She raised an eyebrow.

"This is your day off, Megan. Why the hell are you here?"

She looked shocked, and more than a little hurt, the smile he was so fond of fading away. "I had to work on the opening statement for my case."

"That case doesn't start for another three weeks."

"You know how I like to prepare."

"You're obsessive," he corrected, smiling even though his words were slightly confrontational. "You need to get out more."

"I get out fine. I went out last night?"

"Yeah... where?"

She paused, her mouth open and moving, but no words coming out.

"See?" he said, giving her a look.

She smiled, finally rolling the statement off her back. "I appreciate the concern, Nathan... I really do. But I don't need it right now. Don't want it. All I really want is to work and get my mind off everything else. Can you just let me do that, please?"

Nathan frowned, then nodded, although he made a grunting sound in his throat. It was the same sound he made in court when a judge overruled his objections, something only brave judges did anyway. "I just don't want this job... or me, as you superior... to be a reason for you to regret this, later in life. You're still young, Megan."

"I'm not going to have any regrets, Nathan," she said finally, trying to sound as upbeat as possible. "And if you want to help me, find me a case before this one starts."

Nathan sighed, then started moving toward the door. When he opened it, he was surprised to see someone standing outside it, his eyebrow rising high. "I think your next case just found you."

Megan looked up. When she saw who was there her eyes bulged in shock.

⋏⋏

Mike walked Cathy and her sister Trina right to their front door after school, something he and Xander had made a point of doing just to make sure they got there safely. Trina went inside without a word, but a quick smile in his direction let Mike know that she appreciated his kindness. The second that the door was closed behind her the lovers sat down on her front stop together, ignoring the cold of the concrete in favor of the warmth of each other's company, and rare treat for the pair. Their hands linked, and after a moment their lips did as well, both of them sinking into a long, wet kiss that seemed to make their frustrations dissipate into the night air. After several minutes they parted, each one with a smile the other would have described as goofy.

Mike let out a happy breath, leaning back on his hands. "Some times, huh?" he said, almost laughing at the absurdity of their lives of late.

"Mmm," she hummed in agreement, leaning down and resting her head against his chest and curling up close, putting all of her weight on him, both literally and figuratively. He kissed her lightly on the head, one of the subtle gestures the couple had come to give one another in their time together to let the other know it was okay to unload. "It's never going to stop, is it?" she asked, although it wasn't a whine or a plea, more like a general statement.

"Doesn't seem that way, does it?" he heaved, wishing he had a better answer for her.

"I guess I kind of always thought that if we got through this thing, and the next... and the thing after that... and then the *other* thing... that someday we'd... I don't know..."

"You thought we'd win," he finished for her, having known the outcome of the sentence immediately after she'd begun it.

"Exactly," she said, swirling her finger in circles against his chest. "I guess I thought things were going to be the way they were. That we'd be happy again."

"You're not happy?" he asked, leaning his head back to see her face.

She grinned. "I am right now, silly," she chimed, kissing him. "I mean in general, though. Just... no drama anymore, you know? Or at least, *regular* drama. Teen stuff, the stuff we should be worried about."

He kissed her head again. "Yeah, I know."

"So, how do you deal with it? I mean, other than Xander, you see more of it than anyone. Maybe more. How do you deal with how much we've had to change just to survive this world?" She sat up now, looking him in the eye.

"Because I believe it will get better," he said honestly, and she could tell in his eyes it was true.

There was a brief silence, and then she shook her head.

"How can you say that, when it seems like everything is just getting worse?"

He reached out and touched the side of her face. He pulled her in for a short kiss, then out again, playing with the nape of her neck. "Because of you," he said finally, stroking her cheek with his thumb.

She tilted her head by way of asking for an explanation.

"There was a time, back when all this started, that I thought the same way you did. That I had to get through this thing and the next and the next... not for me," he stressed, emphasizing his points by touching his chest, then hers, "... but for you. I thought I had to make this world a better place for you, and all my energies went toward that. Then, somewhere along the line, when you and I were apart -- that all changed."

"How do you mean?"

"I used to look into your eyes and want to make the world a better place. To save the world so that it would be a place fit for someone like you to live in... now I look into your eyes, and see the world through you... and I don't think the world needs saving anymore. When I'm with you, everything's perfect. So I know it's going to get better... because the world is, for the most part, a good place. You showed me that."

Her lips trembled, and she leaned in and kissed him passionately. "I love you," she said when they paused, their lips still only a centimeter apart, noses rubbing.

"You'd better."

They kissed again.

CHAPTER ELEVEN
DESPERATE MEASURES

The elm tree's leaves turned from the sun.

No matter how much light it gave they would not take it, hiding instead against the threat of the cold. It burned at them and the shivered back, and the elm lost all its protection from the biting wind. The heart of it became cold with each breeze that slunk through the gaps in the leaves, slicing at it until even the truck forgot what warm even felt like.

Mike closed his locker door and let out a deep sigh that ended in a chuckle and a grin, shaking his head back and forth. He gave himself one last moment to enjoy the memory of the kiss Cathy had given him, then picked up his book bag and slung it over his shoulder. He started to walk down the halls toward smoking section.

He opened the doors and the cool winter breeze hit him instantly, sending goosebumps shivering up and down his spine. "Cathy?" he called out, squinting against the sun's reflection on the snow. "Hun, you out here?"

There was no sound at first, then a small giggle. It sounded like something that would come from a small child. He grinned immediately, wondering what kind of game she was playing with him now. Ever since they were kids, she'd never gotten tired of hide-and-go-seek, only lately his prizes for finding her had become much more rewarding.

"What're you doing out - " he started as he turned the corner, the smile stopping as quickly as the sentence did.

Calla McFadden was leaning against the snow-covered brick wall of the school, her jacket wrapped tight around her as she held her thumb and forefinger up close to her mouth, which was drawn up like a bow, sucking the last few puffs out of the joint that she had meticulously rolled, trying to get as much out of it as possible before it got down to the filter she had hastily made out of the cardboard from a pack of Marlboro's. Her eyes were wide at first, the both of them wondering what exactly the other thought they were doing, but not knowing how to ask. When the shock wore off, Calla's thin eyebrows lowered into a scowl as she tossed what was left of her joint into a snow back, exhaling a puff of blue smoke. She gave him what she referred to when amongst her friends as 'the elevator' (looking a person up and down, usually for the purposes of either checking them out or seeing if you could take them. Or both,) then started to walk past him. She stopped when the both of them were shoulder to shoulder and turned toward him so that her lip was dangerously close to his ear. "You're cute for a spaz," she drawled, snickering a little as she, turned the corner and disappeared, leaving Mike to just stand there bewildered.

Calla walked through the snow with her feet long past cold and approaching numb after standing in it for so long. The door opened before she got to it and Cathy came out, shivering once at the sudden change it temperature. Calla once again gave the elevator, smiled in approval of what she saw, then continued through the doors. She turned before they closed, again giving Cathy the elevator from behind, and again smiled.

Cathy rolled her eyes and blushed, then spotted Mike coming out from behind the smoking area, an expression of shock on his face. "What happened?" she asked, almost giggling as she turned to make sure that Calla was gone.

Mike said nothing for a moment, as if formulating his thoughts, his eyes moving back and forth searching for the answer. Finally, they met hers. "I honestly don't know."

She giggled, then reached down and grabbed him gently by his collar (something she could so rarely do, but her elevation on the concrete step allowed for it) and pulled him up into a kiss. It lasted for well over a minute before she let go of his shirt, and a few more moments after that before she touched her hand against his chest and nudged him away. "What've you been doing all day?" she asked cheerfully, sitting down against the steps.

He moved to sit down beside her, sliding one arm around her shoulder without even thinking about it, pulling her to his shoulder. "Not a whole lot," he sighed, "Went to gym, played doubles with Tommy for a bit, then went with him to get Gatorade. Didn't like physics after that."

"You never like physics after gym," she noted.

"I don't like sitting all sweaty. Even after a shower, it's just not comfortable. Anyway, got bored of that fast. Left class to go to the washroom and didn't come back, hung around with the juniors for a while then got another shower just to make myself wake up and feel human a little, then came out here."

"That's why you smell so good," she cooed, snuggling in.

"That's why I'm frigging freezing out here."

She laughed and placed her arm around him, partly in an effort to warm him, partly just because she wanted to. She paused, just enjoying her lover for a long moment, then spoke. "Have you heard any news today?"

He thought a moment, then shook his head. "Julie called Tommy, they talked a few hours. Nothing major, but she mentioned you and Xander barging into her boyfriend's place a few weeks ago."

Cathy blushed, then turned her face into his chest to hide it.

"Any reason you didn't mention that?" he asked, shaking her shoulder playfully, enjoying her embarrassment.

Xander looked at Cathy as their lips parted, almost laughing. She looked back up at him, her hand still rested on the back of his head. She wasn't laughing.

"This probably isn't a constructive course of action," he chuckled, moving off of her. He felt her hand tighten, and stopped.

"Yes it is," she whispered, pulling him back toward her. Their lips met again as she wrapped one leg around him, pulling his entire frame into her.

"No," she said quietly after a moment, then turned to look up at him, raising her voice so that he could hear. "No reason."

"Hmm. Well, she's doing good now anyway, according to Tom. New boyfriend..."

"Met him. Seems like a tool."

"Not him. New one since him, he said she says he's really nice. Seventeen, looking at a full scholarship next year. Even helping her out, apparently she's been getting As on her last few exams."

"Wow," Cathy said, legitimately surprised. "Never would have thought."

"I know. Tom said she's still having problems dealing with... some things, that's why she wants to stay away. But when she thinks she's ready, she's planning to visit us."

"That's good..." she said, trailing off a little. She looked around, still visibly agitated. She shuffled her feet from side to side, then turned back to Mike. "He's not coming today, is he?"

Mike frowned, then shook his head.

ʎ⟨ʎ

August Styles sat on her back porch, hunched over and in tears again. Her mother was in the kitchen, screaming at someone on the phone.

She was talking about her baby.

She took a sip from her glass of juice even as tears started to come down again, and she tried to make sense of everything. She remembered that Cathy girl, and how nice she'd been. She said that she lost a baby once, too...

and even though that would be bad, it would still be all right in the end.

She threw her head into her knees, moisture falling from every hole in her face as she fought the urge to throw up.

"August," came a familiar voice.

She looked up, only to see a man standing at the entrance to their back path. He was tall and thin, with shaggy brown hair and thick, black-rimmed glasses. He had an overbite, and his face and shoulders were covered in acne. His expression was grim and determined, and both his fists were clenched so tightly that they were shaking, their knuckles white.

"...Timmy...." August said, her face full of shock, and just a taste of fear.

CHAPTER TWELVE
ESCALATION

Xander knocked twice on Cathy's door, then opened it. He felt safe doing this. He'd been coming over to play since he could remember, to the point that Mr. Kennessy would get mad at him if he "made him get all the way up and come to the door." He wiped his shoes clean of the snowy slush they'd accumulated, then stepped inside and turned the corner into the kitchen. "Cathy?" he called out, noticing the time on the wall and realizing that it would be getting dark soon.

"Here," Cathy said from around the corner in the dining room, curled up into herself sitting on the table, her feet on the chair at its head. She looked somber and worried, a look usually reserved for when something was happening to either him or Mike.

"What's wrong?" he blurted, immediately thinking of Mike's injuries. "Is he okay?"

Mike stepped around the corner, a phone pressed against his ear, raising his index finger to Xander to indicate he'd be done in a minute.

Xander turned back to Cathy, whose expression (although worrisome) was mostly blank. She didn't know what the call was about either, but it was safe to say that it wasn't good. "Sorry to cut it so close. I know we're going to have to go pray soon," he apologized, tapping her knee to try and break the uncomfortableness.

She smiled. "By the looks of him," she sighed, motioning to her boyfriend, "We might have a long evening ahead of us anyway."

He nodded, a million things flashing through his mind at once as he tried to think of what the call might be about.

"Where'd you go?" she asked after a moment, her hair bobbing as she turned to him.

"To get help," he answered simply and vaguely.

She cocked an eyebrow. "How'd it go?"

"In progress," he grumbled, making a scuff mark on the tile floor with his boot, for the purpose of scuffing it back out.

She nodded.

"Okay," Mike said, speaking for the first time since Xander arrived, raising his finger again. "Okay, thanks. That's good man... and Tommy... thanks, dude. You're the best." He hung up the phone curtly, then joined the both of them in the dining room, putting an arm close to Cathy.

"Tommy?" Xander asked, a little confused by the mention of that particular name. "What's that about?"

"Did he have anything on August?" Cathy chimed, hopeful.

"Not exactly," Mike said, his voice low. "August and

that boyfriend of hers, Tim... they both ran away from home tonight. Nobody knows where they are."

"Fuck," Xander grunted, rapping a knuckle against the table. "We've got to find them."

Mike nodded.

There was a silence then, as Cathy looked from one of her men to the other. "Pardon me for saying this but... is this such a bad thing?"

Neither of them spoke.

"I mean, we'll definitely find them, but this might give us the chance we need to be able to help her. Find out if he's the father and exactly what went on, maybe even stop her Mom from going through with the abortion thing. This could work out for us... right?"

Still, neither man spoke. They both looked at one another, knowing they were thinking the exact same thing, their faces a mixture of dread and anger that seemed to switch back and forth between both friends.

"What?" she asked, putting both her hands forward, not understanding. She looked from one to the other in question. She thought for a moment, and it was only when Mike looked at her and she saw the fear in his eyes... and even more in Xander's when he looked, that she really understood what they were thinking. "Oh," she said in a hushed voice, bringing a hand to her mouth in shock, her eyes glistening in terror.

Mike grabbed his coat and slung it over his shoulder, nodding quickly to Xander, who headed toward the door. He gave her a quick kiss as they headed for the door in silence, closing it behind them just as Trina came down the stairs from her room.

Cathy's hand was still on her mouth when Trina approached her, only now she was fighting off tears as well.

"What is it?" Trina asked, automatically concerned when she saw her sister and pieced it with the boy's unusual abruptness. "Oh my gawd, what's wrong?"

Cathy looked at her sister, almost in shock. "Derek's going to kill that girl," she said in a hushed voice.

CHAPTER THIRTEEN
WATCHERS

Jennifer Bradley sat on her living room couch, letting the material fold and distort underneath her as she reached down to the floor and pulled up a brown and orange afghan to wrap herself up in. She shoveled a mouthful of popcorn into her mouth while flipping channels aimlessly, not even really wanting to watch anything. Behind her, her mother stepped in from the kitchen and watched the channels that flickered by for a moment. "Jennifer, did you eat your chicken?" she asked as she dried a dish.

"Mm-hmm," the girl responded, never taking her eyes off the screen. "Wuz good."

"Thank you," the older woman responded politely. "Oh wait, stop there honey."

Jennifer flicked back a channel or two, halting at her mother's requested stop.

"... olice force that was already assembled to look for escaped murderer Derek Smith, have now been forced to divide their efforts, also searching for missing local teen August Styles. Styles and her boyfriend Timothy Brassington disappeared from their Coral Beach homes approximately two hours ago, and have not been seen since _"

"Isn't it just awful, Jen?" she said in a hushed voice, putting down the plate and cloth on a nearby table. "I wouldn't know what to do if that had been you."

Jennifer stared at the screen, its warm glow reflecting off her pupils as the images danced before her.

Mike turned down a nearby alley as Xander followed, looking for anything that might give them even the slightest clue of where the pair might be. "You seeing anything?" he called out, checking a nearby sunken entrance to a Chili's.

Xander frowned. "I lost their scent about three blocks back. Been trying to find it again ever since."

"And?"

"Got a couple of quick whiffs, nothing enough to say for sure it was them... and they were too far apart. I think they must have got a cab or a ride or something."

Mike looked down at the shorter man, becoming satisfied, in a frustrated way, that there was nothing here either. The pair began to walk back down 52nd street and would soon move to 53rd (King Street, as it had been renamed last year), having decided to take a grid approach to their search. "Is it possible that they were... taken?"

Xander shot him a look. "If there's one scent I'm sure I'd recognize, it's his. Haven't caught so much as a trace of him since we started, or I would've told you."

"Fair enough," Mike sighed, running both his hands

through his hair. "We've checked everywhere I would go. Everywhere you would go... now we're just walking around, man."

"I know," Xander agreed, reaching for his cigarettes and then stopping himself for the third time, not wanting anything to dull his senses. "But we've got to remember, these two wouldn't think like us. I know they're our *age*, but we can't really get into their heads like we could someone else."

Mike clenched a fist, slammed it once against a brick wall, then continuing his walk as if nothing had happened. "Think. What about the motels? That seems like a good option. It's late, they're going to need a place to sleep."

Xander nodded. "Cathy's been calling them ever since we left. She hasn't turned up anything so far, but if we think they got a cab maybe we should call her and tell her to check the ones in Coral Cove, too."

Mike's eyes bulged as he realized how wide their search area was getting. "We suck. We need new brains. I mean, where would they go? What kind of state of -"

Xander raised a palm quickly, stopping his friend in mid-sentence, raising his head as high as he could, then taking a long, circular breath in through his nose.

"Anything?" Mike asked, hopeful.

Xander frowned. "No. Thought I caught her for a second, but it was gone. The window must have been down in the cab or something, she's scattered everywhere."

For a brief moment, Mike thought of what would happen if Derek found them first, bringing a certain literalness to the statement. He forced the thought out of his mind. "You going to be okay?" he asked. "I want to mind these kids, but if you're starting to feel womb-y, we'll take a time out and bring you to the church."

Xander shook his head. "Even if you did, I'm not sleeping tonight."

Mike nodded.

Xander stopped again, raising his nostrils high and stretching them to their utmost.

"You have a boogy," Mike said under his breath.

Xander shot him a look, as his eyes returned to their normal, human-coloring again. He ignored the statement. "They stopped here. There's a big stain of them here, and then nothing all of a sudden. And motor grease. They were definitely in a taxi."

Mike took out his cell phone and slid it open. His large fingers lumbered on the keys as he typed check local cabs and then pressed send. "Why would they stop here?" he asked, doubtful. "There's no spot to rest or get food within two blocks."

Xander looked all around, surveying the buildings around them, finally stopping when his eyes found something across the street. "I think I'm finally getting into their train of thought," he grumbled, and started to cross the street without further explanation.

Mike turned, looking ahead in the direction he was walking, and sighed. It was a quaint little specialty store, called Baby Bash. He grinned despite himself, then jogged to catch up with his friend as they both reached the entrance. "Of course. They're getting ready. They're kids, they probably don't even realize how far off the baby actually is."

Xander nodded, cupping his hands around his eyes to

peer in through the glass door.

"It's closed," Mike said, trying the knob despite himself.

Xander lashed out, smashing through the window with one swift strike that sent shards of broken glass flying in all directions. He grinned at Mike as he turned the latch from the inside, ignoring the blood that traveled down his arm and dripped onto the street below. "I have a key."

Mike sighed even as he opened the door. "You're a tool. I have a key... who says that in real life... I have a key."

The pair stepped in, Mike being mindful of the broken glass.

Xander ignored him.

The shop looked like it had once been a video store, the way the shelves were built and aligned, the 'employees only' section in the back having been the 'adults only' section in its previous incarnation. There were blue and pink stuffed teddy bears and rattles and many items featuring Winnie the Pooh all along the left side of the store, with more practical items like diapers, clothing, and cribs along the right. He leaned back his head and sniffed, his eyes growing wide. "They were here."

Mike shot him a surprised look, even as he picked up a pink bear, squeezing it's tummy to make it produce a squeaking noise. "You weren't sure? Next time, how about being sure before all the breaking and entering."

Xander stepped toward the back room, and Mike followed after only a moment's pause. Xander twisted the knob to the room, finding it to be locked as well. He twisted hard to the right. The bolt inside snapped with a loud crack. He opened the door and continued in as if nothing had happened.

"More breaking and entering..." Mike grumbled, although he had become aware that he was talking to himself.

Xander looked all around the small room quickly, finding what he was searching for quickly on the table. It was a small lock box. He produced a single claw from his index finger, slid it inside the lock, and pulled. The metal shattered into pieces on the floor. "Just don't make 'em like they used to," he said, opening the box and ruffling through the paper inside. He pulled out a large wad of bills, each one separated by a different rubber band depending on their value, and tossed it aside, instead picking up a pile of receipts and fumbling through them.

"What are you looking for?" Mike finally had to ask, eyeing the bills and feeling temptation, which he immediately brushed away.

Xander stopped, taking one receipt out of the box and then closing it, with a loud clang. "This," he said, handing him the large line of paper.

Mike scanned over it, finding there were easily a hundred items on the list, ranging from diapers to toys to a crib. It was timestamped just a few hours before, probably as the store was closing. "And what does this tell us?" he asked, putting the paper in his pocket.

Xander started to march out in much the same way he had come in, only this time Mike was right there with him instead of jogging behind, both men fueled by the fact that they were still on the right trail. "Tells us we don't need to widen our search. Before we were looking for two kids on the run. Now we're look for two kids on the run carrying over a hundred baby items. That's going to make their job harder... and ours easier."

"Makes someone else's easier too, may I remind you."

"You don't have to," Xander said, as the two kept walking down the road side by side, turning the corner onto King Street.

CHAPTER FOURTEEN
DETECT

It was like watching a volcano erupt, or a hurricane grow from a gust of wind into a force of nature.

I curled into Mike and covered my eyes, as if not seeing would in some way protect me from what was going on. His cologne rubbed off on me, and it allowed me a seconds release. But only a second, because that was exactly how long I could look away.

Adam Genblade jumped onto the table, shattering the pitcher of water that had been on it into a million tiny jagged shards. I have a very clear memory of this, the glass falling as water began to pour out, glimmering light as it went. The water hit the floor first, then the glass. It broke and splashed at the same time, and for one instant, I couldn't tell the difference between the two of them. The glass had become fluid, the water hard.

Genblade screamed something as this was happening, I have no idea what. It snapped my attention back to reality, back to him. His orange prison jumpsuit clung to his heavy, muscular body with sweat, and I could smell his BO from the back of the courthouse. He looked dirty and menacing, his teeth that were filed down to serrated edges, his gums bleeding even though he had done nothing to them.

I chanced a look at Xander. I didn't think he could see me from where he was, there were too many people there. His eyes were glued on Genblade, and his mouth was an odd shape somewhere between shocked and enraged. His fists were clenched so tight that his knuckles were pale, and small driblets of blood oozed down them. I had never seen him so afraid in all my life, but I have since it once or twice since. He spoke, and even though it was a whisper, I knew exactly what he had said: "Genblade's free."

ʎ✕ʎ

Cathy sat alone in the smoking section, her hair a mess and her face conspicuously devoid of any sort of make-up. There were bags under her eyes, and if asked to describe herself, she probably would have said 'road-kill,' or something of the like.

She let out a long, tired breath and stared up at the graying sky. *Don't you dare snow on me,* she thought spitefully, willing the weather to cooperate with her today of all days. It seemed that nothing else was going to.

"Is this a private sulk, or can anyone join?"

She turned her head without parting it from the brick it was leaned upon. She was surprised at how comfortable it was. Maybe it was that it reminded her of Xander, but somehow the moldy old wall had grown on her... although not literally, she hoped.

Tommy smiled, both hands thrust into the deep pockets of his jeans.

She turned away, giving no sign to dismay his presence, which he took as encouragement and sat down next to her. "Have you heard from them?" he asked, getting comfortable as he found a dry spot to lean.

"No," she said blankly, shaking her head. "Not since they called and told me to check the cab companies."

"Same here, asked me to call hotels in Coral Cove. Got nothing. You?"

"Nada," she droned, staring at the skyline. "We're losing them, Tom."

"It's only been a day."

"I encourage you to remember that *last* time we said that about a missing child."

"Wasn't always that way, though. Mike and Xander saved that little boy from Malcolm that one time."

Cathy nodded. "You're right. With those two on it, that girl's got a hell of a chance."

"With those two around, we might have a chance, too," he smirked.

"Nice to know we're appreciated," Xander said, even as he came around the corner, a lit cigarette already between his lips and being inhaled.

"Anything?" Cathy asked. She stood up and hugged Xander without even thinking.

"No," he said, giving her a friendly squeeze before they parted. "Mike's getting some coffee, this wasn't his first all nighter. We got a lead, spent the rest of the night chasing it. Didn't come up with much, but we're going again in a minute... we just came to check in."

She nodded, stepping away from him as the nicotine

itched at her nose.

Xander turned to Tommy then, as if only now fully realizing his presence. "You two get anywhere?"

Tommy shook his head. "They haven't been in any motels. I even got..." he paused to choose his words carefully, "... our friend in the Cove to make a few calls to places that aren't in the phone book, but she came up with squat."

Xander nodded. "You tried, that's all that matters."

"What did you find?" Cathy asked.

"One place they visited. They bought something, looks like a direct payment bank card or some shit. We're going to try to use it to narrow our playing field."

She nodded.

"You two get to class," Xander said, tossing his cigarette into the snow.

"You can't just do that!" Tommy protested, his arrogance and anger coming through, something that was rarely seen in him anymore.

"We care about August, too," Cathy added, flicking Xander on the forehead as if to make his brain start working.

Xander looked at her, expressionless. He turned to Tommy, then back again. "I know," he said finally, in an obvious tone of voice, as if he did not know where their attack on him was coming from. "You guys are helping. Most of the best intel we have right now came from in there," he said, motioning up at the school. "Someone in there knows where she is -- or at least knows how she got in her current situation -- and I want to know who."

Cathy nodded, followed reluctantly by Tommy.

"Get to class."

She nodded and walked past him around the corner.

Tommy moved to walk past too, but Xander stopped him, placing a hand against his chest.

"Not you," Xander said simply.

Tommy almost laughed, shrugging the hand away and moving to go past. Xander grabbed him by the arm and threw him to the ground, nearly beating his head off the brick wall.

He knelt down to become on equal eye level with Tommy, who was hissing in sharp pain and clutching his arm. "Not you," he repeated, casually, as if the short burst of violence had not even happened.

"What the fuck is the matter with you?" Tommy glared.

"I want to make sure whose side of the game you're playing on," Xander stated, lighting another smoke.

"What?" Tommy yelled, moving to get up only to be held back by Xander again.

Xander shoved him, hard, and Tommy decided not to try to move again. "You been on the fence for months. Some days it seems like you're with us, some days it seems like you're against us... most days doesn't seem like you care. Truth told, I didn't really care either... but it's different now. Derek's loose, and that means new rules. I need to know where you stand... so *I* can decide whether I stand with you, or if you're just another person I'm gonna put in the ground."

Tommy looked up at him, his face somber with just the smallest bit of spite.

Xander raised an eyebrow as smoke curled around his

head, awaiting a response.

"I'm with you. I'm with Mike," he said, and Xander finally released his hold and let him rise to his feet.

"Good!" Xander said happily, slapping his back warmly but forcefully. "Because if you're wondering why you're staying here why me and Mike go do the grunt work... it's because I need someone I can trust to protect Cathy, just in case Derek shows up and decides to go Columbine again -- Can we trust you?"

Tommy nodded.

"Good."

Putrid black liquid sputtered from a hidden nozzle and splashed into the small paper cup as Mike batted two packets of artificial sweetener against the palm on his hand, trying to loosen the contents within. The machine groaned with effort, the slop it spit out looking less like coffee and more like axle grease. He pushed the thought aside and poured the sweetener in, using a small wooden tongue depressor to stir it. He lifted the cup to his mouth and took a long chug, his face curling with disgust when he stopped long enough for the taste to really set in. "Ugh," he grunted in response to the bitter concoction, then took more.

"How you can drink that, I have no idea," came a calm, soothing voice from behind him. He didn't even have to turn around to know that it was Gallagher.

"As I understand it, you have quite a taste for coffee yourself, sir," Mike said, a little less politely than he usually would have. The lack of sleep was beginning to effect his personality.

Gallagher slid five quarters into the snack machine next to Mike, then stepped back a pace to make his selection. "That," he responded, motioning to the cup, "is not coffee. That is what is left over *after* the coffee is made. It is coffee's refuse, my son. What I have in my office, that is coffee." He pressed the button to make a cereal bar plop down, then reached down to pick it up.

"Agreed. Can't be that different, though."

Gallagher stood back up and smiled mischievously. "Not all on its own of course, no. But if one were in a position to, say, bless the water he used in his coffee every morning..."

Mike raised an eyebrow. "You'd do that?"

"I trust my secret is safe with you, my son?"

Mike chuckled, nodding. "It's Mike... sir."

Gallagher looked at him quizzically for a moment, then nodded. "I am sorry, Mike."

Mike frowned, downed the rest of the coffee, then tossed the cup in the trash. "Not nearly as sorry as I am, sir."

Xander entered the cafeteria. He smiled warmly at Gallagher when he got close and fixed his collar. For some reason being around the holy man always made Xander very aware of how presentable he was. "Good morning, Father."

"Good morning, my son."

Xander shot a look at Mike motioned toward Gallagher. Mike shook his head. Xander rolled his eyes.

"Am I... missing something?" Gallagher asked, quaintly amused by their little charade.

"We were wondering if you'd heard anything about the girl," Xander said, causing Mike to turn and slam his head against the coffee machine. "What?"

"Way to be subtle," Mike groaned, rummaging about his pockets as the need for more caffeine came upon him.

"No, I haven't..." Gallagher said after a moment. He took one last bite of his bar then disposed of the wrapper. "... I was wondering if the two of you were looking for her as well. Have you found anything?"

Xander produced the receipt from his pocket and showed it to Gallagher.

Gallagher glanced over it, then looked back at them. "Where did you get this?" he asked.

"Uh..." Mike stammered, as more coffee droned out of the machine.

"Say no more," he interrupted, raising his hand in objection. "I've just decided I'd rather not know."

"Hear no evil?" Xander smirked, amused.

"Exactly," Gallagher grinned. "Although I don't know how much good this will do you."

Xander placed a hand on Gallagher's shoulder, taking back the slip of paper. "Plenty, with your help, father."

Mike shot Xander a look.

ʎ⟨⟩ʎ

Xander sat down at the computer in the Guidance Office and made himself comfortable. The desk was small and the keyboard was completely covered with file folders. Xander stacked them on the floor next to the desk and frowned. He turned back to Gallagher, who was pouring up three cups of coffee. "You don't even know how to use this, do you?"

Gallagher started to protest, lost his words, then gave up. "Sometimes I think that machine is the antithesis of everything I have dedicated my life too."

Xander smirked, switched on the monitor, and waited for it to warm up. He squinted to see it as it did, seeing a flashing red exclamation point next to the mail icons. "You do know you've got, like, a hundred unread e-mails from Principal Shnieder in here, right?"

"What?" Gallagher gaped. He handed Mike his coffee and set another next to Xander.

Xander picked it up absent-mindedly, took a long sip, then put it back down. "Yeah. Something about more student files, electronic ones... they don't have physical files yet, taking too long to print. They're for when you're done with the physical ones."

Gallagher turned to the still-growing stack of physical files that populated his desk and huffed. "I hate that man," he said finally, his shoulders slumping.

"This is amazing!" Mike said between sips.

"There's more," Gallagher smiled, motioning back to the full pot with his mug.

Mike's eyes bulged happily, as his knee started to shake from overdose of caffeine.

Xander shot Gallagher a look that the older man recognized as 'cut him off soon.' He'd learned the look well when holding Easter mass. The cardinals would always give it to him in regard to a particular Bishop that always seemed to overestimate how much wine they should bless and have to drink it afterward.

"So what are we doing exactly?" Gallagher asked,

leaning in over Xander's shoulder to watch.

"Mmm," Mike agreed, not bothering to take his mouth away from his mug to do so. He sat on Gallagher's desk and got comfortable.

Xander twisted, a tightness forming in his chest as Gallagher got into his personal space, but decided to say nothing. "You know all that crap at the bottom of the receipt when you pay for it with a bank card?" he asked rhetorically, tapping the paper twice. "Well, it's not just gobledy-gook, it's actually a code that's specific to that card. If we can trace the card, we can see if it was used anywhere else, and for what, and try to get a good idea of where these kids are hiding out."

Gallagher nodded, impressed. "I didn't know my computer could do that."

Xander made a side-to-side motion with his hand, even as he opened up the Internet browser. "It can't, not really. But I can use programs on the Internet that can."

Mike raised an eyebrow, finally taking his coffee away from his lips. "Um... I'm a little more tech-savvy, and I'm pretty sure there's no web-site called www. Please enter a interac code so you can track it .com."

Xander grinned. "Remember when my computer melted a few months back?"

"Vaguely."

"Well, I lost everything. All the programs I'd spent years creating and working online with people all over the world to create... pft, gone. So, when I finally got my computer back and started to rebuild, I decided to load everything up onto an ftp site periodically so that it wouldn't happen again... which also means I can access those files from anywhere with an Internet connection."

"Ftp?" Gallagher asked absently, watching in amazement as Xander typed something long and incoherent in the address bar, seemingly from memory.

"File Transfer Protocol," Xander explained, eyes now glued to the screen.

"I almost don't want to ask this," Mike sighed, rubbing his temples. "But since when do you own a ftp site?"

Xander grinned. "I don't."

"Then - "

"I'm using someone else's so that it won't be traced back to us. I'm not going to copy the program to this computer, just activate while it's on the ftp. That way, if anyone -- say, the police -- wanted to track who was entering the banking database without permission, they'd just wind up chasing the owner of the ftp site."

"And whom, pray tell, is that?"

Xander smiled devilishly. "It's located within the FBI server that tracks the illegal hacking of bank sites. They wind up chasing their own tails, and they keep looping on themselves forever, until they give up. I did it the second I figured out Tim White's username and password."

Mike laughed and slapped his knee.

Gallagher raised his finger. "I take it that's not... legal."

Xander stopped, looking from Mike to Gallagher silently.

"I understand. I was never here."

"Yeah, that'd be smart," Xander nodded.

"And practice it more," Mike added, patting the man's shoulder. "You'll be needing that little speech a lot around him."

Xander rolled his eyes. "Three times that happened. Will you let it go?"

The icon in the top right hand corner of the screen spun slowly, then eventually a web site that looked like any other folder filled with files came up. One file was marked 'code-breaker,' another 'mac-clone.' He double-clicked on the icon of a cartoon money sign with a smiling set of teeth on it labeled 'money-mate.' A simplistic program popped up on the screen, with vacant spaces one could type in. The spaces were not marked, something that the creator (a friend of Xander's from overseas) had insisted upon so that if it were ever found, there was a plausible denial for what the program was used for, which there wouldn't be if the program had been labeled with fields such as : 'stick in card number.'

Xander typed in the long string of numbers at the bottom of the receipt, his fingers gliding over the number pad easily. He lost his place only once, recounted the digits, then entered the last five and stopped. He clicked exit.

"What the hell?" Mike asked.

Gallagher shot him a look.

"...heck?"

"It's a failsafe the designer implemented to make sure nobody that shouldn't be using the program could. If you click enter it'll lock your computer and download roughly fifty trojan horses from the net. The commands are all re-versed. It's pretty keen, actually."

A dollar sign appeared on the screen and rotated clockwise, eventually stopping when a long list of trans-actions came up. Xander quickly scrolled to the bottom of the list and began to read. Mike took out a pen and jotted down the locations.

"Okay, after Baby Bash they went to a convenience store at 67 main street and got some milk and eggs and stuff like that. Then they spent forty-six dollars and seventy-two cents at The Candy Shoppe," he said, rolling his eyes. "Then they went to a sporting goods store on Plymoth avenue and got... sleeping bags... and then --" he scrolled down some more. His brow furrowed. " -- they went to two movies... and another one this morning. And that's the last entry."

Mike looked up, perplexed. "What, they didn't sleep anywhere last night?"

"I didn't say this was perfect."

"No, no this doesn't make sense at all. Did you check with their relatives?"

"If you think the police and their parents didn't do that you're high."

"Then where are they?"

"I don't know. Where's Derek?"

Mike glowered.

Xander pushed the keyboard away from him. It clacked against the screen's base.

"No, this doesn't even make sense when you get into their mindset."

"Not that we can."

"No, we can. Think about it. How did they get into a movie carrying a hundred baby items, groceries, *and* two sleeping bags? Where would they have put it all? There wasn't enough time between one and the other for them to have dropped it somewhere else."

Xander's eyes sparked. He closed the bank program and clicked in the address bar again, calling up a mapping web site and clicking on a link that read 'plot points.' Immediately a screen asking for an area code and city name popped up, which he typed in quickly, trying to move as fast as his train on thought did. A virtual map of Coral Beach snapped up with a tiny compass in the bottom left and a small graph for the height of land. "Okay, here's where that baby needs store was," he thought aloud, clicking on the location and marking it with a red dot. "Where was the corner store again?"

Mike looked back through his notes. "Sixty-seven Main."

Xander marked it too, and now a line automatically was drawn between the two locations.

Gallagher watched this intently, intrigued.

"Okay, and the Candy Shoppe?"

"Thirty-six Plymoth," Gallagher stated, causing both parties to look at him. "I have a sweet tooth."

Xander shrugged and clicked on the building. Two more lines were drawn, linking all three together to form a triangle. In a blank field at the top of the screen Xander typed the word hotel. Five blue markers flashed on the screen -- none remotely close to the triangle.

"Damn," Mike cursed, resulting in another glance from Gallagher. He shifted uncomfortably.

Xander raised a finger for pause, even as he deleted the word hotel and put in theatre. Three blue dots flashed on the screen, one close to the school, one across town... and one smack dab in the middle of the triangle. He grinned and clicked on the dot. "The C.B. Cinema. First established in 1972," he quoted proudly as he scrolled down the page.

Mike flipped through his notes. "That's the one they went to all three movies at, all right. I think we just narrowed our search field."

Xander shook his head and highlighted a sentence at the bottom of the document. "I think we just ended out search."

Gallagher leaned forward to read what it said, squinting his eyes. "Purchased after bankruptcy -- five years ago -- by Steven S. Brassington. Isn't that Tim's last name?"

"And wouldn't you know it, it was once an apartment complex that got renovated in the seventies -- still some vacant apartments below the theatre. Wonder if any of the members of the Brassington family members have a key and store stuff there?"

Mike got up from the desk, scuttling his notes into the garbage and downing the last sip of his coffee. "Come on," he said sternly. "It might be day, but that won't stop Derek if he finds them first... or any of the other lunatics in this town, for that matter."

"I'm coming too," Gallagher announced, grabbing his coat off the hook in the corner. "Those children are scared, and she knows me... she may need guidance."

"A guidance councilor that gives guidance... that's a first for this school," Xander said as he closed out of his programs. He glanced at the time as he did so, then bit his lower lip. "Fuck. I can't come," he stated, slamming a fist lightly against the table.

"What?" Mike exclaimed, spinning around.

"You go on without me, I've got something important

I have to do," he explained, digging into his inside jacket pocket. "You two go, it'll be fine."

Mike nodded, then turned briefly to Gallagher, and both men headed out the door.

Xander stood alone. He looked up at the wall and saw a cross tacked there carefully, the visage of Jesus being crucified upon it. He frowned at it as the womb-organ within him flared, just slightly. "No rest for the righteous," he said to himself, then started toward the door.

ᚠᚠᚠ

A leaf fell from the elm, and then another.

No longer green, they were deep deep red that penetrated the gaze of all those that looked upon them, dry and arid and cold. They felt like paper and fell apart, with no more consistency than air. More fell, until the elm was bare in the gaze of the sun, everything it once was in pieces at its feet.

ᚠᚠᚠ

Megan sat at the bar of the Rusty Nail, again playing with the spear in her martini, although this time it pierced an onion heart, not an olive. Her hair was down and messy from running her fingers through it the entire day while sorting through files and notes. After an entire night of it, she had decided that Tony had been right -- Jillian Mayer did need to be fired. She vowed to do it at the end of the week. She turned to look around the bar as she took another long sip of her drink, scanning the accumulated masses for a certain face and not finding it. She sighed, cursed, then turned her back.

"Hi," Xander said, holding out a five dollar bill to the bartender. He had been sitting right next to her.

"Fuck!" she exclaimed, clutching at her chest. "If you don't stop doing that, I'm going to put a collar with a little bell on you!"

"It's been tried," he smirked. The bartender took the bill. Xander pointed to the Pepsi cooler. "I try to get it off with my hind legs and wind up limping around for days. Have you given any thought to what I asked?"

She gave him a wry look, glanced him up and down, then took another swig. "I have."

"And?" he pressed. He nodded in thanks as he was passed a cola, then took a long drink.

She sighed. "I can't do it. The case starts *tomorrow*, and I usually take weeks to prepare for one. Not only that, but this would be a slam-dunk case for someone right out of law school, and the Styles mother has hired the best. She really spared no expense in this... I hear she had to borrow money. She really wants this. I'm also not fond of doing a case pro-bono when I'm sure that I'm going to *lose*."

Xander nodded, pretending to consider her points. "Then don't think of it as pro-bono. Think of it as paying me back for saving your life and helping you win the case that made your career."

She growled deep within her throat, glaring at him over her glass.

He sank. "I need help, and you're the only one I can come to," he admitted. He shifted in his chair. "You'll have to help me here, I'm not used to asking for help... and I've had to do a nice bit of it these past few days."

She gave him a sympathetic look, then rolled her

eyes at what she was about to say, knowing full well she shouldn't. "I could get Nathan to help me out, I guess. He's a great lawyer, and he loves any chance to get good PR."

"Thanks," Xander smiled, pushing back a strand of her hair with one finger and accidentally brushing against her cheek. "I mean it."

She smiled at him. "One day, I'm going to tell the bartender here just how old you are, and he's going to shit a brick then throw you out on your ass."

"I'm pretty sure I could take him," he replied smugly, finishing his drink before standing.

She grabbed his arm. "One last thing," she said. "It looks pretty bad in this sort of case when the defense shows up to court without a *defendant*."

"Already taken care of," Xander said as he headed toward the door.

She watched him go, and couldn't help but shake her head and smile.

CHAPTER FIFTEEN
LOWER LEVELS

Mike hopped down the last three stairs leading to the basement of the C.B. Cinema, landing next to Gallagher. "You sure we've got the right place this time? I'm not too keen on stepping into another rat trap," he sighed, looking at the chipped purple door in front of them.

Gallagher looked at the post-it in his hand, then at the surrounding buildings. "When one has tried every other venue, whatever is left, no matter how improbable, must be the correct option."

Mike gave him a blank stare, then motioned toward the door. "So... this is it, right?"

Gallagher nodded, heaving a low huff. He reached out and tried the knob, twisting it in one direction and then the other. "This one is locked."

Mike cocked one eyebrow and grinned mischievously. "I happen to have a key," he chimed as he raised a foot high and thrust it forward, just as Gallagher got out of the way. The rusted bolt snapped and sent splintered wood flying in all directions.

"First hacking, now breaking and entering... how many crimes must I commit with you today?" Gallagher spat before composing himself.

"Just a few more, I promise," Mike drawled. Stepping inside, he raised his voice, "Okay kids, party's..." he took stock of the situation. It was just one room and a bathroom. Food and baby care items were stacked and crowded all over the place, along with wrappers and cereal boxes. And in the corner, looking quite terrified, was August Styles... her face staring up in fear, with tears streaming -- and Tim Brassington. Tim stood between she and Mike, both his fists clenched. "Over," he finished, his voice considerably humbled.

Gallagher brushed past him, stepping into August's view. "My child... are you all right?" he said calmly, and even Mike was soothed by the tone of it. It had an ethereal quality.

August said nothing, but turned her head just slightly toward him. There was soot on her face. She burst past her boyfriend and into Gallagher's arms, tears wailing down her cheeks as he patted her on the back, trying desperately to calm her. "They - want - ed - to - take - my - baby!"

"I know, sweetheart... I know," he breathed. He flashed Mike a quick thumbs up.

Mike allowed himself a small moment of relaxation, then turned to Tim, who had unwound his fists. "Hey," he said, presenting his chest and trying to look as macho as possible without actually causing any damage to the frail young man.

"Hi?" Tim responded, backing away just a little.

"I need to ask you something," Mike said, wrapping

an arm around the boy's shoulder. "You know what sex is, don't you, Tim?"

"Michael!" Gallagher protested, looking up in anger but still holding the girl.

Mike raised a finger for silence, then met the boy's gaze. "Do you?"

Tim nodded, blushing a little from embarrassment and refusing to make eye contact.

"You didn't have sex with August... did you?" he smiled, trying to look as sincere as he could.

Tim shook his head. "No, she doesn't even know!"

Mike smiled, "Good boy," he released the boy, then started to walk away. "Come on, Rev... we better get these kids back to their - "

"I tried to tell her!" Tim spat quickly, the words all jumbling together.

Mike's eyes went wide, and he turned back to the boy. "I'm sorry?"

"I tried to tell her what sex is," he repeated, still almost incoherent, but slower at least. He spoke like a deaf person would, and Mike was having a hard time understanding him completely. "She said it wasn't true -- she said what I said was something else."

"Really?" Mike smiled, stepping back toward the boy. "And what, pray tell, did she call it when you told her about sex?"

Tim looked more nervous the more Mike paid attention to him. "She called it studying."

Mike processed that for a moment, then nodded. "Thank you, Tim."

He walked back to Gallagher, who stared up at him

quizzically. "So, that's it then?" he wondered aloud, more to himself than to Mike, "It's over?"

"Not by a long shot," Mike corrected. "Now the hard part begins."

CHAPTER SIXTEEN
FLASHBACKS

The door to Xander's home wriggled on loose hinges as Cathy stepped in. She slid off her shoes and placed them to one side of the porch before stepping onto the dusty-rose colored carpet. The floor was ice cold. A shiver went up and down her spine. She sighed, then decided to leave her jacket on. "Xander?" she called out, tilting her head to look up the stairs toward his bedroom.

There was only silence in return for a long moment, and then she thought she heard a slight shuffle from the upstairs hall. She raised an eyebrow and began to walk up, stopped, then placed one hand on the banister. She turned. Everything was still and tranquil, like a Norman Rockwell painting. But the air was sticky and thick despite the cold, like wading through half-frozen honey. There was smoke upon it, and since Xander didn't smoke in the house, it was fair to assume that his father had been here not too long ago.

That, or somebody else who smoked.

She turned and looked back at the porch, and remembered a day months ago. The house had been cold that day too, even though it had been mid-September. Sticky, too. There had been a coppery taste in her mouth as Derek had thrown her to the floor. She recalled the feeling of Mr. Drew's gun in her hand as she pulled the trigger, sending a bullet straight through Derek's shoulder and out the other side, spattering blood and bits of flesh everywhere. Mrs. Drew had tried for forever to get the stains out, but if you looked at the wall from the right angle and in the right light, you could still see it. Xander once told her that his senses could even still smell it, the scent of Derek Smith's blood... which meant that if he were in the house, Xander might not notice.

Slowly, she inched her way back down the stairs until she was on level floor again. Keeping one eye trained on Xander's bedroom door she turned and went into the kitchen, fighting to urge to run as much as she could. Running made too much noise, and she'd announced her presence enough as it was. Checking around the corner and the blind spot created by the stove, she avoided the entire area where her confrontation with Derek had been to make her way to the cutlery drawer. She pulled it open and shoved aside spoons and works, rustling about frantically for anything that could be used as a weapon. She found nothing, and had to fight not to slam the drawer shut, moving down a foot and opening up the dishwasher. A foot-long butcher knife with a black plastic handle was perched at one side, jutting up at her like a sword in a stone. She picked it up, still stained with bits of ham, and turned back toward the stairs.

She stopped for a moment and observed a note left

against to toaster from Xander's mom, telling him she would be at the hospital with his father for most of the evening. She leaned her head back slightly so that her hair fell back and away from her eyes, then crept her way back up the stairs.

Immediately there was another shuffling sound, followed by a skittering and then a plunk.

Sweat began to drip down her face and chest as the floor boards began to creak, and she bit her lip as she willed them to stop. She reached the top of the stairs and looked both ways, examining all of the doors that were closed securely, taking heart that she should be able to hear if someone came out of one behind her. She headed toward Xander's bedroom door, placed her back flat against it, and brought the blade up with one hand while slowly reaching for the knob with the other...

-BA-RIIING!-

The sound leapt out from her hip and even shook it with vibrations, making her jump nearly out of her skin. She dropped the knife to the floor. It landed blade down and sunk a quarter-inch into the wood. She jolted downward to pick it up as she reached for the cell phone at her hip. There was a noticeable scuffle inside Xander's room, and a moan.

"Hello?" she said in a hurried whisper, backing away from the door a pace or two now.

On the other end, there was only silence.

"Hello?!" she repeated, forgetting to quiet her voice.

"... Cath?" came the strained voice from over the line. If voices had been something physical, this one would have been put through a cheese grater before speaking.

"Xander?" she responded, unsure. She flipped the phone closed and stepped back toward the door, opening it quickly.

Xander lay on the floor, his skin an opaque grey as he stared in dismay at the telephone which lay a few feet from his head, now making an annoying beeping sound at him. His clothes were tight against his frame from sweat and the expansion of his musculature. A pool of black liquid had gathered around his head, seemingly coming from his mouth and nose, and a similar large black stain was on the crotch of his pants. His eyes were once again completely black, but lacked their particular shine, no longer resembling oil but now more that of unpolished coal. His lips were cracked and dry, and the rest of his skin didn't seem far from it. He let out a haggard cough, resulting in even more black liquid. His hands did not have claws on them yet, but instead seemed to be permanently disfigured and distorted to look like claws, his fingers twisting out in all directions. One of his legs was bent back near the breaking point, something she had seen before during his transformation, and seemed to imply that he became double-jointed after a transformation, to allow for the more fluid movement of his alter ego.

"Oh my god," she said, dropping the knife again. He looked amazingly like a steroid-infused albino drowning in tar.

"Don't..." Xander gasped, black blood bubbling from his nose. "You'll need that..." he said, desperately motioning toward the knife she dropped.

"Not likely," she tisked, taking a second away from her horror to debunk his suicidal tendencies. "If I won't let you do that on your own, you're even more stupid than I think if you expect me to help."

He sighed, looking defeated.

"How did this even happen? It's not nearly time for the Womb to come out."

He coughed again. "Been getting tired more often, at weird hours," he said as he turned and pushed off the floor slowly, trying to get to his feet. He found it hard, as if he were chained to the floor. "Like it's trying to make up for all those months of hibernation O'Toole put it in. Like maybe those treatments were never intended to be stopped... stopped --"

"Once they started?" Cathy finished, taking pity on the boy. She helped him to his feet and into the seat next to his computer.

He managed to nod his head once.

Cathy got the distinct impression that had his eyes been visible, they would have been bloodshot. "Actually, I did a wikipedia search on some of the ingredients mentioned in O'Toole's files. I don't think any of them were for the mixture itself, just to make it transmittable by touch."

"So he could easily administer it," Xander agreed.

"Exactly," she smiled, getting a tissue from off the desk and using it to wipe some of the black bile off of his chin. "One of those chemicals was lysergic acid."

"The fuck is that?" he said, reaching for a half-empty glass of orange juice on the top of his computer's tower and literally pouring it down his throat, seeming to get more and more of his strength back the more her presence awoke him.

"It's what LSD is synthesized from."

Xander's eyes went wide, locking with hers for the first time since she came in. "Come again?"

"I think you're having drug flashbacks."

"That's beautiful," he responded sarcastically. "It's like the gift that keeps on giving."

"Mmm," she hummed. She cleaned the last bit of ooze and noticed that his skin pigmentation had returned to normal, but that his eyes remained very dark, only now showing even the slightest sliver of white along the edges. She wondered briefly if it was the Womb or the drugs causing it. She reached into his desk drawer and produced a pair of cheesy eighties-style sunglasses and handed them to him. "Think you can make it to the church?" she frowned, raising one eyebrow.

He nodded, took the glasses, and allowing her to help him to his feet.

"I should," he half smiled. "We've got a big day tomorrow."

⋏⋏

The gavel slammed down hard, creating an echo heard throughout the entire courtroom, and all present felt its reverberations.

The room was hot and humid, a stark difference to the blistering cold outside, making the windows steam. It hit all that entered and made them feel even more weight than the mere situation itself presented, as if their physical surroundings were mirroring their emotional ones. The courtroom itself was small and seemed much older than the one that had housed Adam Genblade's trial a few months before, though it was in the same building. The walls and seats were not kept with as much care, and as Xander's enhanced eyesight picked up spots where paint had been touched up and his nostrils inhaled dander and cobwebs from under the seats he recognized as being months old, he worried that he and his friends may have been the only ones taking this case seriously.

Megan brushed a strand of hair away from her face as she stood at near-perfect attention, taking the opportunity to spare a glance back at him and remind him that this was not the case.

"You may be seated," Judge Walton said after a long pause. He was an older man and the fluorescent lights gleamed brightly off of his balding head as he leaned forward to straighten his robe and prepare to sit, the loose skin around his cheeks shaking like gelatin. It was clear that at one point he was not as slender as he was now and that his skin had not yet caught up, making it appear loose and saggy. It belied his age, though he looked over sixty, Xander knew him to be not yet forty-five. His father had played bridge with him when he was young.

Xander felt a tap at his arm, and he turned to look at Cathy.

She was grinding her teeth and giving him an annoyed glance, her eyes widening by the second.

He raised an eyebrow to her at first, then realized that he was the last person standing and took his place. "Apologies, your honor."

"None needed, Mr. Drew," Walton replied in a nondescript fashion, barely even giving the boy a glance as his eyes strained through his bifocals to see the small print of the file in front of him.

The smile Xander had pasted on for the Judge faded as he scanned the room. There were very few people present, on either side of the seating area. Cathy and Mike were there. Tommy had wanted to come as well, but Xander had given him a look and he somehow had known not to show up. Tim Brassington was there with his parents -- probably as witnesses for either side -- as well as a man Xander recognized from his stay at the hospital as a doctor, and a sniveling little man he was sure was one of Tony's psychologists. Principal Shnieder and Mr. Miles and Mr. Calender were there as well, showing their support for the school, though for which side, Xander did not know.

"Why am I here again?" Mike whispered softly, leaning over Cathy to Xander. Their seats were directly behind the defendants booths, where Megan, Nathan and August sat.

Xander frowned, keeping his eyes on the Judge's reactions as he went though the papers, trying to discern from his facial expressions which part of the report he was at. "You're here in case we start to go under. Megan will call you up to testify that when you found August and Tim, they seemed fit and prepared for a child."

"Oh, I see," Mike nodded. "You want me to *lie*."

Xander shot him a look.

Cathy frowned and pushed the boys away from each other and back into their upright positions. "I think he's about to start," she hushed.

Judge Walton looked up from his papers, first at Tony and Martha Styles and then over to August, Megan and Nathan. "Interested parties may rise," he said dryly.

Tony was wearing a dark blue pinstripe suit with a red tie that he seemed to be constantly adjusting. His hair had been sliced back and his face perfectly shaven. He looked almost exactly as he did the day of the Genblade trial, save that he seemed taller, now, somehow.

Martha Styles was about forty-five herself, the same age as the Judge. Her hair wasn't quite yet silver, brunette traces still throughout, giving her a distinguished look. She had a round shape to her body and wore an afghan shall over the shoulders of a business suit that Xander was sure Tony had picked out for her, as it seemed nearly identical to Megan's although in opposing colors. Her face was covered over well in make-up, but it was uneven, and looked like it had to have been touched up repeatedly.

Megan and Nathan wore matching dark grey suits, the only difference being that Megan's shortened into a long skirt, allowing her the range of motion she sometimes needed. Her hair, much like Tony's, looked to have been professionally done no more than a few hours before, and she had made every effort to make herself attractive while still being professional to a point.

Nathan looked smoother than the last time Xander had seen him.

Xander realized that he was wearing make-up as well, to cover up a few facial scars no doubt gotten during childhood accidents. He chuckled.

The only one out of place was August. She was wearing a plain white t-shirt and black jeans with a clip instead of a button, which had probably been the best Megan alone could convince her into. It would not have been so bad had the shirt not gotten stained somewhere along the way. She had not stood at Judge Walton's request, and while he had said nothing toward it, it clearly bothered him.

We're off to a great start, Xander thought, rubbing the bridge of his nose. All at once the Womb flared up and he had to fight the urge to buckle over in pain.

Cathy immediately brought a tender hand to his arm. "Are you all right?" she asked, her voice deep with concern.

Xander nodded. "It's just more of the... the..."

"Lysergic acid?" she finished for him, careful not to be in ear shot of anyone who might have recognized the word.

Xander nodded, though he was beginning to perspire. "It'll pass."

"I would like to begin by stating," Judge Walton began, pausing briefly to clear his throat. "That it is a sad day whenever a matter such as this has to be settled in a courtroom. However, under the circumstances, it has been deemed necessary. With that in mind, I would like to hear the opening arguments, starting with Mr. Jones."

Everyone but Tony sat. "Thank you, your honor," he said politely, allowing himself a nod that was almost a bow before stepping around his desk. He poured a drink of water, but did not take a sip. Megan rolled her eyes at this, doing her best to hide the impulse from Judge Walton. He shot her a sideways glance, then moved toward the center of the courtroom.

"Your honor," Tony began slowly, clasping his hands together and scuffling his feet, like a car revving its engine before really taking off. "I've been a part of a number of child custody hearings in my day, as I'm sure you have," he paused, waiting for the judge to nod, which he did. "And I'm sure you'll agree with me when I say that they are almost always a gut-wrenching procedure. Fathers and mothers combating over their children, children having to decide between parents... or worst yet, cases in which neither parent is capable for properly caring for the child. Situations like these are *crimes* against the children of the world your honor, just like any other crime."

Megan once again turned and looked at Nathan, and then Xander.

Xander frowned, realizing that she recognized where he was going with this, and that it was no place good.

"Last month I was the prosecutor in the rape case upstate, and all I could think was : no matter what I do for this girl, it won't make her un-raped. The same with a murder: you can jail the murderer, but we cannot give that person their life back. We cannot give the mothers their children back, and we cannot give their children their father back. It's a justice system I whole heartedly believe in," he said, actually placing a hand upon his heart to illustrate. "But have no issue saying there are flaws in."

"Objection!" Megan barked, standing up so fast it made the blood rush to her head. "He's comparing having a child to a crime, your honor, it's not - "

"It's a hearing, not a trial, Miss. Greene," Judge Walton interrupted. "There is no jury present. Your objection is noted but unnecessary."

"Thank you, your Honor," Tony said, again doing his mock-bow. "The point is this: a child growing up in an unsafe or unsuitable environment is a crime, just as much as rape or murder is. We have laws to protect these children, but so often they are only enforceable *after* the damage is done. We can only take a child away from abusive parents *after* they have been abused.

"Today, your Honor, we have a once-in-a-lifetime opportunity: we can stop a crime before it happens. There is no way that August Styles can properly care for the child that she's carrying. Her mother is not fit to care for the child that she's carrying, by her own admission. Rather than put this young, innocent life through custody battles, foster homes, abuse and neglect... we can stop the cycle right now. We can end this with one punch. August will survive the terrible ordeal of losing her child. She will heal. She will move on. Her child will not," he paused, turned from Walton to give one last look across the room, finally resting on Nathan. "That is all, your Honor."

"Thank you, Mr. Jones," Judge Walton said. He made one last scribble on the folder in front of him, then turned his attention to Megan. "You have the floor, Miss. Greene."

Megan got up, smoothed the lines of her suit briefly, then smiled at the Judge.

Behind the defense station, the womb-organ flared up again, only to die back down.

Martha Styles whispered something unidentifiable to Tony, who nodded.

"Your Honor, in the past thirty years we as a people have made wonderful strides in how we treat others, specifically the less fortunate. There was a time, not all that long ago, when if a white man got a black woman pregnant, not only could he force her to have an abortion... but he could initiate it himself with his fists.

"Gladly, we no longer operate like that. One of the great foundations of this country is the people's right to choose their own destiny. We have foundations and laws set up now to protect minorities against such treatment... laws which are being ignored here today. Blatantly. If this were any other fifteen year old girl at that school, this would not have even been a question. It is the fact that she had Down syndrome that she is here, and it goes against so many of our society's fundamental beliefs that it is un-believable.

"Mr. Jones talks about preventing the crime before it happens," she tilted her head to one side, "A promising argument. The problem with it is that you don't know when somebody is going to kill. You don't know when somebody is going to rape. And we do not know that Au-gust Styles will be a bad mother. She may have a lot to learn -- every new mother does -- but the point is that her presence here today proves that she is equipped with the only tool a good mother really needs: unflappable love for her newborn child.

"It's true that August was coerced into sexual inter-course. It's true she was convinced to run away from home, though it had crossed her mind anyway. But the fact that she maintains her position on keeping her child even though these same people want to take it from her just strengthens my resolve. She will make a good mother, if we let her." She turned to the Judge. "Someone had to give your mother a chance at some point, right?"

She turned back toward the court, walked to her place, and took a seat. This time she did not even look at Tony.

Cathy smiled, nodding to herself.

"Impressive arguments, both. I'll see first witnesses, starting with yours, Mr. Jones."

Again, Tony stood. "Your honor, I call Mr. Mike Harris."

Mike's eyes went wide and he shot a look at Xander. "Wasn't I subpoenaed for August's side?"

Xander frowned. "He knows you're our trump card. He's taking that away from us."

As Mike rose to his feet, Megan rubbed her eyelids with her thumb and forefinger.

"What does this mean?" Cathy whispered softly.

"Means we need a new trump card," Xander spat.

Mike took the witness seat next to the Judge and felt small for the first time in years, leaning the microphone in close. He glared at Tony as the lawyer approached the stand, smiling wide at the boy.

"Please state your name, for the record," he said politely, fixing his gelled hair.

Mike shuffled uncomfortably. "Don't I have to put my hand on a Bible or something?"

Tony smiled. "Only if a Jury's present. This is just a hearing. It's a common mistake, though," he grinned, and somehow Mike got the impression that it was a shot at Megan for her objection earlier. "Now then, name, please?"

"Michael R. Harris," he responded, speaking as clearly as he could into the microphone. His nervousness seemed to fade the closer Tony got to him, replaced instead with anger.

"Mr. Harris, can you recount for me the events that happened yesterday evening?"

Mike smiled. "I would, but I don't think Cathy would appreciate it. Some things are left private."

"Order," Judge Walton said calmly, hiding his grin.

"Regarding Miss. Styles," Tony corrected.

"Oh. Gallagher and I went looking for her when we heard that she'd run away from home. We found her in one of the basement apartments of a movie theatre owned by a relative of Tim's. We found them and brought them home."

"Why were you looking for them?"

Mike did not notice Xander's repeated attempts to gain his attention, or he might have known not to drop his guard. "I've been helping the police out looking for Derek Smith, and I was worried that the two of them might be easy targets for him."

"How good of you. What kind of state did you find Miss. Styles in?"

"She was crying and scared -- but that was just because I kicked the door in. I actually feel kind of bad, but I wasn't sure if they were there and every other door had been locked, so we kind of had too."

"And what was she doing there?"

"Getting ready for the baby. They had some things bought, it actually didn't look half bad. I've seen worse."

"You found her to be preparing the way any fit mother would?"

"Yes."

"But by your own admission, even with a killer on the loose, she made no attempt to stop you from entering and potentially harming her and her child, had she had one, if you had been him? She ran away, spent all her money, was living below a theatre and could not protect her child against you?"

Mike's face went white. He finally looked at Xander, whose face was buried in his hands.

"No further questions, your Honor," Tony smiled, sitting back down.

"Cross?" Judge Walton asked, turning his attention.

Megan glanced down at her questions. They had been almost exactly the same, except without the negative spin. "No questions, your Honor," she said, sliding the sheet into her folder.

"You may step down, Mr. Harris."

Mike hung his head, walking back down to his seat.

"If you still got that knife, you could just take the kid out yourself," Xander said as his friend shuffled by. "It'd save time."

"Shut up," Mike said, his voice defeated as Cathy rubbed his leg.

"Your next witness?" Walton asked Tony, raising his eyebrows.

Tony smiled. "We call Dr. Robert Gagnon, the state's leading psychologist in individuals with developmental disabilities--"

The sniveling man that had been seated near the middle of the court got up and started walking toward the bench.

Xander slammed his head against the Coke machine in the lobby, not even noticing the change that shook loose when he did so.

"Well, what would you have answered?" Mike asked, thrusting his arms in the air as he paced back and forth.

"Oh, I don't know. Anything besides: they let me walk right in after I burst in the place because they could have been killed by the worst murderer this town has ever seen!"

"*Second* worst," Mike said, motioning in his direction.

"Not gonna work today," he growled in response. The Womb had finally quieted down now that he was outside the courtroom, and he was beginning to wonder if it had just been nerves. "For future reference, when up against a lawyer, anything they don't specifically ask you for: just leave it out. Lying by omission isn't lying in there. It's their job to get it out, but that doesn't mean you have to hand it right - "

"I get it!" Mike barked, slamming a palm against the Coke machine. His hand landed in a sizable dent in its frame, and he suspected that today was not the first day that it had suffered such abuse.

"That'll be enough," Megan snapped, walking toward the both of them with Cathy. "We've only got a half hour recess, and I do not want to spend it with you two testosterone kings at each other's throats."

There was silence between them then.

"He started it," Mike said after a moment, thrusting a thumb in Xander's direction.

"Hey, Tony, the people I'm defending are unfit parents!" Xander exclaimed. "And I have unpaid parking tickets, too! And while I'm at it, if you'll kindly look in my basement, you'll find the body of a - "

"This never goes anywhere between you two!" Cathy

yelled at the both of them.

"That's because you always interrupt it," Xander stated matter-of-fact-ly.

"We need a new witness," Megan cursed, sitting down. "Not tomorrow, not the next day, *now*. He's burying us in there. That psychologist was trained in every negative statistic ever. He even cited a case in Canada like this where the mother ended up killing the baby, for the love of Christ!"

Mike sighed, silent. After a moment, he spoke. "Are we sure we're on the right side, guys?"

Cathy glared at him, and it was clear to all that that discussion was over.

"Never mind. It's just, the story Megan was talking about. I never thought of it that way before."

Megan started to chuckle. "That's rich. He's convincing the people that convinced me! That's beautiful. Beautiful. We're done. We need a witness. Now." She looked up at Xander. "What about Gallagher?"

Xander shook his head. "Good guy, but picture the complications with Mike times *ten*."

Mike just turned away.

"Great. Guys! Come on! We need something!"

"We need a father," Xander said finally, drawing gazes from all those around. He turned to Cathy with that driven look in his eyes that made you do whatever he said. "Go back to school. You said there were eight other girls besides you and August that got pregnant this year. I want to know who the fathers were. I want to know the circumstances: was it consensual? I want to know the position, for God's sake -- got it?"

"Got it," Cathy nodded, even as she turned toward the exit.

"Get Tommy's help if you need it!" he called out to her, then turned to Megan. "We call the witnesses now, right?"

"Yeah, but all we really had was Mike. We've got a few professionals. The mother won't say anything in our favor, and I'll be damned if I'm putting August on the stand."

"Call anyone. Call the people present from the school. Call me, for all I care. Just buy us enough time for Cathy to find out something."

"What makes you sure she will?" Mike asked, raising an eyebrow.

"I'm not," Xander replied. "But it's almost all we have at the moment."

"Almost?" Megan asked, hopeful.

Xander shook his head. "I don't want to say yet. Not until I talk to Gallagher first."

"I thought you said he wouldn't be any help?"

"He won't. I just want him here for our new trump card."

Megan smiled. "Which is?"

"If I tell you, you won't do it," he grinned, heading toward the payphones as she and Mike headed back into the courtroom.

"He's frustrating, isn't he?" Megan huffed at Mike without facing him.

"You have no idea."

The elm stood shivering, naked a frightened in the

cold. The remains of her clothes lay at its feet, dead comrades who would never visit again. Her skin was gray and ashen and bitter, her once warm embrace reduced to a bitter boney grasp.

"Hey, Trace!" Cathy smiled, jogging up beside Tracy Outmore, still out of breath when she reached the school house.

Tracy was a good year older than Cathy. She'd gotten pregnant around the same time, and they'd talked about it in the washrooms once or twice together, even before Cathy had told Mike or anyone else for that matter. She was tall and pretty with light blonde hair, and she'd always treated Cathy like a little sister.

She was as good a place to start as any.

"Hey, Catty," Tracy replied, finished her Coke and throwing it into a nearby garbage as she sat at the picnic table in the school yard, adjusting her stomach, which was just beginning to really show, so that it went under the table. "You look spent."

"Yeah," Cathy agreed. She sat down and wiped a long trail of sweat off her brow, which had formed despite the chill on the air.

"Thought you were going to be over at the courthouse all afternoon?" she smiled, big and bright.

Cathy looked away. "Yeah, um... I don't know. After all the drama I went through, couldn't much take it."

"Totally," Tracy nodded, rubbing her stomach.

Cathy watched her hand move, a twinge of envy coming over her for a moment, and she had to remind herself that what she had just said had been supposed to be a lie. "Yeah... Mike's been so closed off ever since it happened."

"Aww," she whined, but not mockingly, poking out her bottom lip. "I thought you two lovebirds made up?"

In the distance, Tommy spotted Cathy, raised one of his triangular eyebrows, and started to walk over.

Cathy sighed. "We just decided not to talk about it. But I thought after a while he'd be okay to talk about it, and now, I don't know..."

Tommy stopped, his eyes wide with shock.

"Well, you can talk to me, sweetie," Tracy smiled, laying a hand gently over hers.

"I don't know... Mike says it's just between us... that we should forget..." she felt horrible. She explain to Mike later, if he ever found out.

"I won't tell a soul. Come on, it'll feel better," she smiled again, warm and inviting.

"Well -- maybe if you did first. Is your guy acting the same way?"

All at once Tracy's smile faded. "Yeah. Guys are pigs. Listen, Catty, I've gotta get to class," she said, getting up and pasting on a smile that was obviously fake. "But we'll talk later, okay?" She gave a mini-wave with her index finger, then turning to walk away.

Well, that was suspicious, Cathy growled internally, watching the girl walk away toward the school, then stop and sit at another table, behind a tree.

"What the fuck was that?" Tommy asked, walking up behind Cathy and finally making his presence known.

Cathy turned and glared at him.

"Are you bipolar? Why are you saying all that crap about - "

"I'll explain on the way, you little monkey," she hushed, grabbing him by the arm and dragging him in the direction of the school.

ʎ⋏ʎ

"Objection, your Honor!" Tony drawled, thrusting an arm in the direction of Tim Brassington. "Mr. Summers is leading the witness."

Nathan turned to Judge Walton. "Your Honor, the witness's own mother was just up here. She said it to us all. He's very nervous. I'm simply trying to put the questions in a yes-or-no fashion, so that the defendant can answer them."

"Sustained," the Judge said begrudgingly. "If your witness cannot answer your questions than you should not have placed him on the stand, but I will not tolerate you using this boy as a puppet to say whatever you want."

Xander leaned in to Mike. "It looks bad when the Judge insults you, right?" He grunted a little as the Womb surged again.

Mike nodded.

"See that?" Xander continued, pointing to Brassington. "Still a better witness than you."

Mike said nothing, but his nostrils looked ready to shoot twin bursts of flame.

"Mr. Brassington," Nathan started again, running his fingers through his silvery hair. "Did you go to August's house to get her the night you ran away?"

"Yes," Tim said, smiling wide, in his tone-deaf voice.

"Good. Did you plan this with her before?"

"No."

"Did you force her to go?"

"No."

"What was she doing when you came to her house?"

"Crying."

"Where?"

"On her back step."

Nathan smiled, leaning against the bench in a relaxed manner, trying to put the boy at ease. "Thank you. Why was she crying, Tim?"

"She didn't want to lose her baby."

"And is that why you told her to come with you?"

"Yes. So she wouldn't be sad anymore."

"Thank you, Tim," he turned to the court. "You see your Honor, everything this pair did, they did out of love for each other and for August's child. I only wish every couple were as well balanced and supportive."

"I thought this was a court of the United States, not Care-A-Lot," Tony grumbled from behind him.

"Hmm?"

"Nothing. Continue, with this... whatever," Tony smiled. "I'm enjoying it. It's like Ally McBeal in 3D."

"Councilor," Walton said flatly.

"Withdrawn," Tony said cheerfully.

"Would you like to cross examine, Mr. Jones?"

Tony almost snickered. "Oh, hell – I mean, not at this time, your Honor. We're good."

Megan's cheeks turned red as she fought the urge to throw he briefcase at Tony. She rose from her chair. "The defense next calls Principal Andrew Shnieder."

In the back row, Principal Shnieder sat up straight for the first time since the hearing began. "Me?" he asked, pointing toward himself.

"Yes, sir," Megan smiled.

Reluctantly Shnieder made his way up the hall, tossing cold stares at Greene all the way.

᠀᠊᠀

Gloria Brover was a short, round girl with black hair that had been dyed into two red streaks going down either side of her face. She was a pretty girl, by no means a knockout, but Cathy had always thought it'd do a lot for her self image if she presented herself a little better. Maybe she'd get more dates.

Then six months ago, she'd gotten pregnant.

Cathy sighed as she walked up to Gloria, who was taking a Chemistry book out of her locker. She forced herself the smile and walked up to the girl. "Hey Gloria!"

Gloria glanced in her direction, then back again.

"Gloria, it's me: Cathy!" she smiled again, pushing her hair back.

"Do we know each other?"

"Yeah, you and Mike went out once or twice before we got together."

"Right," Gloria said, smiling now. "How is Mike?"

Cathy's eyes narrowed. "We're fine, thanks. How about you? How are you and Todd doing?"

Gloria frowned. "He left me last month."

Cathy frowned. "Oh, I hadn't heard. Sorry. What a herb though -- leaving you when you're carrying his kid?"

"Yeah, I've got go..." she said, quickly turning and walking away.

Cathy watched her leave, rubbing the bridge of her nose in dismay. *Strike two.*

᛭

"Hey Steph... Dylan," Tommy smiled, lounging up to the both of them as they sat next to the vending machines in the cafeteria.

"Hey, man," Dylan smiled, tapping Tommy once in the arm. "How's it hanging?"

"Pretty good, pretty good..." he rambled, running one hand through his spiked hair around to the back of his head. He scratched idly, clicking his tongue against the roof of his mouth. "Uh... wow, Stephanie..." he started, pretending to just now take notice of her bump. "You're getting huge!"

"Twenty-four weeks," she beamed, even as she and Dylan snuggled into each other.

"Wow," Tommy said, feigning an impressed expression as he tried to mentally calculate how many months that was and failed. "So -- whose is it?"

CHAPTER SEVENTEEN
STUDY HABITS

"Mr. Shnieder," Megan started, holding the last syllable as long as she could. She stole a glance back at Xander as she did. He nodded once, then looked from his watch and then at the door. "You've... started a social aid project at the school to help people in August's position, haven't you?"

Shnieder nodded politely. "It wasn't just me. We had the backing of the entire faculty and the school board, but I helped start it, yes."

"I see," Megan smiled, taking another long pause. "Can you please tell me the reason that you did this?"

Shnieder shifted uncomfortably.

"Is something wrong?" she asked, raising an eyebrow.

He leaned forward, past the microphone in his booth a little. "Why do you keep making those pauses?"

In the back, Tony snickered.

Megan sighed. "No reason, sir. No need to be nervous, just answer the question."

"Ah," he smiled, instantly relaxed. "I did it to help -- well, to help poor girls like August," he said, motioning to the girl, who was playing with something in her chair and avoiding eye contact with everyone in the room. He frowned, then turned away from her and back to Megan, lacing his fingers together before him. "The rest of the faculty and I have noticed an alarming teen pregnancy rate in the last few years. We try our best to educate against it, but it seems the media keeps educating *toward* it. So we set up the foundation to help teens in Coral Beach that we couldn't get through to in time."

"Very good of you. In that respect, would the foundation be providing August Styles with the funds she needs to care for herself and her child?"

"Of course."

"That is in addition to the benefits that she already receives from the state as a result of her disabilities, correct?"

"Yes."

"No further questions, your Honor."

In the audience, Xander bugged his eyes at her for ending it, to which she shrugged.

"Cross?" Walton called out, almost to nobody by now.

"Sure, I'll take this one," Tony said smugly, getting up and walking around the desk.

ʎʎ

Nadine Kissinger walked away from Cathy angrily, stomping her heels as she went. Cathy hung her head and began trying to tabulate the amount of work she'd have to put in to repair her social life. She briefly considered that Xander had known that this would happen.

"What the hell was that all about?" asked Wanda Starsmoore, coming up behind Cathy.

"Nothing," Cathy frowned, turning to smile at the younger girl, when she noticed the open pregnancy test sticking out of her purse. "Actually, maybe you can help me..."

ʎɣʎ

"Hey, Kendra," Tommy said dryly and he walked up to the tall redhead at her locker, rubbing his already swollen right eye. "How's it going?"

She smirked at him. "Better than you. What the hell happened? Did you piss Mike off again?"

"You don't want to know," he said honestly. "Can you help me with something?"

"Sure!" she said cheerfully, closing her locker and turning to smile at him. "What can I help you with?"

"Well, your boyfriend Scott told me you were pregnant..."

Her smile slowly faded. "And?"

"And he asked *me* to ask *you* if you if there was anyone else who could be the father."

The girl's eyes went wide, and she drew back her hand.

ʎɣʎ

"Principal Shnieder," Tony smiled, addressing the educator formally. "Does August's mother receive compensation from the government because of her child's disabilities?"

Shnieder looked bewildered, then shrugged. "I would assume so, yes."

"And she works as well, yes?"

"I believe."

"So while they are by no means well off, she has the means to care for her child. There have never been any sort of investigations as to whether or not August is in good hands."

"No -- she's a good mother."

"But even a capable mother, in full control over herself like my client, can't watch their child constantly, is that correct? Otherwise this wouldn't have happened?"

Shnieder sighed. "Yes, I suppose that's true."

"So it's fair to assume that, although she would have the funds to support her child financially, August would have an even harder time, especially with an infant... correct?"

"In my opinion... I suppose I would have to say yes, reluctantly."

Tony smiled. "No further questions, your Honor."

Judge Walton smiled. "You may step down, Principal Shnieder. I'll see you and your wife at poker next Thursday?"

Shnieder nodded.

Walton's smile faded as he turned back to Megan, his cheeks shaking as he moved. "Do I dare ask if you have another witness, Miss. Greene?"

Megan turned back to Xander, who again looked back at the door and around the room, then shrugged. She sighed, rising to her feet. "The defense calls Mr. Alexander Drew."

A murmur fell over the courtroom, even as Xander got up and Mike lowered his head to between his knees, unsure if this was amusing or terrifying.

The true womb surged as Xander walked past August and up toward the stand.

ⴷⵅⴷ

"Hi, Skyla," Cathy sighed, sitting down next to her.

Skyla raised an eyebrow, then rolled her eyes.

"What?"

"Don't even bother," she said, adjusting her sweater to better cover her bulging mid-section.

"I'm not sure I understand?" she asked, shocked.

"Nadine Kissinger told me you were going through some sort of Postpartum thing, asking all the pregnant girls about it and all that, well you can forget it," she said, turning away. Cathy just stared for a moment, until Skyla turned back to her. "You can go now."

ⴷⵅⴷ

"State our name, for the record," Megan asked.

"Adam Evensong," Xander said, his smile spread from ear to ear.

Megan huffed. "Xander, state your *real* name, for the record."

"Project # 08276."

"That's enough, Mr. Drew," Walton barked. "And this nonsense is not helping your case."

"As my Dad used to say, your Honor, you can't kill a dead horse."

Somewhere in the back, Mike snorted.

"Alexander Drew, state your name!" Walton bellowed.

"You just said it, what's the point?"

"Just do it, sir."

"I object!" Xander yelled, slapping the bench and leaping into the air.

Judge Walton took a long sip of his water... then another. He looked at it evilly, as if he wished it to be something stronger. "Mr. Drew, stop this right now."

Xander glanced at his watch, then held it up to show the Judge. "Honestly, sir, just a little bit longer."

In the back, Gallagher entered and took a seat next to Principal Shnieder. He waved at Xander.

"No further questions, your Honor," Xander said, turning a smiling at the Judge.

"I believe that to be Miss. Greene's line, young man," Walton reminded him.

"Right. Megan?" he said, turning to her expectantly.

Megan stared at him emotionlessly for a full twenty seconds, her face growing as red as an apple. "No... further questions, your Honor."

"Cross?"

Tony snickered, then held up his water and toasted Xander with it. "Aw, hell no."

"Excuse me?"

Tony coughed, composed himself, then stood up straight. "The prosecution rests, your Honor."

"Get the hell down," Walton cursed. Xander happily hopped over the bench, crossed the room in two large bounds, then sat down next to Mike.

"Have fun with that?" Mike whispered to him, tears of laughter in his eyes.

Xander leaned in. "More scary than when I fought Zakron. Plus I took your place as worst witness."

Mike smirked and patted his shoulder.

"Defense," Walton plead, holding out his withered old hands to Megan. "Please tell me that was your last witness?"

Megan smiled. "Just one more, your Honor. The defense calls August Styles."

August's eyes went wide as Nathan tried to coax her out of her chair and to the stand.

"Jennifer," Cathy huffed, her arms crossed as she stood firm behind the girl.

Jennifer's blonde hair was short and she was wearing a tank top that exposed her belly. Heels made her look much taller than she actually was.

"Cathy?" Jennifer asked, raising an eyebrow as she clicked her mirror shut.

"Listen, I really need your help. I'm through playing around, now. August's in trouble. I lost my baby once, and she's terrified that she's going to lose hers now."

"I don't know what you're..."

"I wasn't finished," Cathy snapped, reaching out and grabbed the girl's arm and digging her nails in before she could get up. "Think of what would happen if you lost your baby. Think of how much it would devastate you."

Jennifer's eyes turned downward, and she seemed to open up to what Cathy was saying.

"Now -- think of my boyfriend reputation in this school, and realize that that is what is going to happen to you if you don't tell me exactly what the fuck is going on here," she spat.

"I don't have to listen to this," Jennifer stammered, making a bee-line for the exit.

Tommy stepped in front of her, his arms crossed. Even with her heels, he had considerable height on her. "I really think you do," he said calmly.

Cathy came up behind her again, Jennifer now sandwiched between the both of them. "Tell me... every... last... detail."

"My son," Gallagher whispered. He had moved up and sat down next to Xander and Mike as covertly as he could as Nathan helped August to the stand finally. "Why was it so urgent that I come here so quickly, if you do not intend for me to speak?"

Xander leaned in. "You're a counselor. I think August's going to need that after this."

"What makes you so sure?"

Xander frowned. "I'm counting on it, father."

Gallagher and Mike exchanged confused looks, then turned toward the front to watch.

"State your name, for the record," Megan said, walking up to August.

August said nothing and lowered her shoulders. She averted her eyes from everyone and tried to pretend she wasn't there.

Megan huffed and turned back to Xander.

Xander lowered his brow and shook his head at her.

She paused, then smiled and turned back to August. "That's all kinda silly, huh?"

August's eyebrows rose and she turned to Megan, then looked at everyone else in the room, all looking back at her, and began to curl back again.

"Them?" Megan asked, motioning to the people, and then to the Judge. "Just pretend they're not here. It's just you and me, sweetie. My name is Megan Greene," she beamed, extending a hand to the girl. "What's yours?"

August took Megan's hand, shook it briefly, and then let go. "August Styles."

Xander smiled, nodding.

"Nice to make your acquaintance, August," Megan said, taking a pace back from the child. "Are you going to have a baby, August?"

August nodded.

"I need you to answer, sweetie."

"Yes. I'm gonna name her June."

"What if it's a boy?"

August paused. "Then I'll name *him* June."

Megan chuckled, along with several other members of the court, including August's mother. "How silly of me. Are you going to love your baby, August?"

August nodded, then remembered, and spoke. "Yes. Just like my Mom loves me."

"And are you going to take care of June, August?"

"Yes."

"Forever and ever?"

"Forever and ever and ever."

Megan smiled. "Good. I'm sure she'll love you very

much." Megan turned to the Xander, and then the Judge. "No further questions your Honor."

Gallagher furrowed his brow, motioning toward the stand. "That was it?"

"Give it time, father," Xander smirked, assuring him with a touch on the shoulder. "We're just breaking the ice."

"Cross?" Walton called.

At the prosecution table, Tony frowned, making no effort to hide his glare at Megan this time. He stood up straightened his overcoat with both hands, and approached the bench. "Your honor," he started, addressing first the Judge, then turning toward Megan and Nathan. "I want it stated for the record that the reason I did not call August Styles as a witness myself was that I wanted to avoid the following unpleasantries, but Miss. Greene has left me little choice."

"So noted."

Tony walked over to August, making no effort to smile at her. His gut flipped when he saw her cower back into her ball, but he kept his resolve.

Xander reached out and touched Megan's shoulder, motioning forward toward August.

"August," Megan called softly from her chair. "This man is going to ask you some questions now. His name's Tony, and he's a friend of mine."

August straightened back out, smiling wide at Tony.

He turned to Megan, raising an eyebrow to her.

"August, how do you know when baby milk is too hot?" he asked, as emotionlessly and as loudly as his drill captain in cadet camp always had when he was a teenager.

The question took August aback. "I don't know," she said honestly, her smile faded but not yet gone.

"Where does baby's milk come from?"

"I don't know."

"What do you do if your baby is crying?"

"I... don't know," she whimpered, her smile gone again, and she was beginning to retreat back into her little human ball.

Tony did not stop. "What do you do if the baby's coughing? What do baby's eat? How do you change the baby's diaper? What if the baby gets a rash? What do you do if her lips are *blue*? What do you do if she falls out of her crib? What do you do if she drowns in the tub?" he slammed his hand against the bench in front of her. "What do you do if your baby is *dying*? What do you do?"

"I don't know!" August wailed, tears streaming down her cheeks now, her face half-hidden by the stained white shirt she had pulled over it to hide from the scary man.

"And what do you do if we decide in the courtroom," he asked, stepping back and spreading his arms, as if to encompass the room. "Right now, that you, August are not fit to be a parent? What if we decide to take your baby from you before it's even born. What will you do then?"

"Wait."

Tony turned and pointed an accusing finger at Megan at the outburst, then stopped. She was just sitting there, smiling at him. He turned toward his desk, where Martha Styles sat, tears streaming down her withered face, as she looked up at her crying daughter. "Martha?"

"I'll do it," she said in a hushed voice, then slowly

smiled up at August. "I'll help August look after the baby. After June."

Tony's arms fell to his sides, and once again he turned to Megan, who just shrugged and thrust a thumb back at Xander.

Mike grinned, patting his friend on the back. "Good play, man. Good."

Xander nodded, beaming proudly. "I rather thought so myself."

CHAPTER EIGHTEEN
PAL

Xander drank his cola, taking half the can in one long gulp before coming up for air. The Womb had finally stopped flaring up, but had left him oddly thirsty, and he took a long gulp of the liquid as Mike grinned at him.

Megan looked over, breaking off from her conversation with Judge Walton, Principal Shnieder, and Tony and walking over.

Mike smiled, then got up and strolled a few steps away.

"You knew, didn't you?" Megan grinned, waving her finger at him. "You knew right from the start."

Xander shook his head. He looked down into his cola and then back again, playing with the tab. "Naw," he admitted. "I knew what we had to do, but I never dreamed it would work out like this. It was what I had planned, more or less, but... naw, I didn't think I was winning this one."

"Still, you pulled some pretty risky moves there for the team. If you learn how to stop giving lip to Judge Walton, you might make a pretty good lawyer someday."

Xander smiled. "That's your battlefield, not mine."

She chuckled, squinting at him, "You sound so old sometimes, you know that?"

He laughed. "Feel that way too -- but this one time, I'm glad to say -- no regrets."

She smirked, leaning in and giving him a peck on the cheek. "No regrets," she reciprocated.

"August," Gallagher said in a soothing voice, still inside the closed courtroom. "You did very well today, but we aren't quite done yet."

August was still in her little ball. "You aren't going to yell at me, are you?"

Gallagher smiled warmly. "No, my child. Never. But, the other day... Tim mentioned studying... can you tell me what studying is?"

August furrowed her brow, then looked away.

He sighed.

"It hurts," she said finally.

Tears welled up in Gallagher's eyes. "Yes, angel, I know. But what else?"

"He... said it would hurt. At first. He said that was how you learned. And then when you learned, it didn't hurt anymore. And studying is how we learn."

"I suppose," he soothed, reaching out and stroking the girl's hair, ever so gently. "But who said that?"

"I saw him - - *studying* - - with the other girl, Jennifer. He asked if I wanted to study too. He said I could learn just like she did. But... it felt funny. Funny and hurt. And he said that if I told anyone, it might make me hurt more, because I would forget. And then, he reached out and..."

"I know child, but *who*?"

"It was..."

〽

"Xander," Cathy whispered. She was out of breath and Tommy was just a few feet behind her.

"Can this wait?" Xander asked, pointing to Megan.

"We found it out. We know who the father is."

Xander's eyes went wide. So did Megan's. "What the hell? I just didn't want you in the courtroom when Tony cross-examined August."

"You mean I got beat on by two girls for nothing?" Tommy yelled.

Xander ignored him. "Well, who is it, Cat?"

〽

Gallagher grabbed Mike by the shoulder and spun him around. "My son -- Mike -- we must find Xander and the authorities. Young August has just told me who her assailant is."

Mike's grabbed him with both hands. "You're sure?"

"Positive. She said it herself. The girl can omit truths, but I do not believe she is capable of fabrication."

〽

Xander walked up to Gallagher and Mike with Megan, Tommy and Cathy in tow outside on the courthouse. "You know?" he asked Mike, weighing the expression on his face.

Mike nodded.

"Well, my boy," Walton smiled, waddling up to Xander and patting him on the back. "Tony was just telling me what a hand you had in this case. Aside from the attitude, good work."

"Yes," Principal Shnieder smiled, extending his hand toward Xander. "Excellent work. Though I must admit, I'd rather you had been in class during school hours."

Xander glared for nearly half a second, which was a second more than he had wanted to wait. He thrust out both of his arms and grabbed Shnieder by his shirt collar, then pushed him back and pinned him against the wall of the courthouse. "You insignificant little weasel..." he bellowed, his voice just having a touch of the Womb's. "I'm going to rip you..."

"My son!" Gallagher protested, pulling Xander back off Shnieder. "Violence is never the answer!"

"Thank you, father," Shnieder gasped, composing himself.

Gallagher spun around on his heels, slamming his small fist into Shnieder's nose and sending him to the floor with blood gushing from his face.

"It may not be the answer... but it doesn't hurt the situation any."

"What is the meaning of this?" Walton asked, waving over the bailiffs. "Arrest these - -"

"Yes," Megan interrupted, stepping forward. "Please, arrest him," she said, pointing at Shnieder.

"What are you talking about?"

Megan grinned. "I had August's fetus tested for signs of Down syndrome... the trump card I never told Xander about."

"Hey --" Xander balked.

"How much do you want to bet that the baby's paternal DNA matches yours?" she asked coyly, handing the file to Shnieder, then turning to August and her mother.

Shnieder smiled, getting up. "You'll never make this stick. I'd never touch --" he looked August up and down with disgust. "-- that! It's absurd!"

Tommy smiled. "What about Jennifer Bradley?"

"Or Wanda Starsmoore?" Mike chimed.

"Wanda Starsmoore?" Tommy echoed. "Really? Wow. Way to go Shnieder."

"Tommy," Xander said sharply. He leaned in toward Shnieder, even as the bailiffs approached. "You're missing the point, Shnieder."

Shnieder just glared, not saying a word.

"Besides the fact that all eight girls you got pregnant are under the age of sixteen... meaning that your teaching career is over and you'll have some very nice prison time ahead of you... once you get out, you will owe *each* of those eight children..." he paused.

"Eighteen percent," Megan chimed.

" -- Eighteen percent of any paycheck you earn for child support."

Shnieder's face went white, and he started to sit down, but the bailiffs helped him back up and began reading him his rights.

As the whole group watched them carry him away, Megan leaned in to Xander:

"Now, that's what you had planned all along... right?"

Xander smiled.

CHAPTER NINETEEN
BEGINNING OF THE END

K - click!

"Make sure they're tight, Cathy," Xander reminded her, craning his head back to see her as she rotated the key until it snapped in solid. "We don't want me getting out."

Cathy gave him a droll look, then reached over and tussled his hair. "What makes tonight different than the last few nights?" she asked idly as she checked and then double-checked the bonds.

Xander looked downward.

She turned to face him then, finally taking it seriously. "Hey, what is it?"

"It's the Womb. It was acting funny today in court."

"More flashbacks?"

"No..." he corrected. "No, I've felt like this before, around you. When you got pregnant. It's the same way it reacts to Genblade or Black Heart..."

She moved slowly for a second, taking that in. "Do you think the Womb's going to attack August?"

He lowered his head again, his eyes becoming visibly tired, then raised it and nodded.

"Aw, Xander..." she tisked sympathetically, putting her bag down. He lowered his head again, and she put both of her hands on his chin to try and raise it, but he wouldn't budge. "Look, there's a reason that *you* transform into the Black Womb and not the other way around. That they need to drug you and mess with your head to get it to do what they want," she smiled. "It's because you're a man with a monster trapped inside, not the other way around. And it's the man that Mike and I love, you can't ever forget that. We can beat this, together. We *will* beat this together."

He still hadn't looked up, and she thought she felt tears running down his face.

"Xander?"

His head jutted forward suddenly, already partially transformed. His razor-sharp teeth dug into the soft flesh between her neck and left shoulder even as they protruded from his gums.

She screamed, long and loud, as he began to thrust against his restraints feverishly, their clangs echoing throughout the church walls and back again. "Xander!" she yelled, hitting him with the arm that would still move over and over again, even as it locked in the iron grip of its jowls, still pulling on the restrains.

"You see?" Spider laughed, deep within his subconscious. "It is as I've told you..."

-SNAP!-

Xander's wrist shattered under the immense force of his own tugs, letting his mutilated hand slide free. Instantly it was covered in black blood that started to swarm over his body, making his fingers into claws that grabbed onto Cathy's shoulder for support, making escape impossible. As his legs turning into muscular, powerful things, he brought one up and slashed at her with it as his teeth gnawed, much like a cat, barely missing cutting her right through her if not for her down jacket, which was now spilling feathers everywhere. Gaining the extra leverage, as the ooze almost finished enveloping him, he wrenched his arm free of the second bond and let her drop to the ground.

She fell limply, slumped into a heap with a -flump- sound that, for some reason, did not echo. The creature looked down at her, her jacket and shirt torn open, revealing her smooth stomach. Her shoulder gushed blood onto the floor and her chest. It leaned over her, licked its lips of her blood, and took a long whiff of her, closing its aqua eyes to enjoy the scent. When it spoke, it almost did so in retaliation to the kind words she had said to Xander against it:

"Black... Womb lives."

The creature spun on its balled heels, then leapt toward one of the boarded windows and crashed through it, sending splinters of wood along with it.

For a moment, all was silent.

"Fuck!" Cathy cursed, sitting up and applying pressure to the wound that had been dangerously close to her neck. She examined the blood on her hand, then put it back again. "Fuck!" she repeated, reaching into her pocket and producing a cell phone, quickly pressing speed dial one and putting it to her ear. "Mike," she said quickly.

"Code Black. I'm fine, I'll make it over to St. Claire's alone. Fine, I'll call a cab. Just get after him. He might go after -- she's not? Oh, okay. Just find it, its been going stir crazy, no telling what it might do. Love you too... bye." She pressed end and slid the phone back into her pocket, still holding her neck tightly. "Fuck," she said again, as she started to limp toward the exit.

Officer Aaron Munroe walked down the corridor of Coral Beach Penitentiary, watching the moon rise to its highest through the cells that he passed. He clicked his tongue against the side of his cheek aimlessly as he did so. He took one last look down the hall toward the New Fish cell, smirked, then turned to head back toward the office.

"Urk!" he exclaimed, looking down at his chest. There was nothing there at first, and then he saw spots of blood forming. It was only just before he passed out that he realized they were from his own mouth.

Black Womb dropped the body and stepped over it, then stepped up to the bars of the empty cell he had been next too. It took a long whiff, its triangular nostrils flaring, catching onto a familiar scent.

It opened his eyes again, its almost-invisible pupils searching the darkness of the cell left and right. Finding nothing, it howled widely, then turned around...

... coming face to face with Shnieder, cowering in the back of his cell.

The Womb stepped forward until its nose was touching the bars, then pivoted its body and began to slide through the bars, the wet snap of its bones breaking and then resetting themselves as it made its way in the only sound it made.

"Please..." Shnieder begged, tears running down his face onto his orange prison jumpsuit. "Please, no -- I didn't mean too -- I never will again..."

The Womb -- through the bars now with its left leg snapping back into socket -- walked forward calmly. It never once took its unblinking eyes off of the man.

"I'll never... please..."

With one sudden motion, it jutted its hand forward and stuck its un-clawed thumb into Shnieder's left eye socket.

Shnieder screamed, the sound becoming more a more moist a sound as blood gurgled from the socket and down into his mouth.

It slammed his head against the concrete wall, its thumb still in his eye. Then again. And again. And again.

Its mouth finally opened into something that could have been described on anything else as a smile.

Shnieder finally stopped screaming, his body growing limp, blood splattered on the wall behind it.

And then it started to slam again, faster and harder with each one until finally letting go. It drew back its hand swiftly, sending long, slender trails of muscle and brain tissue spattering against the far wall. "Black Womb lives!" it bellowed, howling at the moon outside. It turned toward the exit... then stopped.

The cell door was open wide now, the security camera just outside it sparking with exposed wires and tape. The lens was shattered. It turned its head slightly to one side, confused, then felt the bat alongside it's head.

"Son of a bitch!" Mike yelled as the Womb hit the floor, not letting up for an instant, swinging the bat around again and cracking it in the face. The Womb tried to get up but Mike kicked its legs, then started wailing on it with the bat again. "I'm sorry, Xander," he said, letting loose another blow that sent black ooze spraying against the walls of the cell. "I really am. This has got to end. Not tomorrow, not next week... now. Now I love you, Xander, but... this is it." He punctuated each sentence with a blow. The Womb raised its claws but Mike again lashed out, successfully snapping one of the talons off. It grunted in pain, finally stopping in its attempts to get away, just recessing into itself. "You hear me, Womb? You're the one going down, not us! This is the last stand -- either smarten up, or get extinct -- you hear me?"

The Womb looked up and Mike stopped pounding. For a second, he thought he saw tears in the Womb's eyes. Then, all at once, the blackness lost its ability to stay together, splashing down off of Xander Drew's naked, shivering body as if it had never been there to begin with, leaving only a thin layer of blood behind.

The tears had been Xander's, and he shed them even more now, pounding his fist against the concrete. "Don't stop..." he pleaded, so low it was almost inaudible.

His face still a mask of rage, Mike didn't realize what his friend meant at first... then looked down at the bat in his hand, the top half of which was covered in black and red. The anger melted away to pity, and the bat dropped to the ground.

Reluctant at first and shaking from the cold and the blood still seeping from his eyes, Xander shot into the arms of his friend and fell to his knees, letting the tears mix with the blood all around him.

"It's okay, buddy," Mike said, ignored the congealed bodily fluids and stroking the back of his friend's head.

But somehow, both men knew it wasn't.

Nor would it ever be.

CHAPTER TWENTY
DOORS

The elm stood in the dark, the wind moaning through her dead branches. They cracked and broke until all that was left of her was her core, tattered in snow and clinging to life as she watched the horror of winter all around her without breath or reprieve or hope of either.

៱៹៱

"Do you think this'll be enough?" Cathy asked, motioning down toward the frozen dinner she held in her hands.

Mike smiled warmly at her, her kindness never ceasing to amaze him. "A crumb would be enough."

"Still," she pouted, looking down at the plate of turkey and mashed potatoes and gravy she had taken from her fridge when they'd passed by her house. It was covered in wrap and looked as though it could have used some heat, tiny droplets of dew clinging to the inside of the plastic. Before getting it, she had hoped bringing food would help alleviate her guilt, but it did not. She'd spent her lunch hour writing, and couldn't help but think at least some of that time could have been spent going to the church to let Xander out of his chains.

He smirked at her. "Did you make it?"

"No..."

"Tell him you did. He'll love every bite."

She smiled. The smile in and of itself was nothing, the expansion and contraction of a few key facial muscles, but the feelings behind it was nothing short of spectacular. For the two of them to have come so far in just a few months, to not forget their mistakes but to build upon them and learn from them, it meant everything in the world to her. Right then, looking down at the plate of thin turkey slivers, she couldn't imagine herself being with anyone else. But then there was Xander. Her smile began to fade away again as her thoughts became more complicated.

"Did I say something wrong?" he asked, looking down at her with concern.

She forced the grin back into its place, but it wasn't quite the same. Like a lithograph of the Mona Lisa, something just wasn't right about the fake. "Never."

"I'll remind you you said that the next time you try to tell me the contrary."

She laughed and slapped his arm. He pretended to stumble backward into the snow, balancing on one foot and holding the offended arm as if in deep pain. Smirking devilishly, she gave him a tiny shove and sent him toppling over for real.

"Hey!" he yelped. He grabbed a pile of snow into his hands and began to walk toward her menacingly.

"Mike, don't you dare!" she scolded and giggled all at

the same time, backing away a few paces down the sidewalk and put a hand outward in a vain attempt to halt his progress.

He said nothing, shaking some of the snow off of his head and taking another step forward, and another, quicker each time.

"Mike!" she screamed as she turned as laughed, running down the street as fast as she could without dropping Xander's dinner, causing peas to loosen from the saran wrap and fall to the ground all the same.

He was gaining on her, and all at once he hurled the large snowball he had made, splashing it against her back. The snow traveled in all directions, a fair portion of it going down her coat and onto her back. He stopped, snickering wildly at her and twisted back and forth, trying to wriggle the snow out.

"Mike, I swear, I'm going to fucking - - "

"You kiss your mother with that mouth?" he jeered, stepping closer to her and grabbing her arms gently but firmly.

"Oh, shut up."

He laughed again when he saw her cheeks, red and livid with anger, her mouth pouting a little and her eyes drawn down in a scowl. He leaned in to kiss her.

"Not likely!" she protested, jerking her head back and wiggling some more, reaching up the back of her shirt and coming out with the last bit of snow. "You jerk."

She leaned in to kiss her again, and this time she let him, both of their eyes closing as they sunk into it. All of a sudden Mike's eyes went wide and he jumped back a pace, beginning to wriggle himself. Cathy smirked at him as he tried to get the snow out of the front of his pants without calling attention to himself, trying to by shaking his right leg. His was hissing from the screaming cold coming from every one of those nerves. "That was vulgar."

He tapped him twice against the chest, as if punctuating her victory. "Don't forget who always comes out on top."

He smiled, shooting her a look.

"Ugh," she sighed in disgust, slapping his arm again. "Why must all men have such a one track mind?"

"We're devoted to that track. We think of it all the time, and we love it. In some ways, it's very romantic."

"Sure," she beamed, pulling him forward and kissing him again. She turned out of the kiss, and noticed for the first time that they were there.

It jutted out of the snow as if it had been grown there. Staring up at its height compared to the buildings around it, it was hard to believe that it had been built by man at all. It's twin towering, pointed peaks seemed to pierce the moisture-saturated clouds that loomed overhead, hiding the crosses that had once adorned both. One had fallen down recently, and was still stuck in the ground bottom up, about five feet from the west end of the church. The church was simple grey brick on the outside, with no extravagant statues or sculptors like in the movies, the bricks seemed to make faces that stared back at you until you looked right at them... like the faces that one sees in the trees. A single stained-glass window added color to the front. It had long since been shattered in by rocks, but the top of Mary's head was still plainly visible, the last pieces hanging onto the frame for dear life.

"I hate this place," she stated, her hair caught in a sudden and timely stiff breeze as they both stared up at the church.

"I know," he said, trying to comfort her but not giving her his full attention as he looked around to make sure no one was watching. "It'll be okay."

"I still can't believe we chain him up in that horrible place."

He turned back toward her, confident that there was no one about. There never was here, really. This part of town had belonged to the Tee gang until not too long ago, and people still didn't wander around the streets too much. "It's a church, Cathy."

"An *abandoned* church, Michael," she said, using his full name as a way of emphasizing her point, "You know what my grandpa said when Trina asked him why this church was so creepy?"

"What?"

"He said that the devil's greedy. He said when God moves out of one of his houses, the devil moves in."

He laughed a little, picturing Cathy's grandfather (who did not look unlike the devil himself, bushy eyebrows and triangular face) telling such a story to the girls. He wondered if his teeth had been in at the time, or taken out for effect like when he'd told them vampire stories as children. "I think your grandfather was pulling your leg, Cat."

She glowered at him, and he stopped laughing. "Say what you want, but it's a bad idea anyway. It's like a band-aid on a tumor, chaining him up here. It's not actually fixing the problem, just putting it out of sight."

At this he nodded, even as he started to walk toward the doors, motioning for her to follow. She did. "I know," he admitted finally.

He reached out and grabbed the brass loop on the door, a few flakes of its rusted surface scraping at the insides of his fingers as he lifted it to the sound of creeping hinges, took one last look at the street outside, then opened it.

Light splashed into the church, casting their shadows long and thin in front of them. No matter how many times they opened it, Mike would always think that the light seemed wrong here. Cobwebs and tattered curtains blew in the air, covering the holes in the walls the way he covered his hands covered his eyes when his mom turned on the lights when he was sleeping in. Sometime since it closed the church had gotten used to the dark, and now hated its passing.

It smelled like week-old vomit mixed with baking soda and mold, and every particle of dust that floated about, catching the sun before their eyes, carried it.

Mike took a step forward toward the curtain which blocked their view of the main hall. Cathy moved to follow him, then stopped. "Something's wrong," she said, again stating it blatantly as a truth rather than an insight.

Mike turned and looked at her. "Nothing's wrong."

"No, Mike. His hearing. His *special* hearing. He should have heard us even when we were out in the street, why isn't he calling out to us or anything?"

Mike rolled his eyes, then resumed his walk toward the curtain, pushing it aside and making a cloud of dust.

When it cleared, the long hall stretched out before them like a black and white sketch with no focal point.

It looked like something they used mirrors to make of television, a hallway that went on forever. Row on row of pews, many of them broken of burnt, lined it on either side; and at the end was a large brass cross. Chained to it was the Black Womb.

Not Xander Drew.

The creature rose its head. Light shone in from a hole in the building's brick, and they could see that a few millimeters of dust had collected on his scalp. His mouth was invisible when it was closed like it was now, but to anyone who had seen it before the memory of it was enough, with row upon row of razor-sharp, serrated teeth that moved freely at the creature's whim, each tooth joined to the jaw at its own joint. The small, round, black scales that covered his body from head to toe rippled up and down, changing color to dark blue and then back again. It was subtle, but Mike had a theory that this was what it did when it really wanted to get a good whiff of something, soaking the scent in through every one of its pores. His chains were red and black with his blood. The talons on his toes were extended, too, which was rare. There were spikes in those chains, Xander's idea. They went right through his ankles, like Oedipus'.

"Told you," Cathy whispered, taking a step forward past her lover.

"Cathy!" Mike hissed, grabbing her by the arm and spinning her around and almost making her drop her plate.

She stopped, looking at him with a confused look.

"You can't go near it. Big sign. Don't feed the bears," he huffed, motioning toward the Womb and her plate of food at once.

Behind her, the Womb made a low growling sound.

"Something's wrong with him," she said, her voice full of empathy as only hers could be. "There's no blood on the floor. He didn't become Xander then come back or something, he's been like this since we left him last night."

He glanced over her shoulder at the floor around its feet, and sure enough, she was right. "Still, that doesn't mean..."

"I'm going to see him," she stated, and he let go of her arm and walked forward with her.

"Just be careful," he said, gingerly caressing her left shoulder where the Womb had ripped into her. "You know what he's capable o--"

"Yes, I do."

"Can I get a sentence o - -"

"No, you can't," she cut off again, but this time she grinned at him playfully. But she didn't turn toward him. To do that she would have had to take her eyes off the Womb, and that was something you never, ever did. If you had and you were telling about it, then you should go buy a lottery ticket.

As they both got closer they could hear its deep breathing. It reminded Mike of when he learned about Pavlov's dog, the way it drooled whenever the bell would ring, excited at the idea of food. The Womb was panting out of sheer, blood-lust-driven excitement, its eyes still transfixed on them like opaque lenses.

It stank like sweat and semen.

Cathy got as close as she dared, with Mike right behind (his hand clasping hers both in encouragement and in case he needed to pull her back) and stared directly at the creature, staying as silent as she could while still breathing.

The creature met her gaze for less than a second before turning away and huffing quickly, as though it were uninterested. It was like the way a dog broke its gaze with you when you were staring it down. It continuing to look to one side for a moment, then glanced back into her pupils, seeing she was still there, and looked back again.

"Xander," she said, firmly but patiently.

"Rakk!" it barked, turning quickly back toward her at the sound of its alter ego's name. Its mouth opened for the first time since they'd come in, showing those teeth she'd been envisioning moments ago and snapping them shut right in front of her face, its mouth disappearing again, as if to say: *don't push it, lady*.

She blinked but held her ground as Mike tried to pull her back.

"Wmmmmbbb..." it growled in defiance, the sound emanating from deep inside of its throat as resonating against her. She could *feel* the sound, the way one felt very loud music or the vibrations a car motor makes when it starts. It looked away again, and this time she grabbed it by the chin and forced it back. Mike made a fearful hissing sound when she did this.

"We could just stab him," Mike offered. "It means his bloodlust will probably triple tonight, but given the circumstances..."

Cathy ignored him as he trailed off and eventually stopped, realizing that this was not an option for her.

"Xander," she repeated, in exactly the same tone as before.

"Wmbbbb..."

"No," she said patiently, if not a little patronizingly. "Not Womb, Xander."

"Black Womb lives!"

"Yes, yes he does. Black Womb lives. Black Womb smash. Black Womb the strongest one there is. But I want to talk to Xander now, okay sweetie?"

Mike raised an eyebrow, unable to believe what he was hearing.

"Xnnndrrr..." the Womb growled, low in his throat, as the aqua starting to drain from his eyes and turn red.

"Holy shit," Mike said, taking a step closer. "It's working."

"Like trying to wake up somebody who overslept," she whispered, smiling to herself. "You don't just walk in and start shaking them, you just nudge them a little until they wake up."

The scales that covered the Womb's body began to shiver then, joining with each other like two drops of water placed too close to one another and becoming one. They did this all over, the ooze becoming less and less solid and more unstable, beginning to drop from his body as he shook and spasmed in what appeared to be a seizure, his claws slowly retracting into his hands. The Womb's mouth opened in what looked to be a scream, but instead of long teeth, the face and Xander Drew peered out, eyes closed and teeth clenched in pain as the darkness finally lost all of its cohesiveness and fell from of his body in one big splash. His body went limp in their chains and he began to breath hard, a thin layer of blood covering his entire body now.

Cathy bent down and touched his matted hair. He jerked back, as if sensitive to her touch.

Mike began unlocking the chains, and as each limb was freed it fell to the floor with no life in them at all. He curled on the floor in that pool of his own blood and bile, staring up at the cobwebbed ceiling with blank, emotionless eyes. In this form his body seemed to be nothing but skin and bones, his stomach concaved like a famine victim.

The wind outside picked up again, and he shivered when some of it reached his bare skin. Cathy grabbed a wool knit blanket her Aunt had made years ago. It was full of different earth-tones like evergreen and dirt-brown, and looked completely natural on him. It almost made him look alright. He blinked hard, and when his eyes opened again, they were almost normal. Now, at last, he was finally awake. He looked around at his surroundings, scared and confused a little at first, and then his eyes rested on Cathy. He looked a little surprised, as if she had just appeared there in his line of sight.

"I didn't hurt anyone, did I?" he asked, his voice hoarse and raspy. It wasn't even really phrased as a question, like he expected to answer to be yes.

"No," she smiled, stroking back his hair, big globs of congealed blood sticking to her fingers. "No sweetie, you didn't hurt anyone."

Mike watched them silently, his eyes focused on her hand on Xander's hair as he collected his clothes, folded neatly on a nearby pew. He hoisted them up, quickly grabbing the socks as they started to roll off the top, and brought them over to the pair.

Xander reached up to grab the underwear once, winced, then tried again and succeeded, sliding them on from under the blanket.

CHAPTER TWENTY-ONE
UTERUS

Calla McFadden stopped in the middle of the hall, staring at a bumper sticker that had been stuck on a locker that read: horn broken, watch for finger. She giggled to herself, then erupted into a full-blown belly laugh. After a moment she forgot what she had been laughing at, saw it again, and giggled once more before walking past it. She felt like maybe the sticker reminded her of something, but wasn't sure. But she was so sure. She felt like the answer was just in front of her, but that her mind was surrounded by a thin fog that she couldn't see through. If she concentrated, hard, it would begin to clear and she could see her train of thought clearly -- but she didn't really care enough to try. The entire reason she'd lit up again was so that she wouldn't have to concentrate hard on anything.

The sound of squeaking sneakers and bouncing balls coming from just down the hallway seemed miles away, the girls volleyball team practicing hard for the next week's game. As she walked past she glanced in at the girls diving for the ball, skidding their knees off the spongy floor, trying hard to keep the ball on the other end of the court. Off to the side, some girls that were waiting to play were bouncing their balls off of the gym wall in lieu of an opponent. She smiled as she watched them, watching one in particular as she wiped sweat off of her brow with her arm, trying to do so without taking her eyes off of the game. It was Samara, her cheeks red and her hair was up in a bun to keep it out of her eyes. Calla briefly put her hand on the door and started to push it to go in, then reconsidered, turning around instead and walking across the hall to the stairwell, sighing to herself only briefly before her smile returned. She started to giggle again as she remembered the bumper sticker.

The silence was broken by the smallest of sounds. It reminded her instantly of the sound that Cindy-Lou Who made in the old Grinch cartoon she loved as a child. *Like the coo of a dove*. But sadder somehow, and longer. It was a sound that grew until it was a dull moan.

Raising one eyebrow, she turned the corner to look down the next flight of stairs and saw him. He looked tiny in comparison to the room around him, curled up into a little ball sitting at the bottom of the stairs, sobbing into his knees. His shirt was dirty, his jeans filled with holes. He didn't look old enough to be going to school here, like he should be in grade five at the most. If he did go to this school, he had to be in grade seven. His skin was a little dark, like coffee with just a little milk in it, and she thought briefly that if he cleaned up a little and bought new clothes he could be quite the ladies man when he got older. She took a step forward and opened her mouth, then stopped herself, unable to decide on what to say, and a little worried that the child would know that she was stoned. She turned to leave the way she came, then back again. "Hey," she said finally, rolling her eyes at the stupidity of it.

The boy looked up, startled, his eyes full of tears. He said nothing, just stared at her like a deer in the head-lights.

"What, uh, what's your name?" she asked, inching a little closer, trying not to scare the boy.

"Jaden Mal," he stated, his voice small and squeaky. He sniffed back a large string of mucus, then wiped his nose with his shirt the way children do.

"I'm Calla," she said, forcing a smile as she sat down next to him. They stayed there in silence for a full minute, which seemed a lot longer to her. "So -- what's wrong?"

He looked away, staring blankly at the knob on the door leading to that floor as his eyes welled up again. "Nothing," he said after a second, then started to cry out-right.

Calla sighed, clenching her hair. "Listen, don't do that. I'm really not good with this sort of thing, maybe you should talk to someone else. I think Reverend Gal-lagher is still in..."

Suddenly the child started to cry even more, a loud wail escaping from his open mouth, and she could see that a few teeth were missing, one with a large cavity in its place. "Oh, hey, I'm sorry -- what, uh crap -- we can talk to someone else. I'll talk to you, just tell me what's happening?"

He turned to her, opening his mouth to speak. It took a moment for the words to come, and when they did, a fresh spring of tears came with them: "Reverend Gallagher is touching me."

Xander stopped dead in his tracks where his walkway met the sidewalk, staring silently ahead at the bright red front door to his house. After a moment his legs began to get rubbery, and he braced himself against his mailbox for support.

Cathy stopped a few steps later, turning back to face him.

His face was as white as a ghost and his free arm slumped loosely by his side.

She crossed her arms in front of her. "You have to come in," she reminded him, clicking her tongue against the roof of her mouth.

He stared at a rock in the walkway a few feet in front of him, mostly obscured by snow. He recalled having tripped over it once or twice, and vividly recalled the time Sara had hit her knee off of it after falling off a skateboard, and then another time when Julie had stubbed her toe on it. He stared at it until the whole world became blurry except for it, then shifted his focus so that the world was clear and it was blurry, then back again.

"Xander - -" she moaned, her hands falling to her sides as the pity she had been trying to keep in check began to overtake her.

"Where'd Mike go again?" he asked finally, still staring at that spot in the path.

"He had to shower sometime," she said glumly, taking a single step toward him.

She was now obscuring his view of the rock, and he

blinked twice before looking back up at her. His eyes were bloodshot and puffy, the way someone looks after they'd spent a long time crying... only she knew that he had not. His hair was a matted mess, and she chided herself for not remembering to bring a comb or brush again today.

"And he doesn't like the bathroom at either of our places," she continued, feeling that she had waited long enough for him to speak, as she had assumed he would have. "He's a bit of a germaphobe."

Xander was still looking at her, then his eyes went to one side in their sockets, and finally, slowly, he nodded. His head lolled to the left until it was looking at the house next to his, the one with Johnson marked on the mailbox. There was a big **FOR SALE** sign hammered into the snow next to it, and all of the lights inside were out. "When did her parent's move?" he asked, almost as if he were saying it to himself and she wasn't even here.

"A month ago," she sighed, taking another step toward him. "It was right after the thing with Circe and... and Mandy. I don't think that had anything to do with it, though. Her dad had been looking for a new job out of state ever since --" she trailed off, knowing better than to finish that sentence.

He stared at the house a moment longer, then chuckled, turning back to her. "You remember that night?" he asked, finally making eye contact with her. He seemed almost relaxed now.

She shuffled from foot to foot, unsure of what to think of his sudden lividity. "The night Sara..."

"No," he said, raising a hand to cut her off again before she said the word. "Do you remember the night that

Derek escaped?" He was still smiling, but now she could see through it, see that it was entirely superficial.

She stared at him for a moment, a dumbfounded look across her face, then she smiled a little. "Yeah, of course."

"I was going to give up fighting. I thought I was in control of the Womb and that I was going to catch one last killer and then call it quits. Ride off into the sunset," he chuckled, reached for a cigarette, then stopped himself. "But it was me, I was the killer, and Derek got loose... and I guess I've been thinking..."

"That when you catch him you can get control of the Womb again, then finally start your life?" she finished, finally closing the gap between then by touching him on the cheek and making him turn toward her.

He nodded.

She tisked him. "You're going to. I know it. More than that, I feel it. You're going to get control -- and whether or not you catch Derek isn't a big deal, just so long as he stays out of our hair and stops killing the people we love. He's gone now, and we'll probably never hear from him again."

He snorted a little at that, his attention more normal now that she was the only thing in his field of vision. "Yeah, because we're that lucky."

She patted him twice on the cheek playfully, then started to walk toward his front door. She stopped again and back toward him, and this time her smile was gone. "About... about what else happened that night, when we found out Derek had - -"

He raised an open palm quickly cutting her off. "It's okay. Not your fault."

"Xander, we both --"

"No, I was just caught up in the moment. I'd..." he trailed off, looking away for a second and then forcibly making eye contact with her. "... I'd never be able to get with you, anyway. I think it was the excitement and the last of O'Toole's tampering and the Womb acting up and a crap load of other things. But, yeah... maybe nobody's fault, but not anything to write home about either."

"Yeah," she said, somberly at first, then smiling back at him. "Thank you."

He nodded curtly, and they both started toward the door together.

He reached out and grabbed the knob, but waited to turn it. For a long moment he just stood there, arm outstretched, as if waiting for something to happen. His brow furrowed after a second, willing something to happen.

"Some people turn those things," Cathy reminded him, raising an eyebrow from behind him.

"Yeah," he agreed reluctantly. "I... I'm just - -"

"Waiting for the Womb to flare up and tell you that Derek's inside, because if we were talking about not finding him, that's just when he'd show up like in some slasher film?"

He turned back toward her, blushing a little.

She laughed. "Come on. Open the damn door."

He did, and they both stepped inside and started kicking the snow off their boots.

"Xander," came a voice from his immediate right. He spun on his heels to face it, almost extending his claws. Cathy brought up a hand to stop him, grabbing his wrist with speed that surprised even him, until he thought back and realized he'd actually been more than a little slow.

Xander's mother looked back at him, her eyes as red and puffy as his had been a few moments ago, but the rest of her face looked pale and withdrawn, and even a little sunk back, somehow. Her short, curled hair seemed to fall limp somehow, but her shirt was bright and happy, with flowers and Hawaiian colors tie-dyed all over it. It reminded him of the wolf from Little Red Riding Hood, trying to look nice but hiding something horrible.

In the background, his father glared at him through eyes that were wetted by tears, both of his fists clenched until his knuckles were white, and a little blood dripping from one of them. There was a hole in the wall next to where he stood, little bits of drywall still crumbling from it. A few feet t his left there were two more.

Now the Womb twitched.

"Xander, honey," his mother began again, fresh tears dribbling down her face. "We have to talk."

Cathy sat in the middle of Xander's bed, his pillows propping her up as she tried not to eavesdrop of the raised voices downstairs. There were screams and there was crying. She heard a loud thud, and thought that Mr. Drew must have just put his hand through the wall again. She closed her eyes tightly, as if that meant she couldn't hear; then so tightly that she began to see brightly colored spots. Sighing, she opened them again and reached for Xander's phone. She picked it up and started to dial Mike's number, getting four digits in before she pressed the disconnect button and tossed the phone back onto the bed. She fell backward onto the pillows again. They were stiff and uncomfortable, and smelled too clean. They had not been slept in since the last time they had been washed, and if she curled into them and breathed deep she could still identify the particular brand of fabric softener.

There was another hard, loud sound from downstairs, and she thought she recognized that one as Xander. She remembered reading once that in World War II, snipers had learned to recognize the individual crack of each other's rifles. She was sure it wasn't *that* specific, but right now, she was quite positive that the last fist to crash into the drywall had been Xander's.

She reached out and grabbed her book bag and hauled it up onto the bed with her. She began to thumb through it, finally producing a wire-bound exercise book with a bright red front and the letters BW etched into the front with a sharpie. There was a mechanical pencil shoved down into the metal binds that held the pages together, and now she opened it to about three-quarters of the way through. She surveyed the remaining pages quickly, hoping that there was another blank notebook in the bag just in case she got in a good groove and ran out of room in this one.

Making a couple of clicks with her pencil to get the lead out, she propped the paper up against the legs and began to write.

I wasn't there for most of it, but Xander and Mike told me the rest. They told me how- -

She stopped and scribbled out what she had written until it was all black. A voice from downstairs seemed to be crying again, Xander's mom, and for a brief second she debated knocking on the floor and yelling to them that she was trying to write. Burying that thought down deep, she took a deep breath and started again.

"But, why would start a rumor like that about Xander yourself?" I had said, and I felt like just slapping Julie Peterson right upside the head. I didn't feel like *asking* her about this, I felt like *demanding* it, and maybe I was, just a little. I could feel my frustration with her giving way to anger, as the redness in my cheeks wasn't just because of blush anymore.

"Well, y'know..." she started, her eyes gazing off to one side like they always did when she was trying to justify something unjustifiable. It was as though this was the first time she'd actually thought about what she'd done and how it could affect others, and it was dawning upon her how stupid it was. "I just thought, like, if enough people thought we'd been together, it might make Alex want to actually be together. Just so it wouldn't be a big lie, y'know?"

I felt for the girl a little, though I wasn't sure why -- not then. Now I know that while I would never try something so stupid, that we were all capable of acts of stupidity in the name of love; each and every one of us. "Xander's not like that," I stated bluntly. After a moment's pause, I realized who I was talking too, and decided I might need to elaborate a little. "He's complex. And he's been through a lot more than you or I realize. He keeps so much of it inside, trying to be brave. But what he doesn't get is : he doesn't need to be brave. It comes naturally to him. Everything he's been trying so hard to be, he keeps thinking that it's just one step away. That if he tries hard enough, he'll be a good man. What he doesn't get is... he was there ten steps ago. He's never going to stop trying to be better. To do what's right. And that's why he'll always be good. He's not just going to jump into bed with you. I'm not saying anything against you, it's just... he has old fashioned morals. He's going to do what's right. For him to get serious with you, in his mind, that would be him 'cheating' on Sara. And he'd never do that. No matter what people say, I'll never believe - -" I stopped and noticed the enlightened look in Julie's eyes. As if the girl just figured out something that had been on the tip of her tongue for a long time.

Her mouth opened, and when the words came out, they sounded true, even to me : "You love him."

She stopped writing, rubbing her hand a little from the strain it put on her wrist. That was how the conversation with Julie had gone, she thought, for the most part. At least that part she could mostly get from memory. The fight with Black Heart a few pages before had been completely fabricated, made up of half-truths from the news reports and what little Xander had told her about it. What she had said to Julie was true: at that point, he had been bottling everything up, even more than he did now. The whole trip to L.A. seemed like such an odd chapter of their lives now, like it hadn't really happened. Maybe that was just because it had been all the way across the country, or maybe it was just because of the weirdness that had surrounded the whole ordeal.

She rubbed her eyes and tried to think of where to go next. After a moment she smiled, then started to write again. She started by writing Later that night... even though it had been at least a week between one event and the next, but she thought that added some immediacy to the tale.

Later that night my phone began to ring. As I opened it and rummaged for the talk button, I remember thinking that it was Mike. That the Womb had come out during the night and done something to him, killed him, that I'd lost the person I love just as Xander had a month before. "Hello?" I asked, and my voice felt raw and unused.

"It's me," came the voice from the other end of the line. It sounded hushed and deep, and there was a lot of static in the background. I felt like I had just gotten a call from Deep Throat.

It took me a moment to place the voice, then finally it slid together in my brain. "Xander?" I groaned, pressing my free hand against my free ear to try and hear him better, even though all the static and noise was on his end, I was sure. "Are you okay? Is Mike okay?"

I heard the silence through the line and recognized it. Somehow, I could picture him making his hurt face, those puppy-dog eyes turned upwards. I hadn't said 'did you hurt Mike,' but I may as well have.

"I'm sorry," I spat, fully awake and trying to get my apology into his head before he had a chance to really absorb the pain I'd just caused him, even though I knew it was too late from that the moment I had said it.

"It's okay. I understand," he said glumly, and the sad part was that he did understand, completely. It's one thing to think those things about yourself; but for me to vocalize them like that had just been wrong. "It's just the rain, it's making me irritable."

I reached up and pulled the window shade aside, kneeling on the edge of my bed and looking out. "It's not raining here... Where are you? What town are you in?"

She continued on writing. She wrote about how they'd first met Mandy on a trip to Coral Cove, and how she'd decided to come back with them. She wrote about Randy and Tommy and Sud for a little, but as little as possible. It left a bad taste in her mouth when she thought of the events leading up to the day that Sud had been shot, and she did not like it at all. Finally, she got to Xander's first real confrontation with the Tees. She sat up in bed and snatched her Cherry Coke out of her book bag, opening it and taking a long swig before starting again, her hand flying over the page at a mile a minute.

He crashed through the skylight that sparkled moonlight down into the warehouse that the Tees used for their headquarters, spraying large shards of glass and black blood everywhere as he fell. Time seemed to slow down, and all ten Tees looked up in awe. And in the center, little Amanda Peterson looked up as well, clutched into herself tightly. The glass spun around the falling black form and sparkled in the low light, catching it and making it shimmer and shine. It made it look like wings, like he were flying to earth instead of falling to it. Deep inside her heart, Mandy felt the desperation melt away and filled with hope.

He finally landed after what seemed like an eternity. He stayed crouched from the impact for a few moments, then arose. The thinness of him made him look taller than he was, all sleek and oiled with long, taunt muscles. His eyes opened, large and radiating red, and the Tees had just enough time to fathom what was about to happen to them before it did.

She stopped, huffing as she reached the end of the last page, then quickly pulled another notebook from her knapsack and opened it to a clean, white page and continued.

Xander - -

She stopped immediately, crossing out her friend's name and starting again.

The Womb reached out with his hand full of razor-sharp talons and grabbed the closest Tee around the neck, making four tiny slits as he did. As he pulled forward he bent backwards, using the momentum of the movement to hurl the Tee back over his head and crashing into another, both men tumbling into the darkness that surrounded the moonlight.

The Womb righted himself again, his scaled form serving as a barrier between them and the girl now, and it eyed each of them carefully, its claws dangling at its sides. One of them lunged at it, spinning a chain around his head with one powerful arm and thrusting it in the heroes direction. The Womb raised its arm quickly but calmly, and the chain hit it and whipped, typing itself around even as the demon gave it a solid tug, bringing the Tee with it. It extended its fist and the Tee's face flew into it. The thug fell into unconsciousness.

"Never knew I was that cool," Xander said, leaning against the door behind her.

She turned, startled, then smiled a little. "That's not how it went?"

He chuckled, wiping his eyes a little. They weren't red

or puffy anymore, but now she got the distinct impression that he had been crying for some reason. It occurred to her how little she'd seen him with his parents. "Not quite," he answered finally, sitting down backward in his desk chair.

She turned and looked back over what she had written, raising an eyebrow. "That's how I see it happening. She called you the Black Angel, so I figured I'd play it up."

Xander nodded, but did not respond verbally. He had that same faraway look in his eyes that he had had outside, leaning against the mailbox.

"Bob the Squirrel..." she sang musically, putting down the notebook and waving her head in front of him comically, trying to cheer him up.

He raised a hand for her to stop and she did.

"Were your parents mad about you being out all last night? You should tell them it was my fault, somehow, it's really the truth - -"

"My mom has cancer," he said, and his eyes started to well up again. His chin crumpled up toward his mouth as it always did when he was about to cry. But he didn't.

Her mouth went slack, and for a moment it just hung there, unsure of what to say.

"She has cancer," he repeated, running his fingers through his hair. When they came back with blood on them, Cathy realized that his talons had been out and grabbed him by the wrists.

"Don't!"

"Cancer. This little shadow..." he chuckled giddily, then thrust his head back in a full laugh. "She has this little dark spot... on her uterus, Cathy." He chuckled again, but the tears were coming freely now. "She has a black womb."

Her eyes went wide with fright, and without even thinking about it, her hand went to her own abdomen.

He noticed, and the chuckling slowly died down. "Everything coming together and falling apart, all at the same time," he said finally, and even though it didn't really make sense, she nodded in agreement.

"How did this happen? I mean, how can she know so fast?"

He squinted and his mind raced as he remembered something.

He climbed in through his bedroom window, still drenched in blood and bile, landing on his floor with a thud. He was glad that the car wasn't in the driveway, that meant his parents were not home. This was the last thing his mother needed to see.

Xander turned around and looked up the stairs. "Mom?" he called upwards to no reply. He sighed and looked onto the kitchen counter. There was a plate of chicken covered in plastic wrap waiting for him. Water vapour clung to the outside of it, and it was frigged cold to touch. Next to it was a short note: Alex, Gone over to the hospital to see the Kennessy's. Eat some chicken, and go to bed at a decent hour. We'll be home late. -Love, Mom.

He looked through the bathroom garbage, pushing aside bits of tissue and empty toilet paper rolls, and a few used prescription bottles, then finally found what he had been searching for...

"Actually, I think it's been happening for a while," he

said quietly, snuggling into Cathy's shoulder. He hadn't even realized that she had started holding him, but that was all right as far as he was concerned. "I think we just didn't notice."

"This doesn't mean anything," she said, pulling back so she could look at him. "This wasn't you, it couldn't have been. You know that, right?"

He said nothing, didn't move. Didn't even breathe, as far as she could tell. She thought that maybe he was in shock, but didn't know how to tell for sure. "I should call her," he said after a long moment, reaching for his cordless phone and depressing the receiver. There was a clicking sound, followed by another, and then the dial tone hummed to life.

"Call who?" Cathy asked, looking down at the phone quizzically. When he didn't answer she watched him dial. He got three digits in and he realized that the person he was calling wasn't in Coral Beach. "No!" she yelled, moving to grab the phone from him, but he jerked it away, finishing the number sequence with his thumb. "You can *not* call her!" she ordered, falling to the floor as she again made a grab for the phone and missed, banging her knee off the wheel on his chair.

The ringing stopped, and Julie Peterson's voice rang out over the line. "Hello?" she chimed, sounding chipper.

Xander's face went white and he just sat there, listening to the sound of her voice.

"Hello?" it came again, more annoyed this time. "Is anyone there? Hell - low - oh?" Finally she disconnected the call, and Xander's ear was once again graced with the low hum of dial tone until he turned the phone off again.

Julie stared at him, her face deadly serious. "What you really love more than anything. You love death Xander Drew... and as long as you do, death will keep following you."

"What was the point of that?" Cathy asked, rubbing the knee she had banged.

He looked at her, really at her, for the first time since he had told her the news, and started to cry again, retracting his claws and burying his eyes into his palms. He sat there on his knees in the burned carpet of his bedroom and cried like a newborn. She reached out to hold him but he swatted her away.

She hit him and then moved to embrace him again, and this time he complied.

Gallagher opened the large wooden door to his chapel just a crack and peered out at who was knocking, then opened it completely and smiled warmly. "Hello, kind sir," he said, adjusting his white collar, more out of habit than of a need to. "And what can I do for you this evening?"

Officer Adrian Extol glared at Gallagher from under the peak of his uniform hat, the smallest twinge of sympathy for the man floating in his eyes briefly, then leaving again. Behind him, another officer leaned against their squad car in the parking lot, its lights flashing blue and red intermittently. He heaved a sigh, then finally spoke. "Robert Gallagher?" he asked, tipping up his hat.

"Yes, I'm *Reverend* Robert Gallagher," he said, correcting the man, but trying not to sound pretentious.

Extol pulled a pair of handcuffs from his side and snapped one loop around Gallagher's wrist, and it snapped shut quickly and tightly. "Not no more, you ain't."

"What is the meaning on this?" Gallagher bellowed, a look of shock overcoming his face as the policeman finished.

"You have the right to remain silent. Should you choose to waive that right, anything you say can and will be held against you in a court of law. You have the right to an attorney. If you cannot afford..."

But Gallagher wasn't hearing it anymore. His face was pale and his eyes were blank as he was helped into the squad car and carted off to the precinct.

"Want to run that one by me again?" Cathy asked, raising an eyebrow as she clutched the phone tightly to her ear.

"Gallagher just got arrested," Mike repeated, his words filled with just as much astonishment as hers, even he was the one delivering the news.

Xander lay on the bed rubbing his eyes with his thumbs, hard. "And today, we continue a long tradition of Guidance Councilors in Coral Beach," he mumbled before plopping his hands down against the mattress and using them to brace himself up. "So, what are we going to do about it?" he asked, loud enough that Mike could hear him, too.

Cathy didn't speak, and there was silence from Mike's end of the line too. "What do you mean?" she said finally, breaking the silence.

"Yeah," Mike agreed, his voice muffled a little as he spat out toothpaste. "Mystery solved, man. Bad guy already in cuffs, good cops probably having a beer already. Not everything has to be a huge drama, man."

"I guess," Xander said, slumping down into himself. "It just seems too easy, is all."

"Tell that to that poor kid," Mike tisked, disgusted. "I never liked that guy."

"I thought he was okay."

"Me too," Cathy said, placing a hand on Xander's shoulder. "But this is too much, Xander. This is beyond even the thought of forgiveness."

"I know," he sighed, then snatched up the phone and brought it to his mouth. "I know," he repeated into the mouthpiece, louder and clearer than the first time.

"What?" Mike said innocently, raising his eyebrows from the other end.

"I heard what you said."

"I didn't say anything."

"Super. Human. Hearing. Don't make me say it again."

"You're a knob," Mike grunted, and there was a soft jingle as he put his toothbrush away.

There was silence then from Xander's side, and Cathy motioned for him to give her back the phone. He ignored her.

"You're gonna wanna talk to him, won't you?" Mike heaved, the frustration in his voice evident.

Xander nodded. After a full minute of no response from Mike, he said "Yes."

"Fine," Mike spat. "But don't act all depressed when

this turns out bad. Because I guarantee you, this will turn out bad."

"Yeah, yeah," Xander drawled, smiling out of the corner of his mouth and before handing the phone back to Cathy.

"You coming over again tonight?" she asked, the former subject closed as far as she was concerned.

"Um, no," Mike replied dumbly. "I think your mom would cut off a few parts of me that I'm rather attached to."

Cathy giggled, then turned and saw Xander staring at her with one eyebrow raised. She coughed. "What are you doing, then? Can I come over there?"

"Actually, I think I'm going to be staying over with Xander tonight."

To her side, Xander shook his head wildly, waving his arms back and forth in negative response.

"Xander thinks that's a great idea," Cathy smirked, winking.

Xander slumped, then mumbled something incoherent.

"Love you too, hun. Bye." She pressed the receiver to disconnect the call and looked smugly at Xander.

"You enjoyed doing that, didn't you?"

"Yes," she chirped, then sat back at his desk to write some more.

Mike put the phone back on its cradle and smiled, the echo of his lover's voice still ringing in his ears. He gave himself one last quick look in the mirror, then rubbed his hand across his chin to see if he'd gotten all of the stubble. He smacked his face then walked out of the bathroom and into his bedroom.

He opened the drawer to his nightstand and started to ruffle through it, pushing aside candies and school papers that should have been passed in days ago and saline solution, even though nobody he knew wore contacts. Finally he withdrew a small scrap of paper, beaten, torn, and worn around the edges, the numbers on it were faded but still very visible.

Megan Greene = 555-5428 ext. 308

He pressed down on the big button in the center of his phone (the numbers on it having long since been scratched off, probably by him while very bored one night when there was nothing on television) and dialed the digits, then waited as the phone rang four times before someone on the other end picked up.

"Hello," came Megan's professional voice from the other end of the line.

"Hi, Miss. Greene, it's Mike..."

"You're reached the law firm of Mayer, Summers and Soul, the office of Megan Greene. I'm not at my desk or working on an important case right now, so please leave your message at the sound of the tone and I'll get back to you as soon as I can... -BEEP-"

He sighed, knocking the receiver against his forehead once before bringing the phone back to its rightful position. "Hi Megan, it's Mike -- Mike Harris," he said, his voice sounding tired and mechanical. He hated talking to machines. "I'm just calling to... to tell you that if you hear from Xander in the next few days, just say no, okay? Really, it's just for the best. I think he's having a hard time and... anyway, it's nothing. Just, don't listen to him if he calls."

"To save your message, press one. To re-record it, press two. To delete, press three."

Mike looked at the phone for a moment, then finally pressed three. He tossed the phone onto his bed, then pulling on his hair until some of it came out.

༺༻

In her office, Megan looked at the phone with one eyebrow raised, her hand still clasping the pen she'd been using to finish her notes on the Styles case file.

"Message not saved," her answering machine informed her coldly, as she leaned back in her chair and tapped her pen against her mouth thoughtfully.

CHAPTER TWENTY-TWO
JUSTICE

It was three in the morning and Cathy was still at her computer, typing away at what she had begun to call 'her manuscript' in her head, her fingers pounding against the keys furiously. She had considered transcribing what she had written in the notebooks onto the computer, then decided against it when she realized where she was in the story. Even though the subject disgusted her while making her want to cry, the words flew out of her like nothing else, each one exploding onto the page with a burst on emotion.

I thought an explosion had gone off next to my head, and a big slab on concrete slammed into me, making me buckle over. For some reason, the first thing that crossed my mind was Genblade. That almost seems silly, now... but not really. Up until that point, he had definitely been the most nightmarish thing I had seen in my life... *up until that point.*

It towered over me, filling the entirety of the hole it had created in the side of the school. It looked human, just larger, but I quickly realized that it wasn't. It had no lower jaw, its mouth just joined with its chest in a maw of teeth and blood red gums. It had the parts of a human, the arms and legs and head; but they swirled and distorted of their own conviction. It was like someone made a sculpture of a person in half-formed Jell-O and it was baying in the wind.

Its claws were massive each easily the size of my hand, one on each of its three fingers.

Twirling, churning tendrils swarmed around it everywhere, each one making spikes and then retreating them, like a lizard sticking out its tongue to sniff the air. Its face turned toward me... not its head, just its face, as through the skin wasn't attached to the bone, and it bellowed, long and loud: "Zakron!"

I felt fear wash over me, replacing blood in my face as it all drained out. It lashed out with one arm and hit me broadside. The bruise was there for over a month, and I felt the brief sensation of flying.

When I woke up three hours later, I wasn't pregnant anymore.

She stopped writing, rubbing her abdomen tenderly and looking down at it. In her mind's eye it looked as though there were a basketball under her shirt, the way she would have looked by now had that not happened. She took a deep breath and waited for tears. When they didn't come and she was sure they wouldn't, she continued.

Her name would have been Amora Jasmine Harris if she had lived, I think...

ʌ‹ʌ

Mike woke up the next day with the church roof leaking on him, a small puddle having formed in the nape of his chest. He groaned and rubbed the bridge of his nose as he picked up his copy of 'The Lord of the Flies' from where it rested against his groin and laid in down on the floor next to the pew he had slept on, wondering what time it was.

"Let me out," Xander said simply, taunt forward as much as he could be in his chains, looking at his friend with grim determination.

Mike arose, blinked twice to adjust to the dank church, then grunted and scratched his chest. After a moment to compose himself he turned and looked at Xander, who was still lulling the bindings as close to him as he could. "How long have you been awake?" he asked, his voice monotone and achy.

"Two hours," he responded curtly. "Let me out."

"No rush, man," he assured his friend after a quick glance at his watch. "We've still got plenty of time before we have to get to school."

"Not going to school. Not right away, anyway." He gave his left chain a good tug and made it rattle. He was soaked in his own blood again, the black ooze on the floor having long since dried and become crystalline, as if someone had just tarred the floor of the confessional.

Mike rolled his eyes, his arms falling to his sides and away from the keys that hung at his belt. "You're not seriously going where I think you're going, are you?" he asked, even though he already knew the answer.

"I have to know. I need to be sure that Gallagher is guilty."

"This may be hard for you to believe," Mike drawled as he removed the keys from his belt loop and fumbled through them, finding the correct one and sliding it into the left arm shackle. "But there was a justice system *before* you became the Black Womb."

Xander looked at him flatly, but did not speak.

"I'm just saying."

"Yeah, well. Feel free to stop doing that anytime you want."

Mike shot him an annoyed look as he finished unlocking the last shackle.

Xander stepped forward a pace or two, stretched, then moved to pick up his clothes.

"You're feeling better today," Mike noted, noticing the bounce in his friend's step.

"Mmm."

"Is there any way I can convince you not to do this?" he pleaded, hands out before him.

"No."

"You're going to kill again," Mike finally said, making a fist as he said the words he had desperately not wanted to. "That's the only way it ever ends with the Womb, you know. Somebody bleeding and dead on the ground. That's its idea of justice. It'll either be Gallagher or that kid or Calla - -"

"Calla?" Xander repeated as he slid into his dark green t-shirt, turning his head and acknowledging that Mike was speaking, finally.

"Yeah, this girl at school. She was the one who convinced the kid to go to the cops."

"She the one that was smoking pot?"

"I never told you someone was - "

"I can still smell it on your clothes."

"I changed."

"On your skin then."

"I showered."

"Then you didn't do a very good job," he mumbled as he put on his black hiking boots, lacing them quickly as he sat on the hard wooden pews. "Let me do this, even if you don't help. Worst case scenario, I find out the cops were right and then let it be."

"That *isn't* the worst case scenario when the Womb's involved," he reminded, pointing a finger to the right side of Xander's gut.

"It's taking my mind off things. Off my mom..."

Mike stared his friend in the eye, then finally relented. "Fine. Go. Be Sherlock Holmes for all I care, just don't do anything that I'll have to stab you for."

Xander saluted, then turned and started to head for the door. Mike watched him go for a second or two, then looked up and the monument of Jesus on the Cross and followed.

The buds of the elm opened and her leaves looked up and saw the sun, but never forgot the cold of the winter night. No matter how warm it got, the winter was in her now.

Cathy looked from side to side at the mostly vacant cells, her nose twitching from the smell of dried sweat and urine as she stared past the bars. One very close to her had blood in it, the little press-on label just to the side of the cell read: Shnieder. She averted her eyes from it as quickly as possible, realizing that Xander was a few steps ahead of her and quickly moving to catch up.

"Hey," came a voice from her side, and she turned quickly to see who it was. A man leaned against the bars of his cell, his hairy arms hanging out of it casually as he looked at her, his eyes darted up and down her body, then ran one hand through his thinning black hair. "My name's Malcolm, what's yours?"

Her eyebrows lowered as she took a cautious step back from his cell, and finally noticed that he was touching himself. One of his hands had been slid down the front of his prison jumpsuit, and was rubbing vigorously.

Cathy balked in disgust and she gagged. She thought that she might throw up.

"Why don't you come here a - - Shut up, Bitch!" he yelled, spinning around quickly and yelling at the toilet, which did nothing to respond to his outburst except drip a little onto the floor. "If I've told you once, I've told you a million times to just shut up! She wants it, there's nothing *wrong* with that!" He turned back toward the bars quickly, pressing his body against them and thrusting his arms out at Cathy, as if trying to squeeze through.

- tap tap -

Malcolm turned to the side of his cage, where Xander leaned against the opposite side of the bars, tapping one slightly raised talon against the metal to get his attention and smiling. Malcolm nearly jumped out of his skin, stumbling backward and slamming his rear end onto the floor. "Christ!" he yelled, then scurried under his bunk and stayed there in silence for a moment, then he mumbled quietly. "Shut up, you bitch."

Xander chuckled a little, then his smile faded as he turned to Cathy. "You okay?"

"Yeah..." she said, still staring at the man under the bed, then finally tore her frightened eyes away from him. "Yes. Isn't that...?"

"Yes, it is. Don't dawdle. Not here," he cautioned, cocking his head toward the far end of the hall and then heading in that direction, followed quickly by Cathy.

She tried not to look after that, but her eyes still strayed from side to side, mostly to the name plates on the empty cells that had yet to be removed. She was surprised at how many of them she recognized, then realized that she probably shouldn't be. Char's name was there, and so was Owchar's. Then, no matter how hard she tried not to see it, was Smith. Derek Smith's old cell.

A shiver ran down her spine and she walked a little faster, until she was side by side with Xander. "Why did I have to be here again?" she asked, getting as close to him as possible without actually latching on.

"You weren't friends with Gallagher," he stated, keeping his eyes straight ahead.

"Only met him a few times."

"You're not biased. I am. I want him to be innocent, I'll

find a way to believe he is."

Cathy stopped, and after a second, so did he, turning to look at her. "What? Don't you think you should talk to the kid instead? No matter what, Gallagher's going to say he didn't do it, Xander. Innocent or guilty, he'll say he's innocent."

Xander gave her a look that made her heart go out to him, and then they both continued walking without a word.

"I hate this place," she said after a moment.

"I think that's the point," Xander mused, smirking at her just a little.

He stopped, turned to his left and staring through the bars of the cell they'd arrived at. At first, he'd thought maybe he'd gotten the number wrong, the man inside looked nothing like Robert Gallagher. His balding hair was sticking off on either side of his head, and an orange prison jumpsuit with numbers stamped across the left breast replaced his black suit and white collar. Then the slight breeze inside the penitentiary changed, and Xander got a good whiff of him. Of the fear that rolled off him like a fog, and knew he was at the right place.

"Father?" he asked, and Cathy raised an eye to him. His voice was softer when he spoke to Gallagher, more child-like. She hadn't heard anything like that come out of his mouth since Sara died. Maybe even before that.

Gallagher looked up, his face drawn down in an exaggerated frown and bags under his eyes. He looked like his face was melting, and the tears only helped toward that illusion. "My son?" he asked, squinting and rubbing his eyes as he sat on the edge of his cot, then finally stood up and started to walk over to the bars.

Cathy stepped back half a pace.

Gallagher looked at her, hurt, then forced a warm smile in her direction. "Miss. Kennessy," he said in greeting, giving her a little nod.

Xander reached up, holding a bar in each hand and looking through them. "How are you?"

Gallagher sighed, and his heart raced for a split second, then slowed again. Xander struggled to hear, and the Womb surged inside him to help, making every footfall of every rat in the building become as clear as day to him. "I'm fine. That awful man down the hall seemed to take an unhealthy interest in me at breakfast, but then he began to yell at someone who wasn't there and wandered off."

Xander nodded. "Tell me if he gives you any trouble."

There was a silence between them then, as both men could only think of questions that they did not want to ask. Finally Gallagher broke it, his heart skipping a beat. "You think I did it, don't you?"

Xander listened, and the man's heart rate was still steady. "I don't know what to think, Father. That's why I'm here."

Behind him, Cathy rolled her eyes.

"And what about you, Miss?" Gallagher asked, raising his head to see over Xander's, getting a full look at the girl's troubled face.

Xander listened, his beat was still regular.

"You don't want to know," Cathy replied honestly. "But I hope you're innocent."

The heart sank, its beat slower again. Depression, Xander labeled it.

"Father, I hate to ask..." Xander sighed.

"No, I certainly did not," Gallagher protested, his cheeks flapping in outrage before calming again.

Pulse was mostly steady, except for the anger. "I'm going to be a part of this, sir, just like I was with August. Is there anything I should know now?"

"No," Gallagher sighed, eyeing the boy. He looked even more depressed than a moment before, somehow. "No, there isn't, Alexander."

His pulse skipped twice there, once around each time he said no. Xander furrowed his brow and shot a pained glance back at Cathy before looking back at Gallagher. "I want you to know something," he almost whispered, mindful of the guards at the end of the hall.

Gallagher perked his ears, his smile clearly fake.

"If I'm in this, I'm in it all the way. If I prove you're innocent, that's great. If I prove otherwise... well, let's just say you'll see a side of me you never have before." He turned on his heels without saying goodbye and marched back toward the entrance.

Cathy stood, eye to eye with Gallagher before turning and running to catch up with Xander.

"What do you think?" he asked the second she got close enough to him.

She gasped, trying to catch her breath between words. "I think he showed a lot of empathy during the Styles thing that I'm not seeing here, and that's got to mean something." She paused, taking another lungful of air. "What about you, Mr. Super-Human-Hearing, what's the verdict?"

"I don't know," he stated angrily as he shoved open the exit into the main hall with Cathy in hot pursuit.

"What do you mean you don't know?" Mike yelled, thrusting his arms out, his blonde eyebrows shooting upward comically. Xander sat on the snow-covered picnic table in front of him, rubbing his own knotted shoulders rhythmically, wondering why the healing factor didn't take of such things for him. Cathy was standing between the two, her arms folded in front of her and staring downward, watching as her foot made concentric semi-circles all around her. Mike took off his jacket, suddenly deciding that he was sweating, and tossed it on the table. It hit Xander. "Super. Human. Senses," he said in a mocking tone, flapping one palm open and closed like a puppet. "Who was it that kept saying that? Was it you, yeah, I thought so. How could you not know?"

Xander looked up, running his hands over his face as he did, stretching it out. "He responded differently to two different questions. He said he did nothing to the kid, and his heart beat was steady, means he's telling the truth."

"So?" Mike said, looking confused. "There's your answer, isn't it?"

"Then I asked him if he did anything to the kid I should know about, he said no twice, his heart did a double-beat both times."

"Means he's lying," Cathy said absently, remembering an episode of some television show where they had the characters hooked up to a polygraph machine, the little marker waving back and forth jaggedly on the page as he lead character lied.

Mike sighed, kicking a snow drift and sending large clumps flying in every direction. Cathy reached out once to touch him, then rethought it.

"Will you calm the fuck down?" Xander said, irritated. "I really don't need it right now."

Again, Mike's eyebrow's rose. "Again, just don't come crawling to me when this one blows up in your face, because it has disaster written across it in bright shiny letters, man."

"Noted," he said, keeping his eyes on the back entrance to the school a hundred or so feet in front of him as he reached into his inside jacket pocket and produced a cigarette, pinning it between his lips and then lighting it.

Cathy coughed, even though the smoke was nowhere near her yet. He gave her a droll look, and she smirked.

"So, what's your plan now, hero?" Mike teased, jabbing his friend in the arm.

Xander took a short drag then removed the smoke from his mouth, motioning toward the door with it. "Already in action," he said, as if that explained all.

Both Mike and Cathy turned toward the door and watched it for a second, then back to Xander. "What?" Cathy said finally, taking the word out of Mike's mouth.

"Hold it," Xander said, smiling wide. "I can smell it. She's coming now."

This time only Mike turned, waited a little longer, then back again. "You having another fever dream, man?"

"Wait for it. Three... two... one..."

Calla McFadden opened the back door and stepped out, glancing behind her quickly, and then reached into her pocket and pulled out a metal case and headed for the smoking section, where the brick wall met the fence.

Xander smiled, his eyes following her until she disappeared behind the cornerstone.

Mike turned back to him, no small amount of panic behind his eyes. "No," he said, and it came out as an order.

"What?" Xander smirked, throwing his smoke to the ground.

"You are not going near that girl," he said in the same tone, folding his arms and stepping up toward his friend. His chest was level with Xander's head, and he used it to try and exert dominance over him, and tactic he'd used many times in their shared youth.

"It's not a good idea, Xander," Cathy agreed, taking a step toward him herself, but still behind Mike. "Gallagher's not worth that."

Xander shot her a look.

"Come on, you know what I mean. Phillips, O'Toole, now him... it's a little too convenient, don't you think?"

"Everything about this is too convenient," he mumbled, then got up from the table and started to walk over toward the smoking section.

Mike stepped in front of him, still towering overhead.

Xander looked up at him, almost having to crane his neck to do so, flaring his nostrils slightly. He stepped to one side and started to walk again, and this time Mike made no effort to stop him, placing his head in one hand and shaking them both.

Cathy sighed, standing on her tip-toes to give her lover a kiss. "Watch him. Make sure he doesn't do anything stupid. I'm going to go find that kid, hope that cooler heads prevail."

"That's likely," Mike cursed, returning the kiss and watching her walk toward the school, then turning to follow Xander.

"That smells like feet," Xander said, causing Calla to twist her head uncomfortably in his direction. She had been in mid-puff and almost dropped her joint. "I could smell it from over there."

The shock wore off her face as she looked him up and down, and became a sly smile. "Want some?" she asked, handing the joint to him and sticking out her tongue, revealing a small pink stud in it not far from the tip.

Xander took the rolled up paper from her and watched the smoke rise from its tip for a moment before handing it back. "No, thanks," he said as she took it.

She shrugged, then brought it to her lips and took another draw. She held it in as long as possible before letting it out. "Your loss. This is some kick-ass stuff."

"I'm sure." He patted his jacket for his smokes and realized that he just had one and stopping himself.

Again her eyes danced over him, sizing up every square inch of him. This time he felt it, and repressed the goosebumps it invoked. "You're Xander Drew, aren't you?"

Xander regarded her with an amount of curiosity. "I don't know you, but you know me."

"I'm Calla," she smiled, but did not extend a hand, just stayed there in her relaxed stance against the wall.

She took another puff, quicker this time. "I was in Evan and Mandy's Lit class. Didn't do so well last year so they let me repeat for credit."

"Huh," Xander grunted, noticing the red streak in her hair.

She smiled at him devilishly. "Wondering if the carpet matches the drapes?" she laughed.

Xander stared at her until he finally got the joke and smirked. "Cute," he said finally. He found himself comfortable around her, but couldn't place why.

She brought the joint to her lips again, and it was getting down to the butt now. She looked over the rising smoke at him. "Sure you don't want any?"

Xander did not respond, just waved his hand once to dismiss the idea. He saw it now. She reminded him of Julie.

She took a last puff, then tossed the roach into the snow and turned back to him, standing to face him now. "So, what do you want?"

"I just want to ask you something about that kid you helped," Xander said honestly, appreciating her forwardness.

"Hmm," she half hummed, half-laughed, coming even closer to him. He almost wanted to back up a little, but didn't. "Can you ask me them in bed?" she asked, again flashing him her tongue ring.

"Excuse me?" Xander asked, perplexed.

"You know -- pillow talk. Can you ask me the questions... afterwards?" she asked, her eyes locked onto his as she reached out and touched him on the arm, gently at first, then grabbing at it.

"Okay, that's enough," Mike said, coming out from around the corner and grabbing Calla firmly by the arm. "That's enough chocolate for you today."

"Hey," Calla protested, her cheeks livid with anger as Mike gave her a polite shove toward the door. "I was - -"

"Just leaving." Mike finished, saluting a wave to her. "I know. Bon voyage."

Calla huffed then cursed loudly, stomping her way through the snow toward the door.

"Thanks," Xander chuckled when Mike rejoined him, there was already a smoke between his lips. "Weird girl, huh?"

"Yeah," Mike smiled, sitting down next to his friend and leaning his head back against the wall, the first time he'd really been relaxed since waking up. "She reminds me of Peterson."

"Which one?" Xander asked, smoke curling around his head.

"Take your pick," Mike shot back. They both laughed.

There was silence for a few moments as Xander smokes, and he ended it as he doubted it. "Listen, man, I'm sorry about..."

Mike smiled, and it stopped him in mid-sentence. "Me too. But we're supposed to butt heads. It's what we do. Don't worry, I think everything's going to be fine."

Xander shot him a look. "You really believe that?"

"No, but it sounds nice."

Xander nodded, then looked up as Cathy came around the corner to join them, her face pale white. "Did you find the kid?"

"Um, yeah," she said, crumpling her brow.

Silence.

"And?" Mike asked, gesturing his hands in a rolling motioned, trying to coax the words out of her mouth.

"He said that Calla McFadden's been touching him."

CHAPTER TWENTY-THREE
FLESH

Cathy flipped the page of the file folder, letting a long breath out from her puffy cheeks. The library smelled like the oddly comforting mixture of stake old book and fresh, newly printed ones, with one scent overtaking the other depending on which section one sat it. The smell of Mrs. Grimes' rose oil perfume was also unmistakable, even though she was all the way across the hall at her desk. "You sure we should be doing this in public?" Cathy asked, glancing at the large stack of file folders they'd swiped from Gallagher's desk before coming in.

"It's not public, it's the library," Xander said, running a finger over the page in a way that he was told helped with speed-reading. "Besides, if she catches us, what's she going to do? Send us to the Guidance Councilor? Or maybe the Principal?"

"Good point," Cathy conceded, turning the page again. "Who is this Nick Carry kid anyway? I don't remember him."

"Dropped out," Mike mumbled, taking a sip of his

coffee but never once taking his eyes off the page. "Some said he transferred, but he dropped out."

"Looks like he had it rough," she sighed, closing that file and laying it aside with all the others they'd already checked through.

"Did he get crucified?" Xander asked, almost completely under his breath.

"No..."

"I win."

She rolled her eyes, then grabbed another unmarked file and opened it. "Hey, I think I got one," she said excitedly, standing up out of her chair.

Xander and Mike both moved to see as she lay the folder flat against the table, a photo of Jaden looking out at all of them, and large toothy grin across his face.

"Says here he said one of his teachers touched him a year and a half ago..." Mike mumbled, pointing to the information as he found it.

"He said Phillips did, too," Cathy chimed in, disgusted.

"Yeah, but he didn't," Xander said angrily, hoisting up the file he'd been reading. "And a few months later this girl said the same thing about Phillips, and they dismissed it citing that kid."

Mike craned his head to see the folder Xander was talking about. From inside, a picture of Greer Donaldson looked back at him sweetly. She had been one of Phillips' victims, and was still in a coma to this day. He cursed.

"Again," Cathy said, having flipped to the next page and pointing near the bottom. "When he was in Kindergarten. He said it was... his parents."

Mike cursed again, slamming his fist down against the table. "Dammit!"

Xander rubbed a hand through his hair, looking down at the kid's file. "What if it's not true? What if I read Gallagher wrong? I mean, the little boy that cried wolf got eaten at the end -- right?"

Mike nodded. "Sad thing is, he probably was abused at some point, maybe even before he can remember, and now all this is just... ugh."

"Transference?" Cathy offered, touching his hand lovingly.

"Thanks, honey," he smiled, rubbing her thumb in response.

Xander again tugged at his hair, then observed the both of them, his face devoid of emotion. "We need help," he said finally.

Λ⟨Υ⟩Λ

"Hello. You're reached the law firm of Mayer, Summers and Soul, the office of Megan Greene. I'm not at my desk or working on an important case right now, so please leave your message at the sound of the tone and I'll get back to you as soon as I can... -BEEP-"

"Megan?" came Xander's rough, scratchy voice; and Megan immediately turned toward the machine, her pen dropping from her hand and rolling along the floor. "Megan, it's me. Pick up."

Her hand shook just a little as she reached for the receiver, then she stopped and frowned. She let out a heavy sigh, then retracted her hand and took another pen from the clay dispenser next to her paperweight rather than picking up the one she had dropped.

There was silence on the other end of the line for a moment, but the machine did not beep, so she knew he was still waiting for her to pick up.

She pretended to look over her case notes on the Bird and Snelgrove trail. She twirled her hair around her fingers, the words on the page becoming one big blur to her.

"Hey," the voice from the telephone said again, a little short this time. "You don't have Mimosas this time of the week until eight, and I know you're not home. Pick up the phone."

She bit her lower lip hard, her teeth playing clear contrast to her red lipstick. She clenched her fist so tight that her nails dug into her palm, but she did not reach for the receiver.

There was a sigh on the other end of the line, and then the sound of the caller hanging up their phone. "-BEEP - message not saved," the answering machine said in its cold, mechanical voice.

She smiled, wiggling a little in her chair to shake off the call, and then turned her attention back to the file. The appeal yesterday had gone well, and she thought that the jury was on her side, but one of the defendants had the mitigating circumstances of his father's recent death and was a single parent - -

RIIING!

She cursed, slamming her pen back onto the desk and turning to glare at the phone, her eyes wide with rage. She was tempted to unplug it, or maybe forward all the calls to her machine at home so she could get some work done, but decided that Nathan would kill her if she did.

"Hello. You're reached the law firm of Mayer, Summers and Soul, the office of Megan Greene. I'm not at my desk or working on an important case right now, so please leave your message at the sound of the tone and I'll get back to you as soon as I can... -BEEP-"

"Hey," came a male voice, albeit a different one. This one was deeper and clearer, none of the scratch of the last one, and sounded more masculine, without the telltale squeak of adolescence. "It's Mike, Mike -- will you shut up?" he said suddenly in a whispered voice, and there was a muffled sound that she recognized as a caller placing the mouth of the phone against his or her shirt to avoid being heard. She raised an eyebrow. "I'm telling her, just -- I'm sorry, okay? I was -- fine, you're right just -- shut up and go have a smoke, you damn idiot." There was a huff at the other end of the line, and the muffled sound of fabric stopped as the caller returned. "Mike Harris," he continued, as if the middle part had never taken place. "I don't know if you got a message from me yesterday, I didn't think I saved it. Anyway, whatever it said -- I was wrong, I guess. Maybe. Just, if you hear from Xander..." again, the muffled sound, and his voice became hushed again. "This is stupid, if she could hear you and she can hear me, why are we being so -- oh, that's nice, man. You can sit on that and spin - - BEEP- message not saved."

She laughed a little at that last bit, trying to imagine what the conversation would have looked like had she been there to witness it. She laid down her pen and rested her chin on her hand, waiting patiently for the phone to ring again.

RIIING! "Hello. You're reached the law firm of Mayer, Summers and Soul, the office of Megan Greene. I'm not at my desk or working on an important case right now, so please leave your message at the sound of the tone and I'll get back to you as soon as I can... -BEEP-"

"Pick it up," said the rough voice again. "Don't make me put Cathy on the phone."

She reached out and pressed the speaker button to open the line and smirked to herself, picking up her red pen and making a small notation in her line of questioning for tomorrow as she did so. "Hello, Mr. Alexander Drew. And to what do I owe the pleasure of this call?"

"Cute," he chuckled, and she could have sworn she heard the crumpling and cracking of that disgusting leather jacket he wore as he leaned in closer to the phone. A pay phone, she thought. "You always screen your calls?"

"Only since I met you," she mused.

"Hey, you're my lawyer."

"To my recollection you have never paid anyone a dime in legal fees, so that would mean that you don't have a lawyer, Mr. Drew," she said, pretending to make her voice as fake as the machines as she finished one last note, then closed the folder and slid it to one side, clasping her fingers together and addressing the phone as she would a client. "Now, what can I do for you?"

There was a pause, then. "I hear a hum."

"See a doctor, not a lawyer."

"No, I mean -- do you have me on speaker phone?"

"Yes."

"Take me off, please."

She looked at the speaker on the phone oddly, weighing the sincerity of his voice. "There's -- nobody else here. The walls are soundproofed."

"Megan, take me off speaker phone, please."

She reached out and picked up the phone and placed it to her ear. "There. Now, what's so important. If it's about August, let me assure you that everything's fine."

"No, I need your help. It's about Reverend Gallagher - -"

She grinned, leaning her chair back until she almost slipped, then righting herself. "I heard. You have nothing to worry about. Tony's on the case, and he's going to made sure that guy never hurts another child again, okay? Mike's right. You should stay out of this one."

"No, no," Xander interjected, and she could hear that grin on his face. It was the same one he'd used on her during the Genblade trial and when they'd caught Shnieder. She called it the 'I'm about to drop the bomb on you' grin. "I think Gallagher's innocent. I know he is."

Megan sucked in a long breath of air, then let it out as slow as possible. Her head started to hurt around the eyes in a way she had begun to associate with his requests. "You can't be asking what I think you are. Even if I had the time --"

"Make time," he said bluntly, and she knew that he had shrugged as only a fifteen year old boy could.

"I can't, Xander. I have an important case..."

"Ask for a continuance, or something."

"This *is* my continuance!"

"This is important."

"So is the seventy-something year old man looking to get justice on the two assholes that broke into his store months back. I don't think he can take much more of this trial, Xander..."

"Suppose I could take care of that?" he said musically, even a little whimsically.

She rolled her eyes. "You don't even know what I'm talking about."

"Ron Snelgrove and Adam Bird, right? Convenience store heist, about three months back?"

She sat in her chair, bewildered. Almost falling again, she decided her high-school teachers had discouraged against leaning them for a reason and stopped. After a moment of sitting there slack jawed, she said "How did you...?"

"Grapevine. Small town, you know how it is. Was going to check on the old man, but when I heard you were involved, figured you had it covered. But I can handle that, you handle this... cause I can't."

"Xander," she plead, digging her nails into her scalp, wishing for it to be five so she could have a drink with this conversation. "It's not a case I can win. They *are* going to make an example of Gallagher. They *are* going to massacre him on the stand, and that kid's testimony is all the judge is going to need to hear to start the trial that'll put your friend away for the rest of his life."

"Testimony?"

"What?"

"You just said something about a testimony?"

"Yes," Megan said, grabbing her coffee and taking a long slug of it. "The trial's not for a little while, but the kid speaks to the judge with the prosecutor and the defendant tomorrow, along with the arresting officer. They want the kid's story on the record so that he doesn't have to appear at the trail. The kid's been through enough."

Xander was silent for a moment, and she could hear him tapping his lip in thought.

"Xander?"

"Be there, tomorrow. Call your boss, Tony, the Judge... I don't care. You're Gallagher's defense, just in case I can't work out something better."

"But my case --"

"You owe me," he said flatly, losing some of his good nature, but not all. She got the feeling this was him without the smiles and lace he put on around her.

"No, I don't. I *did* owe you for the Genblade thing."

"The August case, which you won with my help. The case you did pro-bono, giving your firm no end of good publicity and putting you in your bosses good graces. What's his name again?"

"Nathan Summers."

"Right. Seems nice," he said, and there was a hint of connotation in his voice.

"Yes, he is."

"Good. It's nice that he's so nice."

She paused, and this time it was her turn to put the phone against her shirt. She bit her lip until it hurt, then brought the phone to her ear again. "Fine. I'll be there, Xander. But only tomorrow, and if it looks bad, I'm removing myself from the case entirely, and that'll be the last I have to do with it."

"Thanks," he said honestly, if not a little glumly.

"Don't thank me. It's not going to go well. The second that kid tells the Judge what he told the police, it's over for Gallagher, and you know it. I in no way expect to even get the chance to *speak* at this thing tomorrow, let alone do anything to help. It's over. If you really want to do something to help Gallagher, buy him a cake with a file in it."

"Thanks anyway, Megan. I'll come by the bar sometime and have a drink when things wind down a little. We'll catch up."

"Sure. I've got to go. I should be working on my cases. That's plural, now."

"Thanks again. Bye."

"Bye," she said, placing the phone back on its rest and looking at it for a moment. She put her hand back on the Bird and Snelgrove file and slid it toward her, opening it, then closing it again. Getting up from her chair for the first time in hours, she grabbed her blazer and headed for the door.

She suddenly needed a stiff drink.

ᚨᚲᚤ

Calla stared out the window of the school, watching as Mike, Xander and Cathy walked out the back entrance and out into the world outside the school. She sighed, laying a chubby cheek against her fist as she sun beamed down on her, illuminating her face in a heavenly glow. She turned away from the trio, opening her desk and taking an envelope out of it.

"Hey," came a voice next to her, and she turned to see Tommy leaning in her direction from one seat ahead and to the right. "Can you see where they're goin' from here?"

"What do you care?" she remarked snidely, curling her nose as she looked at him.

"I don't know. Just feel left out is all."

"If you feel left out, it's probably because you *were* left out," she remarked, turning her attention to the sealed envelope on her desk. It was the pure white of any paper right out of the pack and never exposed to the sun's harmful rays, but the edges of it were worn and the corners beaten, like it had been stuffed away in her desk for quite some time. It did not have an address on it, nor any kind of markings whatsoever. She picked up her pen to write on it, then stopped, tapping it against her desk rhythmically as she thought.

"Whatcha got there?" Tommy asked again, nodding his head toward the letter.

"Don't you ever shut up?" she yelled, slamming an open palm against her desk.

Tommy's eyebrows shot up and his head tilted back in shock a little. The outburst drew the attention of Mr. Calender, who stopped writing on the chalk board and looked up at the pair with his hands on his hips. "Is there something you'd like to share?"

"No," Tommy said nonchalantly, beginning to write what he had missed from the board.

Calla shook her head, then put the envelope away again.

"Feel better?" Xander said, throwing Cathy a look as she came around the back corner of The Factory, sipping on a Cherry Coke through a straw.

"Much. Mike's inside, he was hungry. I don't think he's eaten in days. He said his brain needed food."

Xander nodded, trying to remember the last time he'd eaten and deciding it was irrelevant. He sat on the large, circular stone that pressed up against the edge on the building, now just big enough for two as the snow covered it in.

After a moment she joined him, resting the Coke in the middle of her legs between sips. She turned and looked at the big, grey building behind them, which looked kind of like a warehouse from this angle, its siding covered in the mold that the damp of winter brought. "Can't believe this place is closing down next week."

"I killed the owner. It's a miracle her family's kept it open as long as they have," he said, his shoulders sinking.

"You didn't kill Joan."

"We're fairly sure I did. From what Mike found, and all the other craziness that was going on that day... yeah, I killed Joan. I even think I remember it, but I'm never sure. Could just be I've thought about it so much that I imagined remembering it."

"No," she said, touching him on the knee and leaning toward him. All her hair fell to one side, outlining her china-white face with its black, and she looked beautiful. "I meant, *you* didn't kill Joan. The Womb did."

He shot her a look, laughing a little through his nose.

She was silent then for a moment, realizing that he no longer saw much distinction between his two halves, and her body quaked at the thought. She thought back to a time, years ago it seemed now, when they'd both been sitting on this same rock. It had been spring, she thought.

"Oh, look Xander." *Cathy said, schooching to the edge of the stone.*

"What?" *Xander said, grinning as he turned on his heels to see her.*

"A squirrel," *she replied, her lower lip pouting slightly at the cute sight.*

"What?" *Xander repeated, a puzzled and sceptical look passing over his face. He thought this would be another of her made-you-look gags, but turned his head anyway. Sure enough, there was a little baby squirrel, no more than a few weeks old.* "Oh."

"Oh my gawd, he is the cutest thing," *she said, like a child that wanted a toy she knew she could never have. She turned and hit him on the chest suddenly, so excited that she blurted all her words out at once.* "Let's name it!"

"Okaaaaay." *Xander sighed, pretending to be too mature for her antics.* "How about 'squirrel'?"

She tisked and gave him a little slap on the arm. "No! A real name."

"It's a squirrel, Cat. That's why it doesn't have a real name. If your brain is the size of a pea, you don't get a name. It's in the Bible."

"Then why do you get one?" *she shot, brow furrowed angrily.* "You're just saying that because you can't think of a name anyway."

Xander rolled his eyes, taking a single step forward cautiously until they were shoulder to shoulder. "How about Alvin?"

"It's cliché."

"So's Cathy."

She shot him a look. "Besides, Alvin was a chipmunk."

Xander opened his mouth to respond, then closed it and nodded.

As suddenly as before, she turned and backhanded him across the chest.

"Ow." he winced, though she didn't notice.

"Let's name him Bob." she blurted.

"Bob the squirrel." Xander stated bluntly, raising an eyebrow at her.

"Yes. Bob the squirrel." She smiled at him with her big brown eyes and ruby red lips. She knew he was way too uptight to actually get the joke there, which just made it that much more funny. The squirrel gazed up at them, and in the blink of an eye was down on all fours, examining them. "Oh, you little cutie. Come here, Bob."

"He could have rabies." Xander said in caution, gently grabbing Cathy's shoulder to keep her from getting closer.

"Ew. I didn't know squirrels could carry scabies." she said, crinkling her nose as she recoiled from it a little.

Xander burst in laughter, frightening the little animal, although it didn't run.

"What?" Cathy smiled.

He kept laughing, turning his face away from her as he tried to stop.

"What?" she demanded again, pinching his sides to get the answer.

"I said rabies, not scabies." He said, laughing through the words.

"Oh." she said quietly, her face losing all expression for a moment as she filed that away. She shrugged, stepping in close to Bob again, "I don't care about that."

Smiling warmly and making little clucking sounds with her tongue, she reached her hand out slowly and tried to pet him on the head. It looked up at her with large, black eyes as though it were trying to figure her out just as much as she was it. It inched closer to her, its nose twitching and whiskers turning this way and that until finally it turned and bolted back into the woods as quickly as it had appeared. "Oh." She said sadly, as if she'd just lost her best friend. "Bye Bob."

She turned and looked at him, and in comparison to the memory, it was hardly even the same person. So much of the light and innocence had vanished from his eyes, and he always looked tired now. Always looked sad. Quietly, she leaned over and gave him a peck on the cheek.

His eyebrows shot up and he turned toward her, narrowing his eyes in a confused plead. "What was that for?" he said, and he almost seemed frustrated.

Out of the corner of her mouth, she frowned just a little, then ruffled a hand through his bangs to mess them up. "Just wanted to see something," she said, taking another sip from her drink then quickly changing the subject without making eye contact with him again. "Have you figured out what you're doing about the Jaden kid yet?"

"No, I haven't."

"We could talk to his parents, maybe. See what they have to say."

"Kid lives with foster parents. Been in and out of different homes since he was three."

Cathy rolled her eyes. "Wonder how he got molested to begin with."

"Mmm. I don't know, this just isn't the type of thing we're used to. Ever since the thing with Circe and Genblade, it's like there hasn't been anything tactile for me to hit."

"There's no big evil behind it all, it's just evil people."

He groaned, then nodded. "It's just hard is all."

Mike came around the corner, a far-off look in his eyes, as if he were sleepwalking.

"Hey," Cathy chimed, smiling over at her lover.

He did not respond, just stood next to the old rock and looked dazzled.

"What is it?" Xander asked, brow lowered as he got up to face his friend. "What's going on?"

Mike finally woke up, looking for Xander to Cathy and back again. When he spoke, his voice was cracked and dry, and it was as if the taste of them made him sick, his face turning white. "I just had a really bad idea."

٣٧٣

It's probably the worst thing we've ever thought of collectively, and the fact that it started as Mike's idea makes me hate him a little, wrote Cathy, sitting at a one of the booths in The Factory. She'd written about the whole Circe thing, and then Xander's relapse into the Black Womb, and she'd just finished Derek's escape and the search for him. She'd slowed down considerably at the end, and now was close enough to date that she could write things as they happened, and found she liked it. After we figured out how we were going to pull it off, Mike had suggested coming into the Factory, to try and enjoy it a little before it closes.

Xander shook his head, mumbling something about 'paying a debt' while glancing at the sun as it got lower in the sky, taking one of those awful cigarettes out of his coat and lighting it. "You guys go. We'll meet up at the place after dark. Until then, try to relax." He didn't look at me while he was talking, but I didn't feel left out. I suppose one could argue that it's because I'm his friend and he cares for me, and he was afraid of what he might see in my eyes if he looked in them after what we'd just talked about. If that's the case, then he'd been right not too, because he would have seen sickness and disgust.

He walked away without a word, the way he's been more and more prone to doing lately. It's like his only concern is with doing the job. Really, he's just the type of person who needs something to be obsessed about. Before all this it was Sara. Before that, his computer. Before that, Thundercats... the list goes on and on.

Mike slammed his hands against the buttons on the game machine, teeth clenched and sweat pouring down his face even though The Factory is very drafty tonight. He's disgusted with himself, as well he should be.

For the first time, I think that Xander was at least half right. Maybe the lines between him and the Black Womb aren't as clear anymore... but maybe the lines separating us from our darker halves aren't so clear either.

She finished off the last of her drink, put down her pen, closed the book, and started to cry.

A minute later Mike noticed and came over with her.

The Womb landed in the snow ten feet inside the alleyway, its legs buckling backward from the impact naturally, righting themselves almost immediately. Its mouth was open wide, revealing two long rows of jagged teeth and a slender serpent-like tongue. It stood full from the crouched position it had landed in, turning its head hard to the right side until the bones in its neck popped satisfyingly. It stopped then, standing almost completely still, and waited.

Inside the shell of flesh that made up the Womb, Xander Drew could feel the organ in his right side twitching, pumping more of its black blood into its ears, straining them to listen harder. The entire street was pitch black, the moon blotted out by the clouds, but the creature could see just fine.

Further down the alley, something fell, making a soft clanging sound. An empty can from an overflowing garbage bin, perhaps.

The Womb's face turned, then its head. It bellowed long and loud, displaying its teeth once again, and the pair it had been chasing jumped with fright, making their forms clearly visible at the alley's dead end.

"Ron Snelgrove!" it yelled in a voice like broken glass scraped over sandpaper. "Adam Bird!"

The two men shivered beside a trash bin. One, an obese man with a tattoo of a snake covering almost all of his left arm, was covered in soot and grime from where he had fallen trying to outrun the demon a few blocks back, and had landed in a puddle full of butts and garbage. The other was average sized, but his blonde hair was long and straggly, tied back into a pony-tail with a dark blue elastic.

"What do you want?" the fat one (Bird, Xander thought, although he wasn't quite sure) screamed, not trying even though his eyes were glossy with the tears that wanted to come.

Inside the creature, Xander smiled. On the Womb's face, the grin was sickly and menacing, like the way a cartoon skeleton smiles. "Justice," it said, but it came out sounding more like *just this*, which was just as effective as he took a step forward toward the men, springing his claws for the first time since he'd begun chasing them.

Both men's eyes went wide, and now Snelgrove was crying too, his lip blubbering up and down like a child.

Two hours and ten minutes later the Womb landed in the snow again, this time having vaulted off of a lamppost and landing next to Mike and Cathy. He landed on all fours and looked up at the two of them like a dog. "You guys didn't have to come," he said, craning his head in all directions as he spoke, looking out for spectators even though they were well within the cover of darkness.

"Yes, we did," Cathy said, her eyes cast downward.

"I can handle this on my own. I don't really need your support."

"It's not about supporting this, because I don't," she corrected, and she couldn't help her upper lip curling just that little bit in revulsion. "It's about sharing the responsibility for this."

Mike nodded once in agreement, but said nothing.

The Womb finally rose to his feet and looked at the house they were standing next to. They were facing its back end, the odd little dirt road that went along the backs of houses on this street so that dump trucks could collect the garbage without going on the main drag. He turned his slanted red eyes toward the door, two deadbolts located just above the knob. One looked freshly installed, a consequence of life in Coral Beach. There were three windows on this side, two with their lights off, one with it on and the window cracked just a little to let air circulate. The very top of a shower fixture told him that that room was the bathroom. "How long since the lights went out?" he asked finally, never taking his eyes off the house.

"About twenty minutes for the one on the left. The one on the right was off since we got here."

"That's the one, then."

"Safe bet, yeah." he said, clenching his fists. "We could still find another way to do this."

The Womb turned and regarded him emotionlessly. They stared at each other for a long moment, and finally Mike nodded. He turned to Cathy then, who would not meet his gaze. Retracting his claws, he reached a hand out to touch her cheek... and she jerked back immediately. He held his hand there in mid air for a moment, then let it fall, turned, and walked toward the house.

His leap over the fence took him three-quarters of the way through the yard, and a few seconds later another leap put him on the roof. Silently, he leaned over the eve and slid the bathroom window the rest of the way open, then disappeared inside with one fluid movement.

"Heaven help us," Cathy whispered, burying her head in Mike's shoulder.

Jaden Mal lay in the bottom bed on the bunk beds in his room, his warm covers pulled up and around his body tight and his head laid between two fluffy pillows. The last foster kids that the family he was with had taken in had been twins, so now he alternated between beds, even though his foster mother repeatedly told him to just pick one and stay with it so she wouldn't have to do so much on laundry day.

Batman wallpaper lined the wall and if you looked at the images staring at the door and moving your eyes across until you were at the door again, they told a story of Batman fighting the Joker. Except for a dresser with a few cheap toys on the top of it (hand-me-down Transformers that weren't even real Transformers, just Go-Bots) the room was almost completely bare.

Jaden opened his eyes and looked around, a car passing by and its headlights illuminating his room like a flashlight swept across it. Everything was just where he'd left it, just where it should be, and then the light went out again, leaving him in darkness. He turned his head back into his pillow smiling, and closed his eyes.

- Creeek!-

The sound of the floor board bending echoed off the walls quickly, and was gone as soon as it started.

Jaden's eyes snapped open and he whirled around in the bed, his eyes scanning the night frantically. After several seconds of silence that felt like forever, there was another, similar sound, but quicker, like the foot being removed from the board it had stepped on. His heart began to pump fiercely, as if trying to escape from his chest, and beads of sweat began to dot his brow and grow, tumbling into his eyes and making them itch.

There was a small, skittering sound that his mind could not identify concretely, but made many guesses at. It could have been the sound of a rat scurrying across the fake hardwood floors, the sound of claws scraping against a hard surface, the sound of a few marbles falling and then rolling across the room...

A giant millipede clattering across the floor.

The sound stopped, and was followed by a slurping, and that one was unmistakable. He knew of nothing in his room that could make that sound, on its own or with his help. He clutched his covers tight against his chest, wanting to pull them over his head to hide but too terrified to. Too terrified to move.

Outside there was the telltale engine roar of another car turning to come down the street outside his house. This one was accelerating, the low hum growing louder with every mile it went up. The lights hit his window fast, and he barely had time for his eyes to adjust when he saw it. Hunched in the corner, its back turned to him, was something that might have been a man covered in black scales, only the arch of its back and its feet clearly visible. It turned its head as soon as the light hit it, and Jaden saw that its eyes were large and red, and they glowed in competition with the headlights.

Jaden let out a small yelp, and the creature was gone before the light had even left, disappeared in a quick flash of movement as if it had just evaporated.

Jaden was breathing heavily now, his shoulders rising and falling dramatically with each breath. He could feel his heart in his throat and felt like he was going to choke on it, as his eyes again searched out the darkness for some sign of whatever he had just seen.

There was nothing for a long time, maybe five whole minutes. No scratching, slurping or creaking, and no movement from the dark that enveloped his bed. Building up his courage, Jaden closed his eyes and bit his lip... then stepped down from the bed, his feet gradually finding their place on the cold floor, sending chills up and down his spine. He looked around the room again carefully, squinting at every dark shadow or place that provided any shelter, then turned around to face his bed.

There was a sigh from the darkness and he froze, his entire form becoming as rigid as a corpse. He thought he felt hot breath on the nape of his neck but did not turn around, did not make a sound except to swallow dryly, his mouth feeling like a desert. After another minute of nothing, he bent down and looked underneath his bed. There was nothing there, just dust bunnies and a comic book. He arose to his feet again. He reached to his left and fumbled for the light switch. He thought he felt his hand brush against something that ought not to be there, but the sensation was gone after a millisecond, and his hand finally found the switch. The lights came on all at once, startlingly bright and fixtureless, and he had to close his eyes a second even though he didn't want to.

When his eyes opened, he gazed all around his room. There was no closet, a fact for which he was suddenly very grateful. He checked everywhere, his eyes digging like a prospector for any sign of motion or danger, but found nothing. He smiled, then reached for the light, stopped, and decided it was better to leave it on as he curled up into bed again, this time facing the room. After several long minutes his eyelids started to get heavy again and began to close as he drifted off to sleep.

- squeak!-

It was soft, ever so soft, and he had no idea where it had come from. It seemed to have come from everywhere all at once, and again his eyes feverishly scanned every nook and cranny in the small space he called a bedroom for some sign of where it could be coming from. He tried to tell himself that he was dreaming, but he knew that that wasn't true. He'd never seen anything scary enough in his life to make his imagination dream up that thing, whatever it had been. The memory of it, still fresh in his mind, came to him, and suddenly his eyes were not tired anymore.

There was another sound, a kind of frumping noise, and this time it was all too clear where it had come from.

The top bunk.

The slurping sound came again, and he lowered his head into his covers just enough so that only his eyes stuck out. There was a growl, and then a mumble, and the voice sounded like it was a bear trying to say human words, rough and inhuman.

- squeak-

- squeak-

- squeak-

Each sound was stretched out as long as it could go, like nails on a chalkboard, and there was a slight pause between each one. Their close proximity to each other worried the child, whose pillow was now soaked down with tears.

- squeak-

- squeeaa - -

The room plunged again into darkness, and there was a loud smash that made Jaden almost leap from the bed onto the shattered glass. He realized too late that the creature had been unscrewing the light bulb.

There was another frumping sound, then again (shorter, though), and then silence.

Jaden sat up in bed, his eyes wide, waiting for the motion the creature would make when it jumped from the bed. There was none. There was no doubting its presence now. Anything could have made the sounds, and his imagination could have been responsible for the quick flash of black mass he had seen, but there was no scared thought so powerful that it could unscrew a light bulb.

He stared into the darkness as it slowly grew, the light fading from his memory until all he saw was black. He watched it for a full six minutes, a few more tears and lots of perspiration washing over his cheeks, and then let out a small whimper and turned toward the wall, bringing the covers up close to his nose again.

Red eyes opened suddenly, centimeters away from his. They were so bright they were blinding, and so close that they completely overtook his field of vision. He opened his mouth to scream, and immediately felt a cold hand over his mouth, the creature's claws dragging along his cheek but not cutting it as it rolled in one unbelievably swift motion, stratling the child's chest. Its weight felt enormous, and its hand smelled like molded bread.

As Jaden watched, eyes bugged out so far he felt they

might explode, the creature bent down toward him and opened its mouth, exposing bright, glimmering sharp fangs and a long tongue that came out and touched the boy on the tip of his nose. Tears were coming out of his eyes faster than he could make them now, like a dam had exploded inside their sockets.

The creature took a deep breath, then bellowed "DO YOU KNOW WHO I AM?!?"

The boy said nothing. Didn't move, didn't breathe.

The creature brought its other hand forward, a single talon extended, and slowly closed in toward one of Jaden's pupils with it. "Do you?"

Jaden nodded frantically, and the claw retracted just before it would have blinded him.

"Who am I?"

It removed its hand, and the child did not scream, and he had to struggle to get the words out. "You're the Boogy Man."

The demon smiled, showing that its teeth went back at least six inches further than a human's would. Then the smile left and it lashed out with both hands, nicking the boy's earlobe and drawing blood. "Do you know what I'm going to do to you?"

Jaden shook his head, clasping his hands together in a prayer at his chests. His tiny, chubby knuckles had turned so white that they looked like bones.

It slammed its hands against its own chest, digging the claws in deep and then retracting them after only a second. Eight tiny holes were in it, slowly closing before Jaden's eyes, and the creature leaned in until its chest was hovering over his head, letting the one or two drips of black ooze that came out fall onto the boy's cheeks. "I'm going to eat you. I'm going to eat you one piece at a time until there's nothing left."

Jaden shook his head no, but it wasn't an answer, it was a plea.

"Do you know why?"

Again the boy shook his head, the teardrops mixing with the black ooze on his face and dribbling down his cheeks onto his pillows, making mascara-like stains of his face.

"Because that's what happens when you don't tell the truth. Because that's what I do to little boys that lie. Do you know what I'm talking about?"

Jaden nodded, and his tears weren't silent now, they came out it pained little wails because they weren't just fear anymore, they were clouded by sorrow and guilt. When the creature heard them, he leaned back, just a tiny bit. Then it came forward again, extending a claw to its fullest length and lowering it toward the boy's chest...

"I'll do it!" Jaden squealed, closing his puffy red eyes tight so he wouldn't have to see what was happening to him. The words were barely distinguishable, distorted by pain and fear and his wailing. "I'll tell the truth I swear I will just don't hurt me, please don't hurt me please please please please please..."

He opened his eyes and found the creature no longer there, even though he was sure the weight of it was still on him. He looked around, moisture shaking from his scalp with each direction he turned in. After five minutes it occurred to him that the creature had left, after ten he was sure of it. At one point he thought maybe it had been a nightmare, but the glass on the floor and the black smudges on his pillow were all the proof he needed.

He would find no sleep that night, nor the one after.

Again something landed next to Mike and Cathy, and this time it was Xander, not the Womb. Cathy had fully expected him to be in tears, but he wasn't. To the contrary, there wasn't anything on his face at all.

Mike opened his mouth to speak, then stopped. He looked down and cursed under his breath.

"Did..." Cathy began, then stopped as well.

"It's done," Xander said flatly, and started walking away from the house without a word. They followed him and walked in silence all the way home.

They did not chain Xander to any cross that night. He assured them it would be a sleepless one.

CHAPTER TWENTY-FOUR
NOTES

As I lay awake that night, my thoughts kept going back to the boy. Could he have been reasoned with? Could the courts have been convinced with the same evidence that convinced us? Was this the only way to do it?

I kept reminding myself that it was pointless, now. That the damage had already been done, and that no amount of speculation was going to undo it. But every time I dispelled my doubts with that argument, the same recourse came to mind: what happens next time? How far are we going to have to go the next time something like this happens?

As hard as I tried not to think about it, it kept coming back to me.

CHAPTER TWENTY-FIVE
SILENCE

Mike jogged along at a brisk pace, finally catching up to Cathy and Xander as they headed to school. They were early for once, not having to make a detour to unchain Xander at the church. He huffed from lack of breath, his face sweaty even though the air had a biting cold wind on it. "Hey," he said, taking a moment to compose himself.

Neither of them said anything in return, they just kept walking in silence. After a moment, so did he.

As the school came into view, Cathy finally broke it. "We did the right thing, right?"

"No," Xander said, without a moment's pause. "We did the wrong thing for the right reason. There's a difference."

She paused, considering that. "We did do it for the right reason -- right?"

He did not look at her, nor did he answer.

"We'll see when Megan calls us after the meeting with the kid," Mike said, touching her hand gently.

"So, what? The end justifies the means? Is that our

new team slogan?"

Again, silence.

"Maybe it always has been," Xander said, his face glued to the icy sidewalk in front of him. "Maybe now we're just growing up enough to realize it."

Cathy sighed, joining him in his staring contest against the road before them. When she looked up again they were at the school. There were almost no cars in the parking lot.

Mike opened the door for both of them and then entered himself. "What do you have first period?" he asked Cathy as they neared the corner to go to her locker, trying to change the subject any way he could.

"Chem, I think," she said, rubbing her temple. "My brain won't work. I didn't get any sleep last - -" she stopped in her tracks as they turned the corner, her mouth open wide.

Xander and Mike turned toward the source of her shock, and Mike's expression changed to watch. Xander's remained constant, silently regarding the horrific scene presented before them.

Calla McFadden hung from the ceiling, a rough noose made from what looked to be one of the big white sheets for Home Ec. Class tied around her neck. Her head was jerked awkwardly to the right, and there was a red ring around the edges of the sheet. Her mouth was open but here eyes were closed. Her arms dangled at her sides and she swayed in the breeze from an open doorway down the hall. Next to her was a toppled over chair. On her chest a white envelope had been pinned, and there were several names on it but scratched out, the end result being the letter was addressed to no one.

Cathy turned a threw herself at Mike and began to cry again.

Xander took one cautious step forward, noticing the urine stain on the front of her pants and the small puddle on the floor from when she had lost control of her bladder. He closed his eyes and listened, trying to get any sense of a heartbeat, or of any smell except that of death.

He found neither.

⋏⋎⋏

"State your name, for the record," the Bailiff said, and each word was followed by the clacking of keys as the stenographer in the corner dictated all that was said.

The small room just to the side of the main courtroom was dank and drafty. When the other areas of the courthouse had been renovated and redesigned in '86, this one had been left out, as it was so rarely used. There was an old oil portrait of Richard Nixon on the wall behind where the Judge sat at the far end of the table, and it dated the room considerably. Dust was everywhere, making Megan cough every time she took a breath. Nathan had patted her on the back in support the first time, but after that didn't see the point. The room was small, with the large oak desk taking up most of it. Even with one's belly pressed against the table, your back still wasn't too far off from the wall.

"Judge Miriam Pike," she said, crisply and clearly, without bothering to look up from the file before her at the man taking down every word spoken. She was pushing fifty at least, but her curly blonde hair tumbled over her shoulders and down her back and made her look fifteen years younger. Her eyes were big and blue, with long lashes. She had full, pink lips and a tight chin.

"Anthony Jones," Tony sighed under his breath, his hands clasped before him on the desk. He was wearing a grey pin-striped power suit, his hair slicked back and his face so cleanly shaven it might have been waxed. No matter what the case, it seemed, he went all out to dress to impress.

"Megan Greene," she said, trying to sound involved but with her eyes were firmly glued on the boy, who sat between Tony and the Judge on the opposite side of the table. Pushing the sides of her dark red hair behind her ears and wishing she had worn it up, she glanced back down at the few frantic notes she had made after Xander's call.

"Nathan Summers," Nathan stated, his arms folded around the bulking chest of his grey suit, which almost matched the color of his silver hair. He was by far to tallest in the room, and even sitting he came very close to the height of the short, stocky bailiff.

All eyes turned to the boy. His eyes and cheeks were still red and puffy, and his lower lip quivered as he surveyed all the faces watching him meekly. He looked terrified, and had ever since he got out of the car out front. Tears seemed ready to spring forth from him at any moment, and Megan drawled a sigh at the sight. With a face like that, her case was six feet under before the child had even spoken. "Jay - - Jaden Mal."

"Thank you," Judge Pike said, smiling at the boy as politely and warmly as possible, trying hard to put the child at ease with his surroundings. She turned toward Tony and gave him a nod.

"Jaden," Tony coaxed, leaning in to face the boy. "I need you to tell us what happened three days ago, when you were in the Guidance office with Reverend Gallagher."

The boy was silent. He stared blankly at the file Tony was leaning on. It had his name on it.

"Jaden?" Tony said again, coughing discreetly into his sleeve and throwing a quick look to the Judge, then to Megan. In the corner the stenographer typed away.

"I have to tell the truth," Jaden said, his voice far away and tired, as if he wasn't even aware of where he was.

Megan shot Nathan a confused look, who returned it.

"Just tell us what happened," Tony repeated, his hands open palmed in a sort of pleading gesture now.

"Nothing," Jaden said finally, looking from Tony to the Judge. "Nothing happened. He just talked about my foster family and how things were going. He didn't do anything."

Tony's eyes went wide. He looked to the Judge, who had an eyebrow raised to him.

"Jaden, if you're scared..." Tony coaxed, leaning toward the boy, placing a hand on his shoulder in support.

"I am scared. I have to tell the truth, that the man didn't touch me. It told me so."

Megan leaned in, her ears perked.

"It?" Tony pressed.

"The Boogy Man. He told me I had to tell the truth. I should tell the truth."

"Uh-Huh," Tony sighed, watching as Megan took out her notepad and started to scribble down what was happening. "And... who is this Boogy Man?"

Jaden looked confused, turning from Tony to the

Judge, as if the question had been obvious. "It was black... and slimy, and it had scales and black blood. And it had red eyes and a red mouth with lots of teeth and it came into my room last night after I went to bed and told me I had to tell the truth."

Megan looked at the child, her brow crumpled, her mind taking in what she had just heard and filing it away.

"Your Honor," Nathan interrupted, standing to his full, empowering height as he finally spoke. "Is this serious? Because my firm has other cases it's supposed to be handling right now. We are doing this, without cost, because we believe in Gallagher's innocence. If the child says that's true, than..."

"That will be enough," Judge Pike said, motioning for Nathan to sit back down.

"Thank you, your Honor," Tony nodded, sweating a little.

"From *both* of you," she corrected, pointing her pen at Tony.

"Your Honor," Megan said, raising her hand without looking up. "In light of the child's testimony, I move that all charges against Reverend Robert Gallagher..."

"Will be dropped," Pike finished, nodding as she closed the folder before her, tapping it twice against the desk. "We'll process his release immediately. You may leave, Miss. Greene. Mr. Summers." Megan and Nathan rose and began to head for the door. Tony rose as well, but the Judge turned to him and waved him back down. "Not you, Mr. Jones. Your client and I have a bit more to discuss."

CHAPTER TWENTY-SIX
NO REASON

Mike and Cathy sat on Xander's bed, their backs against the wall. Cathy's legs were curled up into her breasts, her chin rested on her knees. Mike looked depressed, occupying himself by tearing loose material from his jeans, staring at a spot or stain on the bedspread. Xander sat backward in the swivel chair at his desk, facing both of them but not looking at them. School had been cancelled, and for good reason. Most of the student body hadn't even made it there by the time word had spread, hadn't even seen the body.

"What did the note say?" Mike asked, forcing himself to find his voice. It came out squeaky and uneven.

"Nothing, really," Cathy frowned glumly, her voice muffled by her pants. "That's what that cop you're were friends with said, anyway. It was three pages long, but it didn't say much of anything. There was no... reason. And the date. It was written three months ago, but the date she killed herself was right there on it."

"She knew all this time?" Xander asked, raising his

head off the back of his chair. "She was planning this? There had to be something that set it off."

"No," Cathy sighed, her lips pursed. "She was just depressed, I guess. She just... decided she didn't want to live anymore. She even said sorry to anyone she hurt or for anything she did, that she was going live her last few weeks however she wanted."

"Why are you doing it here?"

Calla looked down at the clumpy green substance in the baggie, then back up at her friend, an annoyed and comically exasperated expression on her face. "Because when I do it at home, my parents get mad."

"What're you doing out - " he started as he turned the corner, the smile stopping as quickly as the sentence did.

Calla McFadden was leaning against the snow-covered brick wall of the school, her jacket wrapped tight around her as she held her thumb and forefinger up close to her mouth, which was drawn up like a bow, sucking the last few puffs out of the joint that she had meticulously rolled, trying to get as much out of it as possible before it got down to the filter she had hastily made out of the cardboard from a pack of Marlboro's. Her eyes were wide at first, the both of them wondering what exactly the other thought they were doing, but not knowing how to ask. When the shock wore off, Calla's thin eyebrows lowered into a scowl as she tossed what was left of her joint into a snow back, exhaling a puff of blue smoke. She gave him what she referred to when amongst her friends as 'the elevator' (looking a person up and down, usually for the purposes of either checking them out or seeing if you could take them. Or both,) then started to walk past him. She stopped when the both of them were shoulder to shoulder and turned toward him so that her lip was dangerously close to his ear. "You're cute for a spaz," she drawled, snickering a little as she, turned the corner and disappeared, leaving Mike to just stand there bewildered.

The shock wore off her face as she looked him up and down, and became a sly smile. "Want some?" she asked, handing the joint to him and sticking out her tongue, revealing a small pink stud in it not far from the tip.

Xander took the rolled up paper from her and watched the smoke rise from its tip for a moment before handing it back. "No, thanks," he said as she took it.

She shrugged, then brought it to her lips and took another draw. She held it in as long as possible before letting it out. "Your loss. This is some kick-ass stuff."

"It was happening the whole time," Xander mused quietly. "We just didn't notice."

They sat in silence for a minute and considered that, and Cathy couldn't help but think of when she'd found Xander's gun when he'd tried the same thing, and failed.

"There has to be a reason," he said hoarsely, his eyes welling up finally and drawing the attention of his friends. "This can't be it. This can't be all there is. I terrorized a young boy, I've killed more people than I'd care to count, risked my life more -- and this girl just decides she doesn't want to live anymore for no reason? Spends the last three days crying out for help to deaf ears and then does it... for no reason? It can't be, there's got to be more --"

"But there isn't," Mike said glumly.

Xander looked up to meet his friend's steady gave, a single teardrop traveling down each cheek.

RIING!

Xander moved, picking up the phone and wiping his eyes with his sleeve, as if the person on the other end could see them. He sniffed back hard once to compose himself, then answered. "Hello?" he was silent for a moment, then smiled just a little. "That's great. Yeah, sure. Tonight's fine. Bye," he hung up the phone and turned back to them.

Mike raised an eyebrow to him. "Hot date?" he said, trying for lividity, but his voice was still far to sombre for it.

"We won," Xander said, then leaned his head back on the chair.

There was several minutes of silence then, as all three considered the validity of that statement.

"Yay for us," Cathy said finally.

CHAPTER TWENTY-SEVEN
CONFER

Megan Greene sat alone at one of the booths at the bar across from the offices Mayer, Summers and Soul; attorneys at law. She sipped her margarita casually, keeping one eye on the yellow legal folder next to her as she scanned the room, waiting for her guest. She did not know whether or not he would be late, as he had always shown up to meet her of his own discourse, hardly ever by something prearranged. She was still wearing the power-suit and grey skirt she had been in the meeting with the boy, but the suit was unbuttoned now and so was the top button of the white blouse underneath, making her much more relaxed. Covertly, she slid her right foot out of its heel and stretched it. After the meeting she'd spent the majority of the day processing and running back and forth from the Bird and Snelgrove case to the office, and her feet were killing her. She ate the olive from her drink then took another sip, hoping the pain would subside soon.

"Hey pretty lady," Xander said, his voice devoid on the usual upbeat twist it had in these meetings. He said the words as though he were reading lines from a script, rather than feeling them.

"Hey," she smiled, motioning to the beer she had ordered for him at the seat across from her. "I guess that's three I owe you."

"We'll call it even for the beer," he smirked, bringing the bottle's long neck to her mouth and taking a long drink, the smallest bit of it dribbling out of his mouth.

"Sorry I doubted you before. I think this was the easiest case I ever worked, subject matter aside."

He did not respond, except to peel the label off his drink.

She coughed uncomfortably. "Well, Gallagher was released a few hours ago, and the charges should be officially dropped by the end of the week. He should be getting home right about now, actually. The Judge ordered the boy taken out of his foster home and admitted him into psychiatric care, pending further examination. They're worried that one of his other caretakers abused him and caused this whole mess."

Xander nodded, still not looking up, and took another swig.

"They'll find out who, I'm sure."

Again, he nodded.

"I meant to ask -- what made you so sure Gallagher was innocent to begin with?" she pried, trying hard to draw him into the conversation.

He looked up finally, but his eyes were twin black holes. It was like looking at a machine. He tried to speak, then closed his mouth.

Something inside him was broken, she could tell, and

she reached out and touched his hand, wanting to help him badly.

"It was his permanent records," Xander replied, finally finding his voice. "Anyone who had cared to look would have seen it. He'd cried abuse so many times it probably would have been uncovered anyway, if the prosecution hadn't rushed so much."

Jaden closed his eyes and tried to go to sleep, the image of the black man still burned into his eyelids. He shuddered. This time, the room was completely bare, nothing but the bed and the walls around it, no windows except the one in the door the hospital had locked after the lights in the rooms had been turned off remotely.

"I thought so," Megan nodded, frowning. She paused and clicked her tongue against her teeth, then took another drink as she decided exactly how to phrase what she was about to ask. "How much do you trust Gallagher?"

That got Xander's attention. He looked at her, eyebrows raised and pupils sparkling. "What?"

"I'm just saying," she sighed, laying her hands out as if to display her points. "*You* looked through the kid's records and found out that he'd said it before, and knew that he was probably lying. Like you said, we would have probably found this out too, but not before the legalities had ruined Gallagher's life. But didn't he have access to the files too? Couldn't he have seen them, known someone would assume the child was lying, and do this?"

⋔

The lock to Jaden's room door snapped to with a crack, and the door slowly opened on creaking hinges. There was a man in the doorway wearing a uniform with brown hair that went down past his ears and thick braces, smiling wickedly to himself as he took one last look around outside.

⋔

"I trust Gallagher completely," Xander said, but his voice lacked conviction as he thought back to when he had spoken to Gallagher in the penitentiary, and how his reading hadn't come out quite right. It was like Gallagher had been holding *something* back, without outright lying.

"Okay," Megan sighed, forcing a smile and raising her glass to him. "To another victory for team Drew / Greene."

Xander paused, still considering what Megan had said, then raised his bottle as well.

⋔

The orderly sat at the edge of Jaden's bed, sliding his hand underneath the covers.

"No," the boy said, starting to cry. "I'll tell. I'll tell the truth. The man said I have to tell the truth..."

The man snickered, his voice high and nasal. "Go ahead," he laughed. "The more you tell them someone's touching you, the longer they'll keep you in here -- with me."

-clink-

Their glasses touched briefly, and they shared a moment of eye contact that made them both smile. Even though they both had so much on their minds, and they were so different in age and background and... everything, really; they found solace in one another's friendship and drank to it, both of them finishing their beverages.

"You did good work today, Xander," she said, smiling warmly at him.

"No, I didn't," he corrected. His voice was gruff but there was an honest smile on his lips. "But I'll do better tomorrow. Maybe that's the important thing."

"Cheers."

He straightened his jacket, obviously getting ready to leave, then stopped. "How'd it go with the Bird / Snelgrove thing, anyway?"

Megan looked up at him, raising an eyebrow suspiciously. "Curiously enough, they admitted to all wrongdoing at the hearing today. They're going to pay all damages and will be serving at least six months apiece."

Xander smirked. "Somehow, I thought they might," he got up now, touching her hand briefly as he did. "I got to go. I have a previous engagement with Mike and Cathy, and I don't want to keep them up too late. Keep the peace, okay?"

She smirked at him. "See you later."

"Not if I see you first," he said, then turned and headed for the door and out into the night air.

Megan watched him go, then opened the file that had

been at her left side the entire time, and took out two sheets of paper. The first was the stenographer's report from the meeting with Jaden and the rest earlier today.

Jaden Mal: The Boogy Man. He told me I had to tell the truth. I should tell the truth.

Anthony Jones (prosecution): Uh-Huh, And... who is this 'Boogy Man'?

Jaden Mal: It was black... and slimy, and it had scales and black blood. And it had red eyes and a red mouth with lots of teeth and it came into my room last night after I went to bed and told me I had to tell the truth.

She frowned and motioned to the bartender for another drink, then picked up the second sheet, examining in carefully. It was stamped as the official stenographer's report from the trial of Adam Genblade.

Megan Greene (defence): Mr. Genblade,

Adam Genblade (defendant): Please, Adam.

Megan Greene: Adam, do you know the man seated behind me?

Adam Genblade: His name is Xander Drew.

Megan Greene: Correct. And how do you know him?

Adam Genblade: We studied together.

Megan Greene: Really? Where?

Adam Genblade: At the Church of Smoke and Mirrors, of course.

Megan Greene: But how do you know him, really?

Adam Genblade: He is the Black Womb.

Megan Greene: Of course he is. And what is that exactly?

Adam Genblade: A manifestation of a genetic disorder which resulted from meticulous breeding for decades by Engen's top scientific minds.

Megan Greene: What does it look like?

Adam Genblade: It covers your body in a dark, black film with red eyes and mouth.

Megan Greene: Why can't we see it?

Adam Genblade: It exists inside him until blood loss or lack of consciousness or emotional stimulation forces it out.

Megan laid the sheet down carefully next to the first, then looked at them side by side. Black, slimy, red eyes and mouth. Black, filmy, red eyes and mouth. The bartender laid her drink down next to her and she immediately took a long gulp, looking at the door that Xander Drew had just walked through.

CHAPTER TWENTY-EIGHT
LAST

The night air was cool on Julie Peterson's skin, and made her shudder as she stepped out the back porch, realizing she hadn't taken the clothes off the line as her Aunt had asked her to hours before. To add to the chill she was only wearing her yellow tank top and grey pajama pants, and the wind cut through them as easily as though she was wearing nothing at all. Her auburn hair was still a tangled mess from the shower and draped around her freckled face, she huffed as she looked at the long lineup of clothes pinned up before her.

One by one she started picking them in, bending over every now and again to lay them in the clothes basket at her feet.

He watched her intently, especially when she bent, her long legs moving as if she'd been poured into her clothes.

In the kitchen the kettle started to whistle, and she turned back to it, several pins stuck between those thick, ruby lips.

He chuckled softly to himself from the bushes, a high-pitched and whiny sound.

Another gust of wind came, and this time she cursed as it not only nipped at her already freezing skin, but took a shirt clean out of her hands and into the snow below the step. She growled at it, then turned and went back into the house.

He lost sight of her for a moment, beady eyes searching the various windows frantically, pushing away the leaves he stood behind and his own long brown hair aside for clarity. She came into view through the kitchen window.

She took the kettle off its burner, then turned it off, shivered, and walked out of the room.

Again he looked for her, scanning each window within sight.

She appeared in her bedroom, taking an old sweater out of the closet. She started to pull off her tank top to change into something that would protect her better.

He watched her undress, his smile undeniable, but his pulse steady.

When she was done she went back downstairs, then through the kitchen, and finished taking in the clothes. Her mother came in from the living room, and the both of them sat at the kitchen table and sipped tea for thirty-two minutes.

He watched the entire time, trying to figure out what they were saying while watching their lips, often being distracted my Julie's, sweet and supple.

After that they went upstairs and to bed, and he watched her change a second time, and finally she turned off the light.

Derek Smith rose to his feet out of the bushes, smiling to himself as he continued to watch the window, then licked his lips and turned to walk back into the forest.

EPILOGUE

Reverend Gallagher was reinstated as the school's Guidance Councilor, all the charges against him were dropped. I don't feel like we can call that one a victory. The school isn't assigning students to go see him anymore, and very few will willingly. There's an odd logic to it, I suppose. Like, where there's smoke, there's fire. That once someone's been accused of something so hennas, even if proven innocent he shouldn't be trusted again. Still, it almost seems a shame not to count it as a win for our side... we've gotten so few over the past few months.

You can see the hurt in the man's eyes now, too. Xander said it's all natural, that everyone has their own natural healing factor for things like this, as he does for everything else. That the human soul has an infinite capability for regeneration. He said it, but he doesn't believe it. His actions are louder than his words, and every day, more and more, his actions spell defeat. Looking at him now, I think maybe the opposite is true. That maybe our bodies can heal, but our souls can't. That maybe the first stab comes at birth and we all spend the next eighty years bleeding to death spiritually.

Some of us don't even take that long.

When Mike and I chained up Xander for the night, there was that look in his eyes as he slipped into delirium. Somehow, even though his eyes were only just beginning to turn black, it seemed like he was already the Womb. Like the transformation matters less and less, like now that's just who he is. I looked at him, sweat dripping down his brow, and somehow I knew he was seeing things that weren't there.

"Mike?" I said, tugging on his shirt. "Mike, I think he's hallucinating."

Mike finished snapping the chain tight around Xander's hand just as tiny enamel claws began to poke their way out, just breaking the flesh. He turned toward Xander emotionlessly, squeezing his friend's chin to make him look up at him. "It's hard to tell. I think maybe his eyes are rolled up into his head."

"Is he in pain?"

Mike looked at me. His eyes were filled with pity, but not toward Xander. It was like I wasn't getting something that he was, and he felt bad for me. The way you feel bad for mental patients who just can't help that they don't understand. "I don't think he notices it anymore, sweet heart," he told me earnestly. "You go now. I'm gonna stay with him a minute until he transforms."

I turned to go, then stopped. Instead, I planted my feet squarely in front of him, looking into the pools of tar he called eyes.

"Hun, you don't have to..."

"I want to watch," I said, cutting him off. I'm sure I'm making myself sound much more determined and righteous here than I actually was. Maybe.

"Cathy,"

"I want to watch!" I said again, turning to chide him. When I looked back, the ooze had already begun to slither over his body. I use the term ooze only because that's the way he describes it. To me it's more like gel, and I always thought it went over him the way a slinky goes down stairs, tossing itself forward over his body and then pulling itself up, then repeating. Watching it like this, it wasn't hard to see it as a living thing, completely separate from Xander.

But I wasn't looking at the black gel, I was looking right into his eyes. They say the eyes are the gateway to the soul, and I wanted to see if it changed. When Xander became the Womb, did his soul change as well? I thought I'd gotten my answer months ago, when he'd first revealed the Womb to Mike and me, but lately... I just needed some reassurance, okay? Let me do what I want, I'm damaged.

His eyes may have been black, but his face was still his. It made it easy to see how much pain he was in. He turned away from me and mumbled something that I think was in French, which was odd, since Xander didn't know French. I paused for a second to translate internally, and it was something about a blonde.

When he turned back to meet my gaze, I knew. He was thinking about Sara. That was it, that's what he was seeing... and yet it wasn't really. That was part of it all right, but not all. Suddenly it was like I wasn't looking into his eyes anymore, but seeing through them. That's the best way I can explain it, I know it's not coming out the way I mean. I could see what he was seeing, and it wasn't just Sara, it was Julie, too. And Mandy. Poor, sweet Mandy. Kerri Walker was in there too, her tiny corpse rigid and frozen when they found her naked in the woods. For the briefest of instants there was Megan Greene, and Jaden Mal, then his mother, and then there was me. He spent a good long while on that thought, and for the first time I saw myself the way he must see me all the time, and it made me want to cry everything out of me right then and there. Then, at the end, there was Calla McFadden. A girl who had spent her last hours on this earth calling out to all of us for help, and we just wouldn't listen. Who, even through whatever it was she was going through, had stopped long enough to help a young boy crying out himself, astute enough to see something of herself in him.

The gel was almost covering him now, and the place where I was looking wasn't even so much his eyes as dents in his face. I blinked and the link between us, whatever it had been, was gone. I looked around at the old abandoned church we were in, and at the cross behind him that supported his chains, and suddenly it all seemed very fitting. I wondered if the church he'd been in as an infant had looked anything like this. The church, the cross, his background with the foster home and Engen -- suddenly it all made sense with what I had seen in his head. It was Catholic guilt, twisted somehow so that it was his own. I got a mental picture of what Xander's mind must be like. It was just a hallway filled with doors. Like the old lady and the tiger trick, only he's waited too long. There's a lady behind each door, and the tiger's already gotten to them all. No matter what he does, he always feels he was too late. And then, right at the end, he realizes he was the tiger all along.

Two long red slits formed across the two dents I had been looking at, as if they had been cut there, then they opened and revealed themselves to be eyes. Long, curved, triangular eyes. I swallowed hard, then looked into them. The Womb made a shallow purring sound that I recognized as what it did when it did not want to be noticed by its prey. I don't think it realized I could see it just as it could see me. No wonder, not many things would look at it so closely without running in terror.

"Cathy..." Mike started again, but I ignored him.

I stared into those red puddles until I saw what I wanted to see. Somewhere, behind the cat-like corneas and the cones that took in all of the light in the room, I saw it. It wasn't quite Xander, but then I wasn't really expecting that. What it was... was guilt. It was thinking of doing things to me, and somewhere inside it, the Black Womb felt guilty for what it was dreaming.

I felt a smile spread over my lips and leaned in, pressing them hard against him. It tried to open its mouth to bite me, but I wouldn't let it. My mouth caressed his the way it had Xander's not so long ago, its flesh warm and wet against mine. Its flesh felt scaly, and it reminded me of kissing Mike when he had been trying to grow a mustache (something I'm glad to say he gave up on quickly). I cut the inside of my lip against its jagged teeth, then reached up and ran my hand over his bald scalp. I kept my hand there as our lips parted, and I finished my childhood crush on Xander Drew. Somehow, it was over now.

I loved him more than anything, but in that moment, I had gotten everything I ever wanted to.

I turned to Mike as I stepped out of the Womb's biting range, expecting him to look mad or bitter, but he just stared at me with a knowing look in his eyes. He knew what it had been about, and somehow the kiss had made him feel even more secure. At least, I know that's what it did for me. I told him I loved him and asked him to come over to my place when he was done, just as we had the night this all started. It seemed like a life-time ago. Like my soul had bled buckets since then -- and maybe come out better for it.

As I walked home I started to think about the differences between Xander Drew and Black Womb, and as I did, I couldn't help but comment on the differences between good and evil. Lately that line had gotten blurred, to the point where everything was just grey now. Someone had told me once that when you mix black and white you get grey... and no matter how much white you stir back in, you'll never get anything but grey. What we'd done to that boy in the name of good... did a good ending justify a horrible act? By that same measure, does an evil act nullify a million good ones? They say the road to hell in paved with good intentions, and it makes me wonder what the road to heaven is paved with.

Somehow I think I don't want to know.

Cathy hit save, then closed out of her word processing program. The file stared at her from her desktop and Mike looked at it with her, leaning over her shoulder. "That's really good, baby," he said approvingly, kissing her lightly on the side of the head.

She said nothing, just stared at the file. BW.doc looked back at her, each of the capital letters like a pair of eyes staring her down, seeing which of them would blink first. Of course, she did. She brought her mouse pointer to the file and clicked down on it, holding it in her digital grasp as she brought it to the recycle bin and dropped it in.

"What are you doing?" Mike asked, but made no motion to stop her.

She right-clicked on the trash bin and clicked empty. A message came up asking if she wished to permanently delete the file, and she clicked yes.

"I thought you wanted to document everything, so that people will know everything that we did in case something happens -- so that the truth can be known."

She turned around in the chair, looking at him glumly. "Some things are better left not said," she said, not meeting his eye.

He frowned at her and stroked the side of her face with his thumb, then leaned down and kissed her. "I love you," he said, then started to walk toward the bed. He had a feeling they were in for another long night of talking. She seemed to have a lot on her mind.

Even now her brow was furrowed, the way it was whenever she was in deep thought. She bit her lip and stood, walking toward him as he lay down on the bed and started to pick up his DS again. "Promise me something?" she said, and her voice was right there and far away at the same time.

He lay the game back down and looked into her eyes. "Anything."

She lifted the edges of the loose shirt she used as a

pajama top over her head and let it fall to the floor. She looked at him calmly, bare breasted in the moonlight. "Hold me afterwards," she said as she walked toward him, pulling a cover over them both. She kissed him before he had a chance to answer. She'd already known what it would be.

What happened next was many things.

It was a expression of the love they had both felt since meeting one another.

It was proof that they could overcome anything that this world threw at them, together.

It was a search for something good and right in a world that had proven to be the anything but.

It was a symbol of their devotion and trust in each other.

More than anything, it was a door... a door that led only to the future.

ENGEN TIMELINE

With over twenty novels spread over three different series by many different authors, the Engen Universe of titles is growing every day and into genres we couldn't have imagined! From the original ten book *Coral Beach Casefiles* thriller series, its crime novel sequel series *Xander Drew*, our flagship adventure title *Infinity*, or single-novels like *Jacobi Street* or *light | dark*, there's something in the Engen Universe for everyone with more books by more authors on the way soon!

...But how do the events relate to one another, chronologically? While some astute readers have guessed at the potential timeline (some accurately, some not), we're going to finally set the question of the Engen Timeline to rest.

Turn the page for an up-to-date guide of the ever-widening world of Engen, featuring the works of Ellen Curtis, Andrea Hackett, Sarah Thompson, Jay Paulin, and Matthew LeDrew!

In the 10 Years Prior Black September

"Reptilia" by Matthew LeDrew
published in *light | dark*.
Danger descends on a small secluded town in the form of a deadly virus with fantastic and terrible side-effects. Can a small group of doctors escape alive?

Compendium by Ellen Curtis
Three short stories forming the basis for the Engen Universe's ties to suspense, genetic engeneering, and the supernatural. Features the stories "The Tourniquet Revival," "Falling into Fire" and "At Midnight, the Dawn."

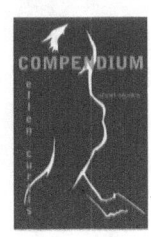

"The Theogony" by Matthew LeDrew
published in *light | dark*.
A tale of young Theo Flaherty of the *Infinity* series and his time admitted against his will to the Black Springs hospital, where he learns to paint, and seeks out his father.

Black September

"Revving Engen" by Matthew LeDrew
published in *light | dark*.
A direct lead-in to both *Infinity* and *Black Womb*, Tasha travels to Coral Beach, Maine on a hot tip about a recently discovered young man with incredible abilities.

Infinity by Ellen Curtis & Matthew LeDrew
Faced with a destiny he's uncertain of, the enigmatic Victor must bring together four unique people with very special abilities… or face the tasks ahead alone. Guaranteed to excite!

Black Womb by Matthew LeDrew
Fifteen years ago, something happened in Coral Beach, Maine that resulted in the present death of a seventeen-year-old boy. Now four high-school students must try to solve the mystery... before the killer picks them off.

Jacobi Street by Matthew LeDrew
When a mysterious painting shows up at an art gallery he works at, Bob must work with Eddie and Sloan to track down its sinister origins and convince the people living on Jacobi Street of them, before its too late!

Transformations in Pain by Matthew LeDrew
When two girls are assaulted and one is hospitalized, the residents of Coral Beach must put their shared tragedies behind them and stop the man responsible, as well as unlock the secrets behind the true nature of the Womb...

Year One: October

Smoke and Mirrors by Matthew LeDrew
The approaching trial of Genblade brings closure to the people of Coral Beach, until people start showing up dead in the same manner they did when he was at large.

"Scarlett" by Andrea Hackett
published in *light | dark*.
Introducing Scarlett, the slightly damaged hunter on a mission to save others from the monsters from her past.

"The Inevitable" by Ali House
published in *The Lightbulb Forest*
A young woman must contend with the
emergence of a frightening new power alongside
the emotional high of a first date.

The Tourniquet Reprisal by Curtis & LeDrew
A man lives in Atlanta, Georgia that people
don't talk about, but everyone knows he's there.
He arrived a year ago and turned a gaggle
of uneducated youth into something new,
something to fear.

Roulette by Matthew LeDrew
As the teen suicide rate in Coral Beach starts to
climb astronomically fast, Xander travels to Los
Angeles to fight his most terrifying adversary
yet… and learns that the only thing worse than
looking for release… is finding it.

Year One: November

Exodus of Angels by Curtis & LeDrew
Victor's enigmatic past is illuminated when
Jaycee accompanies him to visit a new friend
in the paliative care ward of the Black Springs
hospital, where Theo also happens to be
searching for a cure for Leigh.

Ghosts of the Past by Matthew LeDrew
Coral Beach faces its most awesome threat when
one of Engen's past mistakes is unleashed upon
the unsuspecting populous. Friends and enemies
unite to fight a common enemy… but will even
that be enough?

Touch Your Nose by Matthew LeDrew
Simon Monk must infiltrate the San Fransico branch of Shane Industries, a massive company with deep ties to the Engen Universe. Where do his true loyalties lie? And can he get out without causing harm?

Ignorance is Bliss by Matthew LeDrew
After being set through the ringer one too many times, Xander decides that his life with Julie needs a little more attention... which is bad news because a new villain has come to town with his sights set on Adam Genblade.

"Gristle While You Work" by Jay Paulin published in *light|dark*.
A short story centering around the rise of a new, and possibly cannibalistic, serial killer in the Engen Universe.

Becoming by Matthew LeDrew
For months Xander Drew has been doing his level best to keep the streets of Coral Beach clean, which means it's time for the forces of darkness to strike back... all at once.

Inner Child by Matthew LeDrew
Julie is hospitalized with life-threatening wounds to both body and soul. But the real threat comes from the hospital walls themselves, as a demonic presence makes itself known to Xander and his friends.

End of Year One

Gang War by Matthew LeDrew
The Tees, a homicidal gang of evil men, has finally been taken down by Xander Drew. But his victory is short lived, as retired Tees are mysteriously killed. With a town of suspects, anyone can be the culprit... including one of their own.

Chains by Matthew LeDrew
Sociopath Derek Smith has been freed from prison and is praying on the weak; and none are weaker than August Styles: a pregnant girl with Down Syndrome who has run away from home.

"Omega" by Ellen Curtis
published in *light | dark*.
A sinister division of Engen begins a series of experiments on pregnant women in a fashion eerily similar to those that created the original Black Womb project.

The Long Road by Matthew LeDrew
Xander meets the American people — and realizes that the world is harsh and wicked, but can also be soft and gentle, even loving. Xander Drew comes of age on the road, and sets his new direction.

Year Two

Cinders by Matthew LeDrew
Detective Horton enters a violent and dangerous world he didn't know existed beneath the veneer of order and structure that he has based his entire deductive method around.

Sinister Intent by Matthew LeDrew
One of the killers Detective Horton could not catch has resurfaced: a serial killer who flaunts his sinister intent in front of the Los Angeles Police Department, making it so that no one is safe.

Faith by Matthew LeDrew
Xander's mysterious and troublesome past returns to haunt him on the streets of Los Angeles; a place where even more people can get caught in the crossfire of the games of death and deceit that makes up his life.

Flickers in the Night by Matthew LeDrew
Lisa Rowdan is hunted by her haunting -- and powerful -- ex-boyfriend Ryan through a lonely city street. Can she escape him?
One of over twenty great sprine-tingling short stories!

Family Values by Matthew LeDrew
Xander and his new friends Crowley, Lisa, and Tim investigate a series of kidnappings and murders that stretch back decades, all of which have the same similar twist: victims being found after years of being missing.

The Future

Fate's Shadow by Matthew LeDrew
When one of Xander's old cases comes up for trial, Megan Greene returns with it. The former friends are led into conflict regarding her client's innocence. However, they put their difference aside when they both become targets of the vigilante known as Shiro Gilbert.

The Future

"Remers" by Sarah Thompson
published in *light | dark*.
In the not-too-distant future of the Engen
Universe, young athletes are the targets of a
scouting program to create the next stage of super
soldier with cybernetic enhancements.

ABOUT THE
AUTHOR

Matthew LeDrew holds an Honours Degree in English from the Memorial University of Newfoundland with a minor in Anthropology, and studied Journalism at College of the North Atlantic in Stephenville, Newfoundland. He was honoured to be a jury member of the 2018 NLBA awards.

He has written twenty novels for Engen Books: the ten book *Coral Beach Casefiles* series, *The Long Road, Cinders, Sinister Intent, Faith, Family Values, Jacobi Street, Touch Your Nose, Infinity, The Tourniquet Reprisal, and Exodus of Angels* the latter three of which with co-author Ellen Curtis.

He lives in St. Johns, Newfoundland.